fLy

fLy

M.Z.

The Book Guild Ltd

First published in Great Britain in 2018 by
The Book Guild Ltd
9 Priory Business Park
Wistow Road, Kibworth
Leicestershire, LE8 0RX
Freephone: 0800 999 2982
www.bookguild.co.uk
Email: info@bookguild.co.uk
Twitter: @bookguild

Typeset in Garamond

Printed and bound in Great Britain by CPI Group (UK) Ltd, Croydon, CR0 4YY

ISBN 978 1912083 268

British Library Cataloguing in Publication Data.
A catalogue record for this book is available from the British Library.

I dedicate this book to
Sylvie, Natalie, John, Adriano, Zoe, Sofia and Valentina

ACKNOWLEDGEMENTS

I would like to thank William Shakespeare for giving Tristan his moral compass. Tristan often uses quotations from Shakespeare, and in particular in Chapter 17, Tristan uses part of a speech by Leontes from Act II, Sc 1 in *The Winter's Tale*.

1

fLy: I heard it well before Hannah did and then I smelt the juice and it electrified me. Sex involving an aged prodder and a receptive passage was always going to enthral me. But this time I was sitting with Hannah, watching as she sat on the floor outside the door. She has sat there before now; her ear flat against the wood, pressing it hard against the chipped shiny avocado door paint, leaving an indentation from her earring into the nape of her neck. She would notice these imprints as she studied the dry skin around the back of her ears that has plagued her since she first married Tristan. But being the nosy sod I am, I also know that it is not only Hannah that has been envisioning this moment; Sasha too has been fantasising about having an illicit encounter such as this. Sasha, I have to explain, has an English lesson every day in the same classroom with 16 other students. And every evening Sasha thinks about him, 'Sir', as she lies in her bed in the boarding house. She thinks about his voice; the huskiness of it as it passes over his lips and pushes out his slightly stale breath. She thinks about his handwriting and the shapes it makes on the whiteboard. She imagines looking through her marked homework and seeing an unusual note in the margin or on a piece of paper slipped into her file: "I want you". You see as a fLy, a dirty fLy, I can follow anyone I want to and find out their very base secrets. They don't even know I am watching and listening so I wait and I watch and I listen as they push out a turd, talk to themselves in the mirror or confide dark secrets to a friend.

Now let me tell you a little about Hannah. Hannah is older than Tristan and through years of 'Conscious Calorie Avoidance' she has successfully managed to achieve that 'big knee look' and when she turns around to regard her arse in the mirror, one can see that the skin looks oversized for the little bit of fat that creates her half-arse. She uses pots and pots of anti-ageing cream on her pale skin but it does little to rejuvenate her. As a fLy I know she is decomposing and no matter how much cream she slaps on nothing will hide the smell that the fear of ageing emits.

Hannah's social calendar is relatively restricted. She only regularly sees one friend called Fi. Fi also lives on campus as her husband, Raymond Evans, is Head of Economics. They meet up for a cup of coffee or a glass of wine and so I escort Hannah to Fi's house depending on what else there is to do. Often I end up following Hannah as my social calendar is also relatively restricted; I tend to stay with Hannah if I am not in the mood to go into school. Tristan teaches English Literature to children from the age of eleven to eighteen years. I like to watch him whilst he is teaching, not to learn anything or to expand my knowledge of the literary greats but to watch him interact with the students. It is a luxury to be able to look around the classroom at the boys and girls in organised rows at different stages of puberty. Some of them have overly puffy lips and faces displaying plump, scarlet zits in various stages of eruption. Some have brown cornflake scabs capping the small volcanic mounds and some have left their spots alone, all yellow pus, crusted and proud.

Sometimes I will follow one of the girls from class to their boarding house if they exhibit the classic embarrassing signs of being 'on the blob'. I am alerted to this by the way they surreptitiously try to check the back of their skirt and the blue plastic chair as they stand up at the end of class. When they fail to get any assurance from their investigations they try to secretly grab the attention of a close female friend to ask them to assess the 'have I leaked on my skirt?' situation. Having evaluated their feedback, the girl inevitably goes back to the boarding house to change her undergarments and I am rewarded with bloody sights, exasperated sounds and warm fresh fish smells that all excite me and quench my ever-thirsty, basal needs.

Once I have come down from my sensory slake I always take the opportunity to go and spy on Sasha and the other girls that might be in the house; most of them learning how to become the definition of bitches in 3D. In the past I have never stayed on for too long as there was more to be seen in the boys' boarding houses but this year it is different; or I am.

Currently, I want to know more about women, well, those associated to Hannah; so more often than not I return home and follow the apple of my eye to Fi's house.

Fi, in my opinion, is great. She has a very faint damp piss smell about her which she tries to mask with a lavender-scented body spray and her default expression is a farty, flaccid smile that she employs every time she finishes a sentence or looks at her kids. And even though she relentlessly tells her kids to have a good wash and flannel their faces after cleaning their teeth she doesn't seem to be able to do the same thing. If she were to die in a car crash the one identifiable thing that her next of kin would look for is the ever-present opaque jelly, her eye bogey, in the outer corner of her right eye.

Fi is married, happily she would say, to Raymond. Raymond gives Fi her outline; he is her support, her exoskeleton. This doesn't mean that he is a tower of strength; on the contrary he is a bully and a manipulator. Raymond is rigid and rarely shows Fi any form of compassion or warmth; even when they are 'doing what married couples do' he has to time himself. He often regales the same story to his few friends that on the two occasions he impregnated Fi he recorded his 'PBs' (Personal Bests) for stamina whilst on the job. Fi is not sure whether getting the stop-watch out is the turn-on for Raymond or the sight of her naked, doughy pendulous breasts. I know that it is the former because when he has a wank in the shower it is a definite game-changer once he looks at his Casio Mudman G-shock watch strapped to his wrist. He likes to calculate the time 'costs' or 'expenditure' with many activities; this being one of them. As soon as he gets the shower water at the optimal temperature he steps in under the spray, slaps his four fingers and thumb around his parsnip-coloured penis, puts his mouth around the watch face and in unison he commences wanking as his teeth press the button on the side of his watch face. He then races the clock; tugging at his crudité with vigour until he triumphantly sees the resulting cock flob get swallowed thirstily by the silver-mouthed plughole. He has a theory that if you can climax with speed when masturbating using a very tight grip, then you can prolong your lovemaking sessions because your member is in the less constrictive birth canal. How do I know this? He told Bruno at a barbecue I once went to.

Fi and Hannah are close friends. Their common ground is the School and the fact that they both have husbands working in it, otherwise I am not sure that they would have been 'natural' friends. Without their friendship though, I would not have been privy to most of the background information I have on either Hannah or Tristan.

I remember well one of the first times that I had followed Hannah. She walked briskly, her breasts pushed out in front of her, her head lowered and shoulders swinging, to Fi's house. Fi opened her large old wooden front door after Hannah had knocked, only once, with the heavy, antiquated brass knocker. She greeted Hannah with a big wide flabby smile with her eye bogey glassy in the late morning sun. It was easy for me to pass into the hallway without being heard or seen as Fi made so much unnecessary noise as she enthusiastically welcomed Hannah into her house.

At this time, the smell of the dusty carpets was still noticeable in the hallway and in the kitchen I could smell the tiny slices of rotting cabbage peel and bacon fat that coated the inside of the plughole in the large white porcelain sink. It was a pleasant house and the kitchen was vast with high ceilings. A lamp on the end of a long metal rope dangled over the kitchen table and thin fluorescent tube lights were fitted under the eye-level kitchen cupboards.

Fi trundled over to the kettle which sat on its own on the imitation grey granite worktop. She enquired as to whether Hannah wanted a tea or a coffee whilst Hannah positioned herself at the sturdy oak table that was tattooed with burn rings from overly hot saucepans. The legs of the table were painted in cream and the six surrounding chairs were painted cream to match. On the underside of one of the chairs was a crusty old bogey that had a single nasal hair caught into the middle of the grey-green, yellowy lump and around the bottoms of the chair legs were the odd flake of milk-dampened cereal and crumbs of morning toast.

The floor was made of mahogany parquet blocks that had been polished for many years, their patina near deep-plum in colour which reflected the four metal window frames that allowed the sunshine to fall into the kitchen and then bounce off of the polished surface to fill the room with natural light. When the deafening noise of the kettle about to come to the boil ceased and Fi had plated up the Rich Tea biscuits, she pulled a melamine tray out of a narrow cupboard that was adjacent to the fridge. With caution Fi put the two mugs of hot drinks and biscuits onto the tray and shuffled over to the table. It was, I had decided, the height of the ceiling which made talking audibly offensive; the echo was very tinny so Fi tried to compensate by doing a sort of fat-tongued whisper, her lips working overtime.

5

Fi: *So tell me, Hannah, how did you first meet Tristan?*

fLy: Fi took one of the ten biscuits and dunked it into her drink, watched it for a few seconds and sucked with her floppy lips at the sodden biscuits as Hannah regaled her story.

Hannah first met Tristan whilst he was studying English at University about ten years ago. He used to play his guitar in the Railway Guard pub and in return got free drinks. I wasn't there for this event so the details are vague; the smells, the people, the half-truths all a mystery. All I can do is regurgitate that which Hannah divulged to Fi.

According to Hannah, she was with 'Big-Eared Git' who reckoned he was a talent scout for up-and-coming bands. 'Big-Eared Git' motioned to Tristan to come and join them in between sets. Tristan and 'Big-Eared Git' started to chat and his demeanour captivated her and his rasping voice 'spoke to her' (what else does a voice do?) and all the while he kept smiling at Hannah. Allegedly 'Big-Eared Git' ignored Hannah most of the time so Tristan's interest was very welcome. Hannah was slim then, as she is now, and had blonde long hair with a centre parting. Whilst 'Big-Eared Git' was talking and smoking, Tristan started to twirl Hannah's hair around his fingers, biting his lower lip and ever so slightly narrowing his eyes as he did so. At this point of the story Fi muttered, "Oh wow, that's hot." As a fLy I don't see it but Hannah nodded in agreement and took a big breath and carried on. Supposedly whilst 'Big-Eared Git' went to get another round of drinks and a further packet of cigarettes from the vending machine, Tristan asked Hannah if she knew what 'cunnilingus' was. With this part of the story Fi looked stumped; but Hannah thankfully continued. Hannah told Fi that at the time she knew it was something to do with sex and foreplay but had no real idea on what part of the body it was performed. When 'Big-Eared Git' returned with twenty Marlboro Lights, four pints of Guinness and an ex- girlfriend called Camilla, Hannah knew it was time to quietly suggest to Tristan that they should leave to go and look a certain word up in the dictionary. Tristan assured Hannah that he would rather show her what the word meant instead. He then spent the next twenty-five minutes with Hannah's bum on the bonnet of her silver Ford Fiesta car with him kneeling on the tarmac car park floor giving her Juicy Lucy a good licking!

Fi: *Did you like it?*
Hannah: *To be honest I was so worried about being seen for the first fifteen minutes I couldn't relax but once Tristan started groping my boobs that was it; all the neon lighting and dipped headlights were forgotten.*

fLy: Unfortunately for me, the phone rang, Fi jumped up like one of those surprisingly agile chubby ballerinas and grabbed to answer it. From the sounds of things, it was Felicity Grayson, who was involved with the PTA (Parent-Teacher Association) and Fi was making a 'humpfffnn' sound as way of response or contribution to the conversation every thirty seconds. It was remarkably annoying; Fi's noises and the fact that Hannah's story had been interrupted.

A few months later on when Fi and Hannah's friendship had become more concrete, bound by soft secrets and dull gossip, Fi invited Hannah round to a PTA brunch party. Hannah was unable to go, so I thought it best that I went instead. The brunch was laid out in Fi's sitting room on a picnic table of sorts that ran parallel to the left-hand wall. The room had two blood-orange sofas with green worn velvet pillows and blue, floor-length polyester-mix curtains. The floor was similar to the kitchen's but it was paler, more scuffed and less polished. There was a set of metal-framed patio doors that hid behind one pair of the blue curtains. They led out onto the slightly uphill garden. The garden had no flowers or shrubs in it or around it but was made slightly more interesting as it was on two levels. As one would step out from the house onto

7

the crazy-paved patio area a few steps presented themselves which curved slightly to the right. After scaling the four unevenly spaced concrete steps one would encounter the lawn which was full of dense, vibrant-green, squishy moss. Around the perimeter of the garden was a thick bushy hedge of conifer trees. In the left-hand corner of the garden was a chestnut tree that cast a long shadow over the lawn and towered over Raymond's barbecue area and on the far right-hand side of the garden was a shed that housed the white plastic garden furniture and giant Jenga set during the winter and wet spring days.

The men that attended Fi and Raymond's brunch 'party' were quite similar to Raymond. That day they all wore stone-washed blue jeans, white trainers with black flash emblem, collared T-shirts and some sort of multipurpose watch on their wrists; you know, black plastic, digital, ridged strap with four different function buttons on the side. Raymond would always adopt the same stance; legs astride and arms folded. Under his tree, surrounded by the men, he would quaff his isotonic cucumber and apple juice whilst recounting his PBs for various activities and reinforce why he is ultimately a genuine role model for his own kids and those he teaches too.

On this particular day he was warning the other men of the perils of not keeping a close eye on the changing habits of their wives; especially during the menopausal years. He used Fi as a point of reference and her increasing friendship with Hannah; Raymond didn't refer to Hannah by her name, instead choosing to label her as A.N. Other. (How clever he is… what an original name.) He said that his concern was that Fi would think it 'ok' to drink during the day and 'ok' to wear unpractical shoes. He admitted that he liked to see Fi in her calf-length skirts with a belt and nice blouse; thirty-denier flesh-coloured tights and light brown flat shoes. He said he enjoyed this homely image of a woman and it reassured him that practical clothing was a priority not the flashy, fashion-aware side. What he didn't divulge was that the flat shoes meant he was still taller than Fi when she was wearing them and the tights gave him his morning 'fix'. His fix, to briefly explain, was that before taking his shower, Raymond would rifle through the Evans's washing basket to find the knotted, shrivelled-looking, slightly dirty, thick, flesh-coloured tights. He would frantically look for them like a ravenous pig hunting for truffles, desperate to smell the crotch of her tights and delight in the sweaty, peppery, pissy, fishy odour that swam up his hair-clogged nostrils.

Raymond said that A.N. Other would wear toeless, high-heeled, strappy shoes that allowed her painted toenails to be seen. How could shoes such as these allow a parent to look after a child or children responsibly? Whilst A.N. Other was childless, he couldn't allow Fi to think it 'ok' for her to do the same. Practical shoes had to be a woman's priority; ones which would facilitate having to run after the children or get up or down stairs with greater speed and safety. All of the other Raymondites nodded in agreement, uttering small grunt noises and then shaking their heads from side to side, tutting and then looking lost as if trying to find an additional comment somewhere in their bony domes to add to the futile conversation and impress Raymond, Lord of Twaddle.

Bored, I looked across toward the patio doors and there in the sitting room, perched on the edge of the rather sad-looking sofa, were the women. All of them hugged their mugs of tea out in front of them as if warming their ageing hands, their elbows balanced on their knees and their faces fixed. Their expression reminded me of Tristan's face when he is trying to hold a fart in during a lesson; lips pursed, eyes intense with concentrated stare. I decided to go and have a listen inside to see if the conversation warranted the many vacuous expressions. After a brief time, I realised that Alice O'Grady's halitosis, vaginosis and ingrowing toenails were no longer the source of any substantial interest so now the conversation drifted in and out as to whether they should try and raise money for the local state school by doing an 'Abstainfrom-Facebook-a-thon'. It was time for me to go home and enjoy the underside of the upstairs toilet seat where the congealed piss and puke sometimes hung; a much better way to pass the time.

I didn't have to wait for many days until Fi was once again in the company of Hannah but this time they had convened at our house. Fi slipped off her shoes as she came in through the front door and her sweaty feet left little shiny footprints on the pale strip wooden floor as she strode toward our sitting room. The soft sticking sound of her moist feet stopped as she stepped onto the deep-pile cream carpet that marked out where the sitting room was and where the open-plan kitchen began. Fi made herself comfortable as she sat on the cream leatherette sofa with its off-white scatter cushions, relaxing as she chatted to Hannah as Hannah made the coffee. Once Hannah had brought over both coffees she sat by Fi's side, turning her body so that she could face Fi whilst Fi bored on. I too looked at Fi; I was bewildered. How could someone with lips as loose as hers drink hot liquid and not dribble all over her front? My attention was regained from pondering this, and what hidden delicacies may hide in Fi's cleavage, by the mention of Raymond's name. Hannah was asking Fi if she had ever been concerned about Raymond's fidelity.

> **Fi**: *What makes you ask that, Hannah? I mean, with someone as magnetic as Raymond the thought has crossed my mind, several times to be honest. He is so strong that I am sure many women would find that appealing; but Raymond is a family man and I would be totally unbelieving of anyone that would suggest otherwise. When we have discussed kids in the school going through the mental anguish of their parents splitting up because of an affair, Raymond has always been very verbal in his contempt for a parent jeopardising his family life for sex.*
> **Hannah**: *Do you think you would be less sure of his loyalty and devotion to you if you didn't have children, a family?*

fLy: As Hannah prattled on to Fi about how her and Tristan's childless state was because of Tristan smoking too much marijuana through college and University, I wanted to shout at her and call her a liar. Tristan's sperm could well be swimming in circles but I knew that Hannah was a majority stakeholder in who was to blame.

Every morning, like Raymond, Hannah has a routine. She rolls onto her side and watches Tristan walk out of the bedroom to have a shower. He is always naked and some mornings Hannah entertains the idea of calling him back into bed for a quickie but that fleeting moment of excitement always passes. Most mornings she just stays in bed for five extra minutes staring blankly at the meaningless modern art canvas on the wall. Then Hannah gets out of bed and walks over to the full-length, frameless, bevel-edged glass mirror. She holds her long blonde hair in two bunches out to the side which brings her shoulders up. Hannah then makes sure that she can count her ribs through her very pale whitey, bluey-grey skin. Once she has done that she puts her arms down and releases her hair. She puts her hands on her hips and stands with her legs apart, then shuffles until her inner thighs just touch. She looks down to see the distance in between her feet and measures it with finger spaces. Her ultimate aim is that her thighs don't touch even with her feet together and she has nearly achieved that heroic goal on several occasions. Afterwards, Hannah takes time to listen to see if the shower is still running and if it is, hastily pulls out the drawer on the right-hand side of her dressing table. On the underside, taped, is her contraceptive pill packet. She pops out a small pink tablet, pops it in her mouth, swallows and then puts the drawer back in its rightful slot. As per usual, Tristan comes back in to the bedroom, towel-drying himself. Whereas a few months ago he would have pushed Hannah back onto the bed and made love to her had he seen her totally naked, he now shows no sign of interest at all; not even a hint of a semi. But that is easy to explain.

Every morning for the past few weeks Tristan would wake up after another night of pleasing dreams with a full, thumping erection, the skin around his six-inch cock stretched to capacity. He would put his right hand around it and with his left hand push the duvet off of him and then try to walk surreptitiously to the bathroom. Once in the bathroom he would shut the door and lock it. Tristan would walk over to the sink, put the chrome plug in, turn on the mixer tap and then look at himself in the mirror. He would say, "Good Morning, Sasha," and other times he would say, "Morning beautiful". He would then practise smiling; sometimes with all his teeth out on display and other times with just a hint of his ivories on show. After he had filled the sink with scalding hot water, he would carefully step into the shower putting his right hand out as if guiding someone in with him. Once he had turned the shower on he would administer a large blob of shower gel onto his hand and start rubbing it over his stomach and over his resolutely turgid penis. Tristan would recommence his one-sided conversation with his imaginary friend, asking her to rub him slowly and to let him hold her arse. Soon the conversation would be lost behind a wall of gritted teeth and as he struggled to contain the grunts that coincided with his ejaculation, nutmuck would cascade over the tiled wall behind the taps. The last thing he would say to 'her' was that he loved her. After turning off the shower, he guided 'her' as she tentatively stepped out onto the slippery tiled floor. Once back at the sink he would smile again as he looked in the mirror, but this smile was always the same. Somehow it was a patronising, lips-together, head-slightly-tilted-to-the-side type of smile; one which, I know, would incite a fight in a pub. His words were no longer audible as he lathered shaving crème onto his face but his eyes still danced with the images that distracted him. As soon as he had finished shaving he would rush to get changed, drying as he always did with a towel as he walked. Hannah, like many humans, never paid enough attention to the changes of smell;

she never even noticed the burst of chemical-laced fragrance that the soap and shaving crème offered as he re-entered the bedroom. But I did.

2

fLy: I remember well the day that Tristan came home carrying a white plastic bag. He opened the front door and very quickly, before even taking off his coat and scarf, darted left into his office. He opened the deep drawer of his desk and put his booty behind the last file. Later that evening, after Hannah had gone to bed, he went back to his desk to unwrap his treasure and sprayed some of the aftershave onto his wrists. He sat down on his chair and started to whisper.

> **Tristan**: *I want you, Sasha, to think of me when you smell this. I want this very scent to be a tangible link for eternity to how and what we are today, the undeniable love that holds us steadfastly together. When I first saw you and you walked into my classroom I was blessed. Sure, I was mesmerised as my eyes united with your image but as you glided past me I realised that it wasn't only earth-shattering beauty I was in the company of but that I was in the presence of Shakespeare's 'Hermione'. I recall that day often when I am feeling low or in fact, if I am feeling happy. I can still hear the hinge of the classroom door whine as it stretches open. I look up as a matter of course and my breath is momentarily stopped. The sun is shining very brightly and the finer strands of your pure blonde hair*

14

sparkle. The door closes behind you and you look at me and smile. You are holding your file in your arms close to your chest, as if a baby; our baby. The light seems to change as you step closer toward me and it is no longer the fine strands of hair that are illuminated but the entire crown of your head radiates as if intertwined with crystals. I want to jump up from my desk and grab you by the arms, declaring, "Thou hast the sweetest face I ever looked on, Sir, as I have a soul, she is an angel." But I can't. I feel overwhelmingly smug that of all the people in the world, all the beautiful people in the world, right here in my classroom I have the most beautiful person that ever will be, ever. This person that epitomises grace and majestic sweetness, encompassing all of mother nature's strength and wonderment, has walked in and smiled at me; at me! Sasha, your hair is like vanilla silk, your eyes vibrant and green like freshly washed seaweed, your lips powdered pink marshmallow and your freckles, sprinkled like cocoa on cappuccino foam. And after you, my dearest Sasha, have sat down, I then can smell you. You are wearing a perfume, Chanel No 5, and for now and forever I will have you as that smell and that vision; completely inseparable.

fLy: And he sniffed his wrist again.

I followed him upstairs expecting him to wash the fragrance from him but instead he just cleaned his teeth, undressed and slid into the bed next to Hannah who was snoring. Hannah didn't snore often but when she was really pissed, her mouth would be ajar and a rolling snort would tumble out of her, irregularly for hours. Every so often she would shut her mouth and as the edges of her lips dried, the tackier the flesh would become. She looked like a slowly expiring cod fish on the side of jetty. Tristan would look at her, bereft of emotion, before falling asleep. Then, and only then, I could enjoy the exhaled smell of curdled stomach acid and alcohol.

Luckily for Hannah, Tristan was not one to dwell on or mention such night-time detail as he spent most of his time thinking about Sasha otherwise it could have been a tenable reason for Tristan's dwindling interest in sex with Hannah. Hannah was very open with Fi and when discussing the issue of flailing passion, Fi had convincingly managed to repackage Tristan's disinterest in Hannah as a direct result of stress. She felt that having read a groundbreaking article in a magazine she had read at the chiropodist's, she knew all about a man's libido and how it correlated with life's external pressures. In Fi's mind she knew that Tristan was just another statistic that proved this brilliant theory. Too much stress meant too little lovemaking. Fi announced, forthrightly, that Tristan was being selfish in taking on all of the production, directing and budgeting for this year's school play. Fi felt that there were obvious people to ask for help with it especially as he had decided to do a play based in France and originally in French. Fi also agreed with the article saying that unless they asked round and found help, Tristan would face the very real prospect of a stress-related heart attack. So Fi came up with a plan. She decided to involve Mr Jean Lempriere, Head of Languages, and without children or a wife he could possibly be someone that has less responsibilities and therefore more time on his hands. She would arrange a get-together at her house to help facilitate this. Fi glibly smiled to herself as she realised she had found a solution to a life-threatening situation. Can you see her now, "Is it a plane? Is it a bird? No it's Super Fi," solving issues of magnitude, floating through the sky on a great big air-filled, eye bogey? Where would we all be without her? But moving on…

Contrary to Fi and Hannah's belief, Tristan was very happy and relatively unstressed. I knew this for sure because he and Hannah have a dog called Wallace. Wallace is a Springer Spaniel crossed with a Labrador. Every evening after school, Tristan takes Wallace for a walk. As a rule of thumb I generally go too because sometimes I get left out of the loop with what is going on with Tristan. I find out if there is a school trip, an issue with the week's timetable, classroom maintenance or an unscheduled event at school taking place. Without these walks I would, at times, be totally in the dark as to what Tristan is up to and how school is.

The walks usually last for about forty-five minutes and on each walk that I have ever accompanied Tristan on, I have never experienced angst or worry in Tristan's words; only the wonderment of nature or love-struck rhetoric. Being with Tristan and Wallace is refreshing; they both seem to delight in the same things. When the air is cold and Tristan's breath becomes foggy as he exhales, Tristan will always run his fingers through the grass as soon as he steps out on to it. Wallace excitedly follows Tristan's hands as they ruffle in the green fronds, with his nose, thinking that Tristan has found crumbs of food or a ball. Wallace will look up at Tristan, wagging his stumpy tail, mouth open and tongue lolling out to the left of his jaw as he awaits instruction or a ball that will be hurled along the uneven path. Tristan tells Wallace frequently that he is a very good boy and the best of friends that man could ever ask for. He told him once that his company made him feel as if he had crossed over to a higher understanding of companionship and love; and that it was Wallace that had answered his adolescent question of what life was for.

On days when it is hot and the sun is still quite high in the sky before the shadows become long and thin, Tristan awaits to see the things that delight Wallace. When Wallace starts to investigate a bush looking for the extra-zealous insect that has the fast-flapping wings which vibrate against the seasonal zephyr, Tristan follows him. He too investigates by pushing his nose into the virginal blooms, small and delicately downy. He describes the feelings that start to swell inside of him triggered by the scent. I must say that from my perspective Tristan does well to decipher some of the perfumes that mingle with each other. From the brown sugar, marshmallow and almond tones that create the smell of the white polar star rose to the dusty, charcoal and new leather aroma that the hawthorn puffs out into the countryside air. Tristan delights in what he sees and smells and verbalises this, often talking to Wallace and to his much-wished-for invisible companion, Sasha. The only stress that Tristan experiences is when the walk is over and he reopens our front door, back to his reality of plug-in room fresheners and Hannah.

On our most recent walk, Tristan told Wallace and I about the first lesson of term. Sasha had joined the school to study for her A levels. She had been at another school until she had passed her GCSEs and for a reason unknown to myself and Wallace she had started at our school. Tristan, as you and I know, had been overwhelmed by Sasha's appearance that day but what I had not known was the way that Tristan had tried to 'break the ice' for Sasha within the class. Apparently he had decided to try and merge how to introduce a character into a novel or into a play with how one would try and integrate into a new social scenario. He set the class a task of writing a piece of work to be read out individually to the group, the following week. The idea was to summarise oneself within the confines of a minute's dialogue. He told the class that he too would present himself in the same way that he had asked them to do and in the second half of the lesson there would be a general discussion about actual known character versus written representation. When the aforementioned lesson finally arrived Tristan said that he had started to sweat. He told us that his mouth had gone papery dry from panic and his hands unable to remain moisture-free. He laughed, but not genuinely, as he recounted how his hands slightly shook and his lips slightly stuck onto his teeth as he tried to deliver his carefully prepared self-synopsis. He made the fatal mistake, for him anyway, of trying to be amusing. He told the class that his first love was writing music and his second was the prose of Shakespeare. Tristan said he had even tried to combine the two but had failed and that the modern man should just accept that they can only do one thing at a time. I wondered how many hours he had spent concocting that lame last line. Even as he confessed to Wallace and me of the terrible speech he made his eyes glimmered with hope; he said that in Sasha's one minute she had told him everything that he needed to know. She had said that she was to be turning seventeen within a few weeks and that she did not have any loves or hobbies. On the one hand, so he said, he was saddened that she had not experienced anything to spark the love drug but on the other, he was happy that it was going to be with him that this addiction would be introduced. His happiness was very firmly locked into the delusional, or was it?

When I first met Wallace I liked him immediately. He wasn't a dog that barked very often, to the contrary he often communicated how excited he was through how wiggly his body was. When Hannah or Tristan would return home he would jump up from his slumber and his stumpy tail would dictate to the rest of his body how to move. As his tail wagged in wild abandon his spine would follow; his whole mid-section rolling from side to side, his eyes like headlights on full beam. He was never bothered by me when I used his flank as a bed to absorb the sun's rays as they poured in through the patio doors or when I feasted on the greasy, thin gravy film that coated his blue plastic dog bowl. And on a more superficial level I liked him because of his name. I had always correlated his name with the pioneer of biogeography and the co-discoverer of natural selection until that is, I was in the company of Hannah and Fi one morning.

Fi arrived at our house quite unexpectedly. Hannah had just finished unpacking the week's groceries from her patterned, recyclable bags when the doorbell sounded. Hannah placed the last of her food items away and went to the front door. As she opened the front door both she and I were confronted with Fi, a look on her face I had never seen before. Fi's flaccid, farty smile had gone totally saggy. Her lower eyelids were welling up with tears that had started to melt the caked mascara on her eyelashes (don't worry the eye bogey was still in place...) Her lips looked like grey, over-greasy pastry and her face as if she had just been embalmed. But give her her due, she spoke clearly, which was a surprise having seen the state of her.

Fi: *Oh Hannah!*

Hannah: *Come on in Fi. You go and sit down, what can I get you to drink?*

Fi: *Can I have a glass of wine, Hannah? I know it is early and you know I normally wouldn't but, oh God, Hannah.*

Hannah: *You know better than that Fi, you never need to justify to me needing a drink. You know that! Sit down whilst I get it for you and then you can tell me.*

Fi: *Please promise me that what I am about to tell you goes nowhere.*

Hannah: *Of course.*

Fi: *Well last night Raymond came in from work and he was all excited about getting 'Netflix'. His friend Nathan told him about it and Raymond liked the idea that we could watch any film at our demand for a fixed monthly price. Well one of his favourite films apparently from when he was younger is Braveheart; you know the one with Mel Gibson in.*

Hannah: *Has Raymond got Scottish blood then?*

Fi: *I don't think so; in fact, I am not sure of anything now. Anyway he goes upstairs to wash his hands, I thought, comes down ten minutes later and as usual we sit down for our supper at 8pm. I have already put the children in bed by this time and last night I made a chilli con carne for dinner; it's easy, Hannah, as I make it for the kids and just need to reheat it for our dinner and cook some rice to go with it. By the time I serve the meal in our Mexico-themed dinner bowls, Raymond has already laid the little table in front of the television with our water, serviettes and forks and I sit next to him. All normal. However, when Raymond finishes his chilli, and I haven't finished mine by the way, he presses pause on the film. He takes the fork out from my hand and then wipes my mouth. He pushes me onto the floor.*

Hannah: *Carry on Fi, I am listening and I do care; I sense this is difficult for you.*

Fi: *Well he rolls off my tights and undergarments, sniffs them in a very private place, the gusset actually, and then throws them over his head. He unbuttons his shirt and reveals that he has painted his chest. He must have used the kids' facepaints to do it; his chest was blue with a white cross dissecting the blue, the Scottish flag to be precise. Oh Hannah, it gets worse. He then looks me in the eye and calls me a moron.*

Hannah: *No, he can't have, he must have meant Murron; that's the name of Braveheart's girlfriend that gets killed at the beginning of the film by the evil English.*

Fi: *Ah well, I didn't realise; I suppose that's one thing made a bit better. He then presses play and with that he starts lip-syncing with the film whilst he has intercourse with me and to my astonishment he seems to have timed his climax with the moment Mel Gibson screams "Freedom!" in the battle scene. Oh good Lord, Hannah. Why me? How have I managed to be married, unknowingly, to some sex pervert?*

Hannah: *Did he force himself on you, Fi? Do you feel that he took a liberty or violated you in any way?*

Fi: *Well no, Hannah, because I was feeling rather turned on by watching Mel Gibson in that leathery skirt so there was no problem down there if you know what I mean. He didn't need to force himself.*

Hannah: *You mean you were wet, really moist, it just slipped in, Fi?*

Fi: *Well yes. Oh, Hannah, I am not used to talking like this, about such things on such a personal level. But I am really worried, Hannah. What else might I find out about him? Should I talk to him this evening about it?*

Hannah: *Did he speak to you afterwards or this morning?*

Fi: *Yes, this morning he told me to make sure that the paint came out of his shirt as he wants to wear it for work tomorrow as it is*

*very practical. It is cool and short-sleeved with a handy top pocket
for his whiteboard pen.*

Hannah*: And that was it? No reference to what had happened last
night during supper?*

Fi*: No, nothing, Hannah.*

fLy: So as you can imagine Wallace's name whenever called takes
me into Fi's sitting room that night. Imagine the state of Fi's lady
flaps, if Raymond had plumped for *Gladiator* instead.

I was, and still am, able to disassociate myself from most
stories I overhear. A prime example was when, on one of our
many after-school walks we had ventured out on, Tristan retold
the night that he and Hannah had first met. It corresponded
closely with the story that Hannah had told Fi but the detail
with which Tristan divulged appealed more to my sensory
receptors. He reported back to Wallace how the 'Big-Eared Git'
had sucked the salty peanuts before chewing them and how he
slightly curled his tongue around the orange stub of his cigarette
as he relentlessly dragged the burning ash up toward his mouth.
He described the feel of the tables that were slightly sticky from
carelessly wiped tables and how the varnish on the legs had
bubbled up from the bleach-soaked cloth that was used to clean
them with. He depicted the colour of the dress Hannah was
wearing, comparing it to port mixed with lemonade and how the
amber glow of the car park lights changed the dress's appearance
from burgundy to peach. He meticulously explained how her
hairless, supple and soft mound was like smelling icing sugar
but tasting of fresh sea oysters. He was even able to employ a
quotation from Shakespeare about the scars he still has on his
knees from the tarmac that bit into his skin that night as he
nuzzled, licked and pushed Hannah's clitoris with his tongue: '*He
jests at a scar that never felt a wound*'.

That man had a vocabulary that brought to life a memory
that I so desperately wanted to know and share, but on that walk

22

he didn't explain what it was about Hannah that captured him; that trapped him. I would have to wait for another walk, later that week, to find out what that was.

One evening, again after work and maybe only two days later, the air was still and the temperature was pleasant. It had not rained for two weeks and the ground was hard. The grass was still more green than yellow and the birds still sang; Wallace was his usual attentive and excited self. Hannah and Tristan barely spoke upon Tristan's return from work that evening and once again Tristan employed his baby voice when speaking to Wallace. This infuriated Hannah and she started to shout at Tristan; the voice, in fairness was very annoying but Hannah's reaction was bewildering. She urged him to "Fuck off on a long walk" so Tristan left, myself and Wallace in tow. I, like Tristan, was confused as to why Hannah was in such a mood but as we made our way to the gate at the end of the playing fields, I hoped that I would experience some more aural delight.

Tristan: *Wallace, you must be appalled by her language. I have no idea what kick-started that but in all honesty I have to regularly remind myself of why I ever stayed with Hannah. She is so different now; when I first started dating Hannah I could see that inside of her was this cauldron of fury that I was so attracted to and I wanted to tame it. However, once I had controlled it I wanted to then say goodbye to her like I did with all of my girlfriends but stupidly I made the mistake of meeting her parents. I saw the life that she had and my perception of her changed; she wasn't just someone to have sex with and enjoy superficially; if you like, she was a damaged soul that I couldn't abandon. I remember my reluctance as I approached her front door that Sunday lunchtime. I recall pressing the doorbell and Hannah opening it. She had put on too much make-up and looked like a waxwork figure. Her manner was stilted and she looked tired. I hadn't seen her for three days and had to think back to how I felt about her before the door was opened. She looked as if* she had been sick, the grey under her eyes was still pushing through the thickly spread foundation and her mouth was dry. I followed her into her sitting room. There was a man sitting in a beige armchair. He didn't stand up or welcome me with a cheery handshake and simultaneous slap on the back. He just raised his eyes and said, "So you're Tristan." I had to be polite so I acknowledged him and asked him how he was. He didn't answer. He just carried on looking at me with his hands in his lap. Hannah's mum then rushed into the sitting room followed by her choking floral perfume. She was wearing bright fuchsia-pink lipstick which she had plied over her thin lips and the bottom edges of her two front teeth. "You must be Tristan. I'm Sheila. Well you are every bit as gorgeous as Hannah had described. Now tell me, what has she told you about us?" What a question, Wallace. What should I have said? I wanted to say that Hannah never really spoke of them at all in any context so I just said the first thing that came into my mind and complimented her on the curtains. They were ruched silk, fuchsia-pink like Sheila's lipstick and like her lipstick seemed out of place and egregious. I told her that I thought they really made the room come alive. I cringe to think of it. Throughout the ordeal Hannah barely spoke. But Sheila made up for it; there were no awkward silences as Sheila filled each minute with comment whilst the rest of us ate our Sunday roast. I sat there looking at Sheila, trying to figure her out whilst still looking interested in the monologue that she bored us all with. I was bemused, wondering why I was there; I could not fathom how it was that two deplorable human beings could create Hannah.

Around the room were lots of photographs of Sheila and Stan on various cruises, standing and posing in front of the galleried staircases. On every conceivable flat surface stood porcelain figurines of ladies in voluminous dresses in shades of pink and pearl. I let my eyes wander to the photographs that hung upon the wall directly above Sheila's head. They were all gold-framed images from their wedding day. Stan and Sheila still looked very much as they looked that day. Sheila's hair was short and looked like a spun sugar nest *on her head and Stan had thick black hair with a side parting. Even in the black and white photograph Stan's smile looked slimy and wet whilst Sheila's smile was all teeth and forced. They did not have any bridesmaids but there were people of similar age standing around them with thin ties and ill-fitting hats. I wondered why there were no photographs of Hannah as a baby, or on her first day at school, at Graduation or maybe just on holiday. Even sitting at the lunch table Hannah dissolved into the background whilst Sheila prattled on about something she had read in the Daily Mail newspaper. I kept thinking that Stan would say something, to ask me about what I was studying at University or where I wanted to work when I had graduated that summer. However, the only audible sounds that Stan made were whilst he ate and drank. Before every mouthful of food or sup of wine he would inhale loudly and would then exhale through his nose whilst he chewed. The long nasal hairs would wave like sea grass on a coral reef as his breath whistled through them and in the corners of his mouth little bubbles of gravy foam sat. After Stan had swallowed the unctuous mouthful, his pockmarked tongue would appear and slowly swipe away all of that spitty, frothy juice that had accumulated. He was meticulous in preparing his next forkful and his expression on his face changed from concentration to what appeared to be something sexual as the fork went into his mouth. His hands looked like tacky wax with black, long wiry hairs growing along the lengths of his fingers. He made me feel quite nauseous and uncomfortable.*

One conversation that Sheila was seemingly having with herself was about the time she had used a cheap fake tan before going on a cruise. Sheila had to stay covered up for three days because she was orange. At no point did anyone comment or react to her mindless gabble. It appeared that both Hannah and Stan were quite used to her irrelevant rhetoric.

I started to stare at Hannah's lips as she chewed her food and the way she hooked her hair behind her ears. She sat with a bolt-straight back, regal and majestic in her pose, but her eyes conveyed the anger that grew inside. I wanted to grab her then and there and kiss her till she spewed the words; to free her from the fury and anguish. But instead she controlled herself with slow and measured chewing. I felt suffocated by this middle-class mendacity and I knew that there was a deep-rooted reason for her reserved silence. I found the dynamic of the family very stilted; the way her father was unmoved by his own daughter's silence or his wife's banal conversation; it all made me feel as if I was suffocating and I was longing to get a better grasp of the situation. I can't remember when we left but I was desperate to be by Hannah's side in bed, to try and uncover what secrets she harboured.

The following weekend or maybe the one after that, Hannah and I went up to Holkham in North Norfolk. Pete had offered me his Nan's place, which was in Burnham Overy Staithe, to use over the summer months. You would love it there, Wallace; glorious walks along the creases looking over beautiful marshland and out toward sea. It was somewhere I had always wanted to go since seeing a brochure on Holkham Hall at the library when I was much younger.

Hannah and I must have left home for Norfolk at around five in the morning and had an easy traffic-free drive. After about two hours' driving, Hannah moved her hand over into my lap and she started to rub my cock. As it hardened I had to stop driving because my jeans were getting too tight and I was sensationally cramped. We pulled over into one of the numerous truck stops and with hurried force we managed to get my trousers and boxers down past my knees. The sun was up and there were truckers getting in and getting out of their cabs; chunky men walking around with shaved heads and tartan shirts loosely hanging over their rotund stomachs. I was sitting with my head slightly back, one hand was on the handbrake whilst the other was pushing Hannah's head up and down as I wanted to be sucked so hard. She stopped, sat up and looked me straight in the eye, "Do you want something a little bit dirty; you desperate little fucker?" and with that she slipped her hand under me, past my balls and pushed her index finger up my arse. I was panting in pain and pleasure and all the time she was sucking and gulping and her tongue was strong against me. I came, she swallowed and then she sat up. She repositioned herself so that her back was up against the passenger window, she hitched her skirt up over her hips. She was not wearing any knickers and she rubbed herself between her legs whilst sucking at the fingers of my left hand. In between her increasingly heavy breaths she ordered me to watch her pussy get wetter and wetter. I couldn't help myself but to dive down between her legs and suck the sweet nectar from her as she came.

We carried on with our drive in silence and after another hour or so we arrived at Pete's Nan's place. Hannah and I stepped out of the car; I retrieved our luggage from the boot of the car as she walked casually to the front door. I found the front door keys in the side zip of the black sports bag I had packed and opened the pale blue painted wooden door into the kitchen. In the background the sounds of birds inflated the air with life in an otherwise silent setting. Hannah walked in first and I followed with our cases, pushing the door shut after us. I went through the kitchen, put the bags aside and checked on the contents of the fridge; Pete was right, there was always a bottle of fizz chilling at his Nana's place. I called out for Hannah; she didn't answer. I proceeded into the dining room and then into the sitting room. There she was in her black lacy bra lying back on the white and pink flowery sofa. We had sex and then we fucked and then we made love. I was in love, and, in that moment, I proposed to her. She teased me saying that a way to a man's heart was not through his stomach but through sexual exertion. I laughed. I didn't really think it was that funny but the moment was sweet and I liked the rosy red flush on her chest and glow of her skin. She said that she couldn't believe that marriage was what I truly wanted and that perhaps I should have a rethink when I had a clearer mind. I lied and told her I had been planning to do it that weekend and that moment seemed as good as any as both of us were happy. So she accepted exuberantly and a couple of days later, after a ridiculous amount of sex and champagne, she phoned and told her mum. As she delivered the news I could hear Sheila wailing and crying with joy; Hannah smiled as she listened to the cacophony of noise buzzing down the phone line. Later that day I learned that Sheila was going to throw a party, an engagement party for us. Neither Hannah nor I wanted to have a party, especially seeing as none of our friends would be invited, but we just surrendered to Sheila's want and we arrived three weeks later. The road outside their house was lined with Fords, Vauxhalls and Hondas in varying shades of gold or silver and tentatively we both went in.

I had an idea of what Sheila was like from my first encounter with her at that lunch. However what Hannah and I had to endure next, at the 'party', filled me with a more comprehensive understanding of Sheila, who she was and what she was all about.

It resulted in my complete and total dislike of Hannah's mother.

Stan opened the door to us both and motioned for us to come inside. As Stan turned he said, "Journey good? Traffic ok I trust?" Neither of us answered as we followed Stan into the sitting room. As he opened the door we were confronted with twenty-four sets of false teeth smiling at us and to the right of them, standing in the bay window, was Sheila. She was dressed in what appeared to be a wedding dress. The sun was beaming in and it made Sheila look silhouetted against the garden bushes and trees. There was a hush as all of their friends held their breath, awaiting the reaction from Hannah and me. But true to herself, Hannah did not react; she calmly walked up to her mother and kissed her on both cheeks. Hannah realised that her actions would be scrutinised and dissected by all of the two-faced fossils that surrounded the room. So rather than ask her mother what the hell she was wearing she simply said, "Hello Mum". Stan handed us a glass of cheap Spanish Cava and Sheila raised her glass, "A toast to my treasure and her gorgeous Tristan. I think you will all agree that they make a handsome couple; you can all see how happy they look together and I think I can safely speak on behalf of Stan by saying that when we first met Tristan we were both overjoyed that finally Hannah had met someone we would happily call our 'son'.

When Hannah was about three years old, as some of you here today will remember, we were expecting our second child. Both Stan and I were over the moon thinking that we were going to give Hannah a sibling but at six months pregnant I had to have a termination. Stan and I were distraught. I remember the feeling of loss as if it were yesterday. However, when Hannah called me with the glorious news that Tristan had asked her to marry her it was as if he was the son we were meant to have; he was the soulmate that we had intended for Hannah and one which she so deserves.

Oh how I digress, so back to matters in hand! Now Ted and Margot, Bill and Sue were at our wedding, when I wore this dress for its virgin outing and nothing would make me prouder than to see my Hannah in this dress on her wedding day so I thought how memorable it would be, Hannah, for you to try this dress on today so that your Father and I can, along with our dearest friends, think back to our big day and picture you in months to come. Of course, Hannah, you may want to wear your own dress or trouser suit but for many years I have kept this dress pristine with a dream that you would wear this down the aisle too."

With that Sheila donned a fake smile, took Hannah's hand and walked with her upstairs. I followed the two of them as I could see how utterly awful this was; duplicitous and self-gratifying, the sum of Sheila's parts. As we reached Sheila's bedroom, Sheila turned to me with her lip curled, "Stay out, Tristan." I have never hit a woman, nor ever wanted to until that moment but I stepped back and sat on the floor as I listened to zips being undone and wardrobe doors being opened. Hannah didn't say a word but re-emerged into the 'party' about five minutes later still in the trousers she had arrived in. When Stan looked at her quizzically as she re-entered the lounge, Hannah just said, "Mum is happy."

Soon afterwards Sheila burst into the room and declared, "Well everyone, it seems that Hannah is too big to fit into my dress that I still fit into thirty-five years on! I just never thought of myself as being so slim!"

The gathering recommenced with their drinking and eating of vol-au-vents and smoked salmon on blinis. Sheila's moment had passed, but the memory remains. I couldn't understand how Hannah remained so detached and apparently unperturbed by her mother but this was a part of Hannah that intrigued me and goaded me. Her control seemed superhuman.

We left pretty soon after that performance by Sheila without saying goodbye to anyone. No one there had introduced themselves to us and Stan was unexpectedly chatting to a man of equal age in the corner of the room near the buffet lunch that Sheila had prepared. When their front door shut behind us I truly wished that it was to be the last time Hannah ever had to be involved with her parents. Oh Wallace, you are lucky to be a dog. You are sold as a puppy and given a loving home, never to feel the guilt of your parents or have to ever see them again! Whereas the rest of us damn humans have to bear the weight of failing expectations and tarnish our own character with the brush of parental disappointment.

You see, Wallace, what amazed me about Hannah was that in the time I had known her she had never really talked about her parents, so that day I was given the chance to really see for myself what duplicitous people they were. I never asked her too much about her past because I never wanted her to ask me about mine. However, one weekend after that 'engagement party' we were in the park close to where we lived and having a picnic. It was an honest and charming affair; Hannah, slightly blushing, talking about the wedding and our possible invite lists. We were sitting next to each other as if Siamese twins joined at the hip and we both agreed that our wedding should be a small affair, not only because of the cost involved but we wanted to keep the whole day as personal as possible. We would have to invite Sheila and Stan, her Godparents Trish and Mike, my best mates Pete and Harry but other than that there was no one else that sprung to mind. "What about your mum and dad, Tristan?" So many times, so many times, Wallace, I had managed to stem that conversation, and change the subject but now I just had to answer. I had to say their names and to enlighten Hannah as to why I didn't talk about them or to them. "Ok, Hannah," I said, "seeing as they are now part of today and I know that I can no longer keep you in the dark, let me tell you about Patsy and Nigel Stephens." So I told her, Wallace: "My mum smoked or smokes, I don't know now, but then she smoked about forty cigarettes every day so that she could 'cope'. Her breath smelt of soured milk and coffee and her hair was long and often dirty. She would tie it up into a ponytail that I would watch swish and sway as she walked away from me at school; I was mesmerised by my mum but then I think most boys at the age of six or seven are spellbound by their mothers. At home, though, things were different. She would remind me constantly, even then, that 'these were the best days of my life' and that she had given up her entire life to bring me up and she constantly asked me if I was grateful. I didn't even know what that meant then so I would just nod. She would look at me like I was food that had gone off, milk that had curdled; then she would turn away asking me where she had put her fags. I would help her find them and she would delicately get a cigarette out of the packet and light one, her lips pursed like an asshole around the pale orange butt as she dragged the red ember down the white shaft. I would wonder at night what she would have done had it not been for the cigarettes, saviours as they were. She and Dad would argue all the time and invariably I would hide under my bed along with my comic books. I tried very hard to block out the sound of my dad's anger rolling out of him like boulders cascading down a rock face and my mum wailing in a high-pitched, drilling voice, "I fucking hate you, I fucking hate you!" Mum never seemed to ever say anything else to him when they were arguing and I never knew what it was they were arguing about. There certainly wasn't the quiet after the storm, or the sweet, forgiving lovemaking. Mum would come upstairs sniffing and blowing her nose, dabbing at her eyes. She would come into my room holding a small pile of folded and ironed clothes and put them away in my wardrobe. It was always the way; every single time they argued she would find a reason to come

31

into my room and reiterate, "If it wasn't for you, Tristan, I would have left that prick. But because of you, Tristan, and only you, I am going to stick this out till you are old enough and then I will move out and then we shall see what happens to that shit-sucking bastard. See how the 'Man' copes then." But I didn't want them to stay together. I wanted to have a life like Jake Hemmings had. His mum and dad did stuff with Jake; they did fun things altogether. Mum never did anything with me; nothing, zero, zilch, not even taking me food shopping. She would always leave me at home with my colouring pad and milk. When Dad was home he never played football with me or taught me how to catch. We never watched films together or played games. It was always the same excuse that Dad was too tired and Mum just needed a "fucking break." We rarely sat together to have a meal because Mum and Dad couldn't be anywhere together without arguing and spitting at each other but Sunday lunch was sacred. We would sit around our little pink and white checked Formica kitchen table and eat a roast meat of some sort. When I was about ten years old Dad kept asking me what teams I had made at school that week. Dad knew I could hardly catch or kick a ball let alone score a goal or hit a six in cricket but he liked watching me go red with embarrassment. Once again, around that table, I would reveal that I hadn't made it into a team. It was then that a knot of wire wool would suddenly feel like it was in my tummy and the room would spin. I knew that Dad was being nasty to me and it made me feel terrible and pathetic. Then the same old statement would ultimately come sliding out of my dad's mouth, "You see, Patsy, he takes after you in every way. In my father's day he would be considered perfect cannon fodder. There isn't a sporting bone in his faggot-arsed little body." But Mum never stuck up for me; she didn't chide him for being so horrible to me. She would get upset that I had been likened to her as if it was some terrible slur on her character and start stabbing at her roast potatoes.

It didn't stop there either, if Dad was driving me to school in the car he never used to speak to me. He would just have the radio *on. I would get out of the car once we had arrived at school and with great speed, he would then drive off. But if Mum had been in the car too then it was a totally different story. He would turn on me as soon as we had started our journey to school, "Try and come home today having made the football team, the basketball team, the rugby team, the netball team, the knitting team, for Christ's sake, any team!"*

But on one occasion whilst driving to school things became much worse for me. I was about eleven or twelve years old and Dad and Mum were in the car, Dad behind the wheel, Mum in the passenger seat. As usual he had on his black rubbery driving shoes. On the radio was a Beatles song that to begin with Dad was humming along to. Mum decided to turn off the radio and we sat in silence for about two minutes of the journey. This was when Mum said, "So, Nigel, what words of wisdom are going come out of your mouth today?; you know the type of words that will inspire your son to work hard so that he can follow in his father's really mega-successful footsteps? Or are you going to do what you usually do on our trips to school; call him a poof and me a hooker?" With that Dad slammed on the brakes and with a stony expression stared out of the windscreen. All the cars started to back up behind us and after about five minutes they all started to sound their horns. Stupidly I said, "Dad they are hooting you. Can we drive on to school please?" With that Dad turned in his seat to look at me sitting in the back of the car and said, "Why don't you take your grubby little hands out of your little man's lap and get out of the car and tell them all to piss off? Tell the tosser in the car behind to stop sounding his horn. Go on! Go on!" Dad's face was going purple and where he was shouting at me so much spit had flown out of his mouth, looking like small smashed pieces of ice on his chin. So I got out of the car and walked towards the car behind. All the time I could hear that he was still shouting so I had to prove to him that I had balls. As I approached the red Volvo estate car behind Dad drove off, leaving me in the middle of the junction without my school bag or my school coat. So I had to walk to school. I was very late into school which meant detention; I had no school bag which meant detention and I had no school coat which also meant detention. And as a result I was in detention for two weeks with Miss Tupturn. She was probably the first person I ever had a crush on. She would sit at the front of the classroom behind the teacher's desk in front of the blackboard and tell all of us in detention to remain in total silence. She would then hand out our relevant detention pieces. Sometimes she would bend down to pick up a pencil or a rubber that had been purposefully knocked from our desks and I would be able to catch a glimpse of her navy blue bra and the tops of her china white breasts as her low-cut blouse billowed. I could easily see the little blue veins that would just trace below her skin, silently creeping over the fleshy bosoms. Detention was no longer the punishment I most feared; I loved it. I loved the peace and quiet; the rhythmical ticking of the white and black clock that sat above the classroom door. I loved watching Miss Tupturn with the evening sun catching her hair so that her profile was definite and chiselled. I liked the smell of the revolving floor-cleaning machines and polish that the evening cleaners used on the corridors, the repetitive drone of the brushes buffing the vinyl to almost mirror-like quality. Mum would come and pick me up from the classroom where detention had been held; she would have to sign a piece of paper or register to say that I was back in her custody and I started to hope that Mum wouldn't turn up. I just wanted to spend more time with Miss Tupturn and her creamy silk shirts with loose-fitting knitted jumpers that would allow me a glance of the finer things in life that women offer.

There was one truly awful day, when I went into school, I could barely hold my tears in. On the way to school Dad was arguing with Mum about the same things, I think, again, and a dog ran out from nowhere in front of the car. Mum screamed at Dad to "Stop!" but Dad instead of stopping, accelerated and hit the dog. As the car hit the dog, it flew up into the air and disappeared into the low hedge at the side of the road. It was only then Dad stopped the car. But rather than get out of the car to see if the dog was ok he just grabbed

Mum's face in his left hand and pulled her face close to his face. He shouted, "Don't you ever tell me what to fucking do again! You hear?" Mum's face was covered in his blobby spit and very calmly she just reached into the glove box and pulled out the wet wipes and rubbed her face clean. Mum and Dad were still shouting at each other as we parked in the school car park. I opened the door and slid out of the car without saying a word and walked as fast as I could into school. Miss Tupturn was at the same time coming out of the staffroom when I near bumped into her. As I apologised she looked at me and asked if I was ok. With that I just broke down in tears, sobbing and sniffing, and very quietly she took me by the hand into the Resources Room. She crouched down so that her raw green eyes were level with mine, she told me that it was ok to cry and that she would listen if I wanted to talk to her. I didn't say anything because I was so horrified about what had just happened and that neither my dad nor my mum went to see if the dog was ok and even more so, I was disgusted with myself. Why didn't I even try to get out of the car and check on the dog? I think I was worried that Dad would have driven off and left me there like last time but even so I couldn't tell Miss Tupturn any of this because I never wanted her to think of me as I thought of myself then.

When Mum collected me that afternoon from school we went home by bus. I asked why we were going home by bus and she told me that where Dad had hit the dog it had dented the car so it had gone to the repairer's to be fixed. I asked if the dog had been fixed too and then I started to cry as I could only imagine how badly the dog was hurt. Mum just told me to "Shut the fuck up".

There were other instances which I could have shared that added to my contempt for my parents but I felt exhausted and sad. I explained that after many, many months of contemplation I realised that I could no longer carry the burden of guilt and unhappiness that resulted from their actions. So I decided at the age of seventeen that I would get good school grades and get away, out of my home, away from my parents and start my life again at University.

35

At first I didn't know what I could possibly study at Uni but Miss Tupturn helped me realise that English was one of my passions and that I was rather good at it. It was because of her that my life changed for the better. I didn't even tell Mum or Dad about wanting to go to University; they never asked. So even when I was accepted at Uni I didn't say a thing; I was eighteen years old when I left for University and considered myself parentless. I just left them a note in my room saying that they could rent out my room if they wanted as I wouldn't ever be coming back. And to this day I have not even tried to contact them. The only thing they taught me was how I don't want to be when I am a parent and what I will not expose my children to.

3

Tristan: *I remember looking at Hannah after I had divulged this brief insight to my life as it had been and her face was expressionless. I knew that after telling someone about my parents and what I did there would be this silence but I had always expected there to be a suggestion of rebuilding bridges. But Hannah just sat quietly. I then made the mistake, Wallace, of asking her what the story was with her and her parents; if I had known what she would tell me, Wallace, I wouldn't have asked. I expected Hannah to affirm my assumption that they argued for most of their life as a family and now the father had given up talking to her or her mum. But instead of this she told me about them and the chasm of dislike I had for them grew.*

Apparently Sheila had taken Hannah into town to go and get her ears pierced as a belated birthday treat. Hannah had wanted them done before the party that she was having at home but Sheila had become so involved with cake-making and cleaning that the morning of the party had disappeared, time had run out. Her party came and went and so the following day Hannah had her ears pierced. Hannah didn't mind the day's delay because it meant that she would have yet another thing to look forward to. After having her ears pierced she wanted to spend the day looking at herself in

37

*her mirror and trying out different hairstyles. She was really excited;
she would be one of the first girls in the class to have genuine pierced
earrings.*

*When Hannah and her mum arrived home from having the
small gold balls punctured through her soft young earlobes, she ran
through the house calling out, "Dad! Dad!" Hannah was desperate
to show her dad that she had done it, to tell her dad that it had not
hurt and that they didn't have to queue! But there was no answer
from anywhere in the house so Hannah ran into the kitchen and saw
that the back door was open. She charged into the garden towards the
shed, or 'The Office' as Stan liked to call it. Without knocking she
went into the wooden cabin and standing with his back to the door
was her dad. His dark grey velvet corduroy trousers were hanging off
a hook to the right of Stan's desk and his white Y-fronts were pulled
tight around his ankles as he stood with his legs slightly apart. The
Y-fronts were just above the backs of his brown synthetic leather
shoes which squeaked as Stan, with a startle, turned around. In his
right hand was Stan's erect penis. Hannah had no idea what it was.
Her mother and father were always very reserved and never openly
discussed or alluded to differences between men and women. They
had even booked Hannah a dentist appointment that clashed with
the class on Sexual Education that the school had written to the
parents about. Very soon after Hannah had entered, Sheila came
in. She took one look at the situation and tried to push Hannah
out of the shed. In trying to do so Sheila fell and Stan rushed over
to pick Sheila up leaving Hannah to go over to her dad's desk and
take a closer look. There laid out were the freshly developed pictures
of all of Hannah's friends. Some of the photos had been taken at
her birthday party and some were from before. But oddly none of the
photographs had heads on. The photos had either all been cut with
a pair of scissors or the actual photo taken omitted the head. The
focus of the pictures was varied; there were images of little pubescent
breasts and their swollen, squishy nipples through brightly coloured,
thin vest tops; or there were close-ups taken of her friends sitting*

cross-legged in skirts in front of the television watching the film on television, the focal point on their little pastel-coloured panties. There were enlargements of one particular girl who was doing handstands. Her skirt had fallen to reveal her underwear that was caught in between her buttocks. There was another enlargement of a friend from Nigeria called Adora; the image was zoomed in on her lips as she sucked on a strawberry fruit rocket ice lolly. Hannah wasn't able to digest what it all meant or why her dad had taken such odd photographs, so she turned to walk out. And do you know what, Wallace, that heinous woman, her own mother, reached out and grabbed Hannah by the arm warning Hannah not to mutter a word to anyone about what she had seen, stating that it was no one's business, least of all Hannah's. What her father did in his own free time was of no concern to anyone.

I held Hannah's hand and as no more words came I cuddled her very tightly. Now I knew why I had never met any of Hannah's friends and why her stories of growing up were always void of friendships or fun. How was I going to ever look at Sheila and Stan again without betraying my complete contempt for them? But like Hannah I couldn't comment or pass judgement audibly; I had to follow her lead as I was powerless to change the past but had our future together to mould, to shape, to create. Hannah turned to me and said, "You see now, Tristan, we have two negatives and from this we can have our positive together." It was as if she had read my mind.

fLy: I could tell from Tristan's eyes that Tristan had enjoyed his walk with Wallace and me; a therapy session of sorts I suppose. Wallace always looked happy after a walk which seemed to aggravate Hannah, her body language would become far more brittle whenever they would return. In months gone by she used to ask how the walk was or where they had gone but increasingly she would say, "Don't tell me – you had a great walk and Wallace met up with Digby and they both had a good runaround." Tristan would look down at Wallace and raise his eyebrows. He would walk off to the inner hall and hang Wallace's well-worn brown leather lead and harness over the brass clothes pegs. Next he would take off his all-weather coat and hang it on the same peg. Wallace would follow Tristan until the lead had been put back and only then would he go and sit with Hannah. As ever, Tristan disappeared into the study.

The study room was pale yellow with thick pale cream curtains that had crudely drawn elephants on them. It had been the nursery to the family that used to live here before Hannah and Tristan had moved in. But since Tristan and Hannah as yet had been unsuccessful in getting pregnant Tristan had moved his computer, filing cabinets, bookshelves and telephone out of the sitting room into that room and renamed it 'His Study'. Before he had given that small box room a purpose it existed like an itch that no one wanted to scratch. He hoped that by using the room in a positive way it would take the pressure off getting pregnant and may help in some subconscious way to them both becoming parents. It was a good-sized room for a child; easily big enough for a single bed and small desk; Tristan had even seen some children's beds that had cupboards with a small seating area underneath them. But as an office or a study it was just big enough for his blue high-backed swivel office chair and solid oak desk which had plenty of table space for marking homework and stacking printed worksheets. On his desk he had a mug which Sheila and Stan had bought him for Christmas, which Sheila thought was "a bit of a hoot" because when you filled the mug with hot water the clothes on the buxom brunette would disappear revealing a red pair of lacy knickers and massive boobs which looked like udders accessorised with great purple-coloured nipples. It was Stan's idea to put a silk pair of lace G-string knickers inside the mug. Tristan and Hannah felt uncomfortable with the gift so the knickers were binned and the mug used as a pen pot.

After the walk with Wallace, Tristan wasn't in any mood to

start marking homework or preparing the printouts for next week's planned lessons so he sat just staring down at one file that he opened. The phone started to ring but Tristan carried on looking at the file. Neither Hannah nor Tristan answered the phone so it flicked to answerphone.

Fi: *Hi Hannah, hi Tristan, hi Wallace. It's Fi. Raymond has suggested that we have a barbecue on Sunday and invite a couple of friends. I just wondered if you three would like to join us. If you can come and join us perhaps you could bring a couple of bottles of wine and a salad? Let me know. Hope all is well. Bye for now!*

fLy: Tristan scribbled the message from Fi on a Post-it note and then deleted the message from the machine.

Eventually Sunday comes around and the four of us make our way out of the house toward Raymond and Fi's place. We exit our house via the front door and pass the low privet hedge, along the single cement-slab pathway down toward the road that leads to the gymnasium and over the cricket fields to Raymond and Fi's house. As we approach I smell the delightful aroma of raw meat and olive oil, charcoal drenched in lighter fuel being carried on the thermals. It is a lovely day, very sunny and warm.

That morning Hannah had spent an age deciding what to wear whilst Tristan was out walking Wallace. She remembered that at the last barbecue Raymond had insisted that everyone play Musical Sit-Ups, a game that involved all the adults doing sit-ups and freezing in whichever position you were in and holding it until the music started again. I used to watch Raymond closely, spotting his little raise of eyebrows to signal to Fi when to press 'play' again.

Fi was never allowed to join in any of Raymond's games; she had to be the one controlling the portable stereo hitting the 'pause' and then 'play' button. Raymond loved playing any game where he thought he had a good chance of winning and so at every social occasion Hannah had to be mindful of her choice of clothing.

She opted for jean shorts, white T-shirt, white lacy bra (that way her nipples could still be seen reacting to the temperature), red toenails and flip-flops.

We were all met at the front door by one of Fi's children, and were shown through to the back garden; the child then disappeared upstairs without any form of communication to either parents or to us. We were the first set of friends to arrive and Raymond opened a beer for Tristan and suggested that Hannah go find Fi in the kitchen and grab a drink inside. Wallace had already disappeared as soon as we arrived, galloping down the hallway then up the stairs to the children's bedroom. So it was just me, Tristan and Raymond hanging out around the coals.

Tristan: *Buddy! How goes it?*

Raymond: *Not bad mate. You're looking fit. You been bench-pressing recently? How many can you do? What weights can you move?*

Tristan: *No actually I just did a few thousand sit-ups with a relaxing couple hundred press-ups for fun just before coming, in case you had organised one of your competitions.*

Raymond: *You remember our last barbecue! I said to Fi that I should get a game going this time but she said that it was just too embarrassing, especially for Bruno with his IBS, he still suffers with terrible wind.*

fLy: With this I took my cue to disappear. They were going over old ground and the atmosphere was not relaxed. As I flew away both men were standing mirror image of each other: folded arms, legs astride, beer in hand.

I found Hannah and Fi in the kitchen chopping up lettuce, opening tins of precooked lentils, chickpeas and baked beans, discussing nipple cups and how sweaty they get. I looked at Fi and then understood why the conversation had started. She was wearing big Jackie Onassis sunglasses in her hair (where else?), a maxi dress which seemed to have a type of wide, gathered elastic that went round her breasts with a Moroccan print, and of course, not forgetting the ever-present eye bogey. She had apparently upset Raymond by wearing this dress because he didn't like the fact that if they were to play a game or if she had to rush upstairs there would be the possibility of her boobs popping out. In order to put his mind at rest, she had managed to find her mother's old swimming costume from the 60s which had nipple cups sewn into the bra area of the swimsuit. She cut them out and had cleverly been able to adhere these plastic cones to her two fat boobies by mere sweaty suction. Genius!

Hannah: *I have been meaning to call round, Fi, to ask how things have been since the Braveheart incident and I am sorry that I haven't. Are things all right now, sorted out?*

Fi: *In an odd way things are more exciting, Hannah. Raymond has really embraced this role-playing aspect to our lovemaking. He has identified that his true self stems from an era past so we are experimenting. Last night for example Raymond used his camouflage paints and made us both look like muddied cavemen. I wasn't allowed to talk but instead Raymond insisted that I grunt and point as if I were a cavewoman. I backcombed my hair to give it messy volume and he improvised brilliantly by using his Father's old snooker cue to pound up and down instead of a spear when he was getting excited.*

fLy: Hannah was struck dumb and before an awkward silence befell the kitchen the doorbell rang. Fi rushed out to the hall, pulled aside the net curtains that adorned the window to see who it was, wiped her hands and trotted out to open the front door. A few moments later Fi reappeared in the kitchen.

Fi: *Justin and Peter are here. I had hoped they would arrive late. Peter usually does.*
Hannah: *Who are they?*

Fi: *Peter is Raymond's brother and Justin is his flatmate.*

Hannah: *Flatmate?*

Fi: *Yes, the two of them are inseparable. It is nice to think that Peter has Justin; he has been single for so many years that it is a relief to think of Peter without worrying whether or not he is lonely. There have been numerous Christmasses where Raymond and I have both reached out to him, to get him to join us, but he always declines saying that he would rather be in Brighton. So we have always taken this on board but last year we invited him again and he asked if he could bring his friend Justin with him. Justin really is so nice; he is such a good pianist too. He plays a lot of Richard Clayderman pieces which may not be to everyone's taste but after a big Christmas lunch there is nothing better than 'Ballade Pour Adeline'. Just fits the bill.*

Hannah: *Do you think he will play the piano today?*

Fi: *I hope so; Justin sings too so maybe he will do a few of his Elvis numbers. That would really get the barbecue going.*

fLy: Hannah started putting crisps into various bowls whilst Fi started to load up the tray with plates and cutlery. The doorbell sounded again but this time someone else opens the door. I take this opportunity to go and see what Wallace is up to; I can't imagine there will be much to report on but it is better than watching Hannah scrutinise the calorie and fat content on all the packets that she empties into the decorative bowls. I fLy up the stairs towards the bedroom; the door is ajar so I zoom in. Wallace, with a kid either side of him, is watching a horror movie so I leave them to it and get myself outside. Unsurprisingly, the men are all huddled around the barbecue, Raymond poking and prodding the charcoals, which are now starting to turn white, showing that he is the chief caveman in this little scenario.

A newly arrived couple stroll out and up onto the lawn. She is of average everything apart from her enormous pudendum which gives the appearance that she is smuggling a tortoise shell down the front of her tight beige trousers. She walks over to Raymond with arms outstretched ready for an insincere welcoming hug. Raymond doesn't reciprocate in warmth but instead points and directs her to the kitchen to find the 'girls'. A large smile covers his face as he passes a bottle of beer to the man that arrived with the Tortoise Shell Smuggler (TSS).

> **Bruno**: *Quick word with you gents whilst she has popped inside. Please don't mention the last barbecue to her. I find it all very embarrassing and I am trying desperately to keep my IBS private. It doesn't paint the sexiest of profiles.*
> **Peter**: *What happened last time, buddy?*
> **Bruno**: *Not much to tell but in brief your brother had come up with a new game which involved sit-ups to intermittent music. It seemed that every time the chorus boomed out 'Push it Good', I broke wind. I had been eating foods that I had been told not to, so I am to partly blame, but it was not only the sound that scuppered things but also the smell. It was one of those situations where no amount of air freshener would have helped. I lost the game needless to say and was the brunt of most of the jokes for most of the afternoon.*

fLy: The male group seemed to segregate into subsections after a short while and I flitted in between the ensuing conversations; Justin and Peter talking to each other about getting a new tattoo, whilst Bruno is regaling a tale of when he went punting in Cambridge to Raymond. In a loud, squawky manner TSS re-emerges with a large glass of white wine and Raymond collars her to tell her about different cuts of steak that he has and their suitability for cooking over fire. Fi is still in the kitchen faffing and I am finding the event rather dull; time is moving slowly. I have no idea as to how many minutes have passed when I realise that neither Hannah nor Tristan are outside. With a zing in my wings I fLy around the house to try and find them. I zoom along the corridor again but this time I carry on past the sitting room and towards the downstairs loo. The door is shut, but luckily being a fLy I can carefully pass through the keyhole. And there they are, doing it doggy style. I have no idea what triggered this impulsive show of affection but there Tristan is, banging into Hannah, grabbing her hips and pulling her onto him. Hannah has one arm down supporting her and the other arm is outstretched in front of her against the wall, absorbing some of the impact. As Hannah tries to muffle her exhalations, Tristan starts to groan; the groan turns to decipherable sounds and a single clear word comes out through his clenched teeth as he ejaculates.

Tristan: *Sasha!*

fLy: Hannah is understandably bemused and Tristan insists that he was only thinking about Hannah and how beautiful she is. Hannah says that they should just go outside and try and enjoy the rest of the afternoon; they can chat later on when she is pissed in the privacy of their own home.

What Tristan had just done in such an intimate moment had confirmed her darkest fears. Tristan, in order to try and abate further discussion, held her very tight and kept telling her that he loved her and had never been unfaithful to her. Hannah said nothing. I could see that Tristan felt contrite; his eyes changed shape and his eyebrows furrowed.

They both re-entered the party, each carrying large trays covered with dips and crisps, olives and salamis. The barbecue was starting to chug out a fair bit of smoke so I settled on the table that TSS was standing by. She was discussing her tattoo, which she regretted getting the day after the cling film came off, with Peter and Justin. Fi then staggered over holding an even larger tray of various types of bread and salads, mustards, ketchup and balsamic vinegar. Raymond made his way over to the table from the barbecue with a plate full of medium rare steaks, slightly charred fat, stubby sausages and burnt corn on the cobs.

Raymond: *Ok folks, dig in! You will need your strength so no holding back. Fi, go and holler to Francis and Lesley that grub is up!*

fLy: The five men stood round the table with their legs slightly apart as they tucked into steaks in baps and sausages in rolls. The three women sat at the table, Hannah with her plate piled high with lettuce, Fi with her burnt corn on the cob and sausage and TSS with a steak. Patiently they took their turn in smothering their food with balsamic vinegar.

Justin: *Ladies, I notice you all have oodles of balsamic vinegar on your food. Why? Is there a secret something you are not sharing?*
Fi: *Well yes, it's a great anti-ageing, anti-cellulite superfood. Margot from Pilates told me. She was a dietician to many of the household names, celebs if you like. It's meant to be an aphrodisiac too. The Romans used it hundreds of years ago for just that reason.*
Justin: *Did you hear that, Peter? Best you have a try. I could get lucky, girls!*

fLy: There was a hush as the men stopped chewing and the women ceased cutting. The penny had finally dropped about Peter and Justin's relationship. Justin unfortunately continued, seemingly unaware of the change in atmosphere.

Justin: *I might even get to shout "Just in Peter."*

fLy: As the silence continued, he continued.

Justin: *I beat you all to it! The amount of times Peter and I have had to feign laughter at that quip. In fairness though every boyfriend of mine has had to endure the 'Just in' joke so at least it is still relatively new to Peter; old as nanny's knickers to me.*
Tristan: *As a friend of mine once said, "The path of true love never did run smooth."*

47

Raymond: *What a time to quote bloody Shakespeare, Tristan.*

Bruno: *What sort of English teacher are you, Tristan? Shakespeare taken totally out of context and what's more, calling Shakespeare your friend. How bloody pompous you are; you should have been a bloody politician!*

Hannah: *God save us all from another conversation revolving around Shakespeare. Ladies, I am going in to grab another glass of white. I can take a few empties with me and refill them; anyone?*

Fi: *I'll come in with you, Hannah, with some of the dirty plates.*

fLy: Fi went over to Raymond, hitching up her elasticated maxi dress as she walked toward him. Raymond shoved his plate of half-eaten sausage in a roll at her and gestured to her to take away the dirty raw meat plate that sat to the left of the barbecue. I could see the look that exchanged between them; Raymond, visibly uneasy, shuffled from foot to foot. Justin complimented Raymond on his cooking and said that usually people burn the sausages at barbecues but his were cooked to perfection. Raymond smiled, accepting the compliment but then Justin went and ruined it by saying, "Obviously you know how to treat a quality sausage Raymond; just like your brother!"

Fi grabbed the rest of the plates and disappeared into the house. Raymond turned his attention to gulping beer and scraping at the burnt morsels of meat that clung to the grill with a wire brush on a long wooden handle.

Fi: *Oh Hannah, oh Hannah, we had no idea! Raymond looks like he is in shock and he has just finished his third beer! I don't think I have ever seen him drink more than two and that was on our wedding day. He will be devastated; how will he cope? I mean it's ruined the party; my poor Raymond looks so deflated.*

Hannah: *Well why not tell him to do one of his competitions? He invariably wins and that will bolster him through to this evening.*

Fi: *That's a good idea, Hannah; I told him not to bother as last* *year was just too much but I think we could all do with something else to focus on.*

fLy: So they both left the washing-up and made their way out to the garden. As they reappeared into the garden they were met with the vision of Justin and Peter competing against Raymond and TSS in a wheelbarrow race. Raymond was the barrow and was shouting at TSS to run faster, to get into it. But it was of little effect because Justin and Peter just powered ahead and 'wheeled' across the finishing line that had been made by using the table place mats.

> **Justin**: *Oh Peter! We won, I thought you said your brother was unbeatable; but then we are used to it. You know, you behind and pushing like mad! Not a fair competition in my eyes, Raymond. Another one? A rematch? Tristan and Bruno, what about you two? We could do 'winners stay on' game?*
> **Raymond**: *No, I think we should have a drinking game.*
> **Fi**: *You see, Hannah; it's all going wrong. Raymond doesn't know what he is saying.*
> **Raymond**: *What about it, Peter, Justin? We could time each other necking pints.*

fLy: After about ten minutes Raymond was getting more visibly drunk and shouted that the only game to play at a time like this was 'Twister to Music'. No one had ever heard of this before and no one knew how to play but assumed that Raymond would dispense the 'How to Play Twister to Music Rules'. He disappeared inside the house and re-emerged with two children, one dog and a stereo. He loaded the CD into the player and out boomed *The Best Ever Party Songs Ever 2* and Raymond unfolded the large white plastic mat with its large coloured dots. Raymond ordered Fi to be in charge of the music, explaining to all that she couldn't take part in the game because her dress wouldn't allow it. He also told everyone that there were no rules per se and that when Fi stopped the music you had to find a different coloured spot for a different body part and you were 'out' if you collapsed. Fi didn't seem bothered by her exclusion from taking part in the actual game but looked decidedly chuffed to be given such an important role in the scenario with the stereo, even though that was always her job.

As the adults and kids became more involved and more tangled so the laughter grew. Raymond was giggling so hard, he produced an uncontrollable amount of drool. When Hannah could no longer hold her position on her three spots, she was out and Bruno took her place, and then TSS thought she had pulled a muscle in her arm so in stepped Tristan to join in with the game.

After a further five minutes or so of laughter and stretching and bending, the inevitable Bruno-fart stopped proceedings. Raymond was too close to Bruno's arse, mindlessly laughing open-mouthed. But as predicted in such athletic games, Bruno let rip. Raymond at the same moment was breathing in, which resulted in most of Bruno's gassy poo particles filling Raymond's open mouth and lungs. Raymond stood up whilst retching and declared that he was the champion and that this win was of far greater standing than the unfair wheelbarrow race.

On the way back home Hannah and Tristan were laughing so much, trying to imagine what the fart would have tasted like; they were behaving in the same way as ten-year-olds do. They walked arm in arm, giddy with joy whilst Wallace trotted by Tristan's heel and I sat quietly on Hannah's shoulder.

4

fLy: Upon returning home, I decided to go back to Camp Raymond (unintentional play on words there) because I wanted to know what Raymond would be saying to his gay guests and then finally to Fi. Bruno and TSS were leaving as I arrived. Fi gave them both one of her loose-lip kisses goodbye and Bruno was apologising to Raymond who was shifting from one leg to the other as he waved goodbye. As they drove off down the long drive that weaved its way around the school campus, Raymond ran in and was sick. Fi looked very worried but busied herself in the high-ceilinged kitchen. As the kitchen sink slowly filled with warm soapy water, Fi went out to the barbecue and collected the cast-iron grids. She carried them carefully inside so as not to mark her dress and immersed them in the bubbly, lemon-scented water and gently, ineffectually, she scrubbed them. Raymond appeared and asked where Justin and Peter were. To the best of her knowledge they hadn't yet left but she wasn't sure whether they were hiding in the garden or in the house. Raymond went out of the kitchen and then turned back to Fi, taking her by the hand to go. They both peered out of the kitchen window to see if they could catch a glimpse of them in the garden; it was still just light and the sky was a dusky blue with highlighted lines of pink, white and gold etched into horizon. There was no sign of them. Fi remarked on Raymond's sweaty hands. Ignoring her comment, Raymond led Fi into the sitting room to see if Peter and Justin were there. As Raymond walked in Peter put one of Fi's fashion magazines down and was just about to speak when Raymond interjected before Peter's words made any discernible progress.

Raymond: *So, Peter, you have to tell me what the hell is going on. For years at school I stood up for you; I stood up to Miles Jackson and Andre Cathrow telling them that you weren't gay and to leave you alone. I suffered and I threw punches trying to stop their bullying. I promised Dad that you had a girlfriend, even though you didn't, to reassure him because you promised me that you weren't gay. Now I find out it was all a lie. I don't care that you are gay, I never would have but I made promises and believed you and now it is all so apparent that it was all a sham. I don't enjoy gay conversation or the snide remarks angled to make all those around them feel awkward; maybe the gay people in your surroundings in Brighton do enjoy this banter but I don't, it is crass! I need you to tell me why or when or what made you decide that you could make a mockery of my concern, Fi's concern, when you were 'on your own' in Brighton.*

Peter: *Concern?*

Raymond: *Our concern was such that Fi and I have been actively looking at our finances to get a one-bedroom flat so that you could move up, nearer to us, to negate your feeling of loneliness. A loneliness that you have never expressed but one we had imagined; you in Brighton without a proper family around you. And it is not just that. I feel betrayed, Peter. Why didn't you just tell me? I didn't need your friend Justin to make the various remarks this afternoon; I felt I was being tested or that my nose was being rubbed in it. I don't care about sexuality; I don't care about what people think but I do mind about being made a fool of. I would never have suggested the 'Wheelbarrow Race' had I known; Justin was right, you did have an unfair advantage. And that is another issue in itself, Peter.*

But sportsmanship is not what I am aggrieved about most right now. Did you intentionally let me stand in the firing line, defending you when we were younger, trying to stop you getting kicked and spat at, or were you confused? And before you try to spin me any lines, remember that I love you and that you are not unique; lots of people are gay, lots of people come out, lots of people have to experience all the same issues of acceptance of themselves and from others.

Peter: *Ok, Raymond. I have tried to make sense of it all for many years; my confusion; my dishonesty primarily to myself. Even after my first homosexual experience I still didn't get 'it'; or give 'it' consideration. The first person I ever kissed, male or female, was Mr Knightley the sports teacher. I was the last one in the changing room after swimming and he asked me if I was wearing the correct briefs. I must have been about twelve years old. I could have answered straight away that they were my own Y-fronts but I wanted Mr Knightley's attention. I liked it when he spoke to me, I felt as if Mr Knightley cared for me. He walked over to me and ran his finger around the band of my Y-fronts and then folded the elastic down so that he could clearly see my name sewn into the back of them. All the time I was begging the Lord that I didn't get an erection as I had been dreaming of him so often; but I did. Mr Knightley saw it and took both of my hands into his right hand and led me into the small office in the corner of the changing room. The room, as always, smelt of damp hockey kit and chlorine but I was so exhilarated. He let go of my hands as he quietly shut the door behind us. He sat down on his grey swivel teacher's chair and brought me toward him. I was standing with his knees either side of my thighs. Very gently he closed his knees around me so that I could feel them against my skin. He took his left hand and cupped my chin, he moved my face up so that I was looking straight into his amber eyes. With the most tender of movements he drew my lips toward him so that they were touching his lips, only just, but they were. I pushed my tongue into his mouth, Raymond, and he taught me how to kiss. I didn't think I was gay; I didn't know what I was. All I knew was that I had lived part of* *my dream; I dreamt about Mr Knightley, nightly. I dreamt about him in his tight Speedos at swimming or in the communal showers afterwards. But I put the dream to the back of mind as being fantasy and not reality. None of my friends ever talked about their dreams, their actual dreams, but would talk about having 'wet' dreams and how embarrassing it was that they had to strip the sheets off of their beds before school, putting them into the washing machine without their mums noticing. I don't think it ever crossed my mind that they would be dreaming anything different to that which I was. I have no clue, Raymond, as to why Miles or Andre kept attacking me verbally and why you decided to attack them physically; I tried to stay out of it. I had friends at school, Raymond. I wasn't a loner and their foul mouths didn't upset me; but you couldn't stand it. So don't stand there like some hero saying that you defended me. You didn't. I didn't need defending. I could cope with their gibes and their gossiping. I could have coped with Dad asking me if I was gay. But what I couldn't cope with was you and your never-ending war trying to stop people from saying I was gay.*

I remember Dad asking you why you had a bruise across your cheek and you said that Marcus Bloom had kicked a football into your face during practice and then Dad put an ice pack on it. Why didn't you tell the truth, Raymond? Why didn't you say that Miles had kicked you whilst you lay on the floor? Why didn't you say that Andre had grabbed your ankles as you were running away from him; that you had fallen and you started to cry? It was because you were embarrassed for falling down, for running away from them and of me, so don't stand there saying you don't care about sexuality, whether I am gay or not.

I have lived the past eight years of my life in Brighton, on my own and happy. You have superimposed your feelings on to mine again. Why should you think that I am lonely or that I should tell you I am gay? I have met someone called Justin and I am happy in myself with him. It doesn't mean that I won't meet someone called Justine and be happy with her. This is just how I am, how I exist

54

right now. The only time my sexuality should concern anyone is if they wish to be a part of my adult, sexual life. Otherwise I am Peter, just like you are Raymond; what about you, Raymond? What were you fighting against? Being tarred with the same 'gay' brush?

Raymond: *I am not gay, Peter. Fi can testify to that! I have never dreamt about men; the only time I dream about men is when I am dreaming about being in combat, with oil paint and camouflage. I have never engaged in any form of male sexual contact and I never consider a man to be attractive; sometimes there are men in literature or on screen that I would aspire to be but I am not gay. I only fought with Miles and Andre because I loved you and I didn't like the words they used to dismiss you, to disrespect you; their words were demeaning not just to you but to Mum, Dad and me. There you were, able to cast off their innuendos and their belittlement, and there I was incensed by their lack of human kindness. You are my little brother and I always wanted to protect you. This evening I see that it was all in vain. Why didn't you ever tell me to stop? Why didn't you ever say to me that you didn't mind their derision of you? Why did you let me take the hits and the bruises? Why didn't you ever turn around to me and say thank you? What about Dad, did he ever cross your mind, or Mum?*

Peter: *The reason I didn't say 'Thank you' was because everything you did 'in my defence' was done in your defence. I never once came to you crying and Dad never once came to me airing his beliefs. He went to you, as he did with everything. When Mum died he asked you where we should scatter her ashes. He never asked me. When Mum was ill in hospital, he took you, not me, to say goodbye. So when you ask me why I didn't ask you or why I didn't say thank you, it is because I never mattered; to you or to Dad.*

Raymond: *That is not true! All Dad was trying to do was to shield you from the reality of cancer. Trust you to see yourself as the bloody victim! Yes, he did ask me where to scatter the ashes and not you, but you were only eight years old, Peter. There weren't the advisors and the help centres there are now for how to cope with the horrors of* *cancer; it was just him and his squadron leader to refer to. It wasn't that you didn't matter, it was because you did matter to him that he didn't take you to see Mum in hospital or about where Mum's ashes should be put or, about your sexuality! I never told him what was happening to you at school because I didn't need to. Some of the other parents told him about Andre and Miles and Dad asked me to look out for you; it would be what Mum would have wanted me to do, so he said. All of your life you have never accepted that perhaps you were happy because of the loyalty, support and love you had from Dad and me. Why can't you just acknowledge that and then apologise for not telling me that you and Justin were a couple? Trust me, if I was coming to a party you were holding and I was bringing a friend, I would let you know if they were my partner, regardless of sex. It is called manners. Now at the risk of being rude I would like you and Justin to leave, immediately.*

fLy: Fi was standing agog as she watched her brother-in-law and his lover leave. In one short space of time she had been privy to an insight into Raymond's unknown past and present. He never talked about growing up and she had told Hannah that she had always assumed it was the loss of his mother that had made him resistant to discuss the past. Now it appeared that their past was the baggage best left in the 'Customs Hall'; turbulent pasts were now an unknown common thread uniting Raymond, Tristan and Hannah.

Fi went over to Raymond as he sat on the sofa, and put an arm around his shoulders. As he put his head in his hands, he started to cry and Fi joined in. Her mascara ran, her lips became looser but her eye bogey stayed in place. Thank God…

Raymond: *I can't believe it, Fi. For years I have always felt that I had stood by my brother, thinking that Peter would be forever thankful for the blood, sweat and tears that I shed for him. But now I have realised the error of my assumption. Today has been* *shocking and the most upsetting element, Fi, is the feeling of disgust that I have toward Mr Knightley. I used to look up to him; near idolise him! He was a respectable Professor of Education but today I find out that he violated my brother. He was knowingly behaving in a manner that would incur severe and warranted punishment; breaking the trust that every parent had in the teaching staff of that school!*

Every single teacher is taught that they wield a certain amount of influence and power over the children that have been entrusted into their care and I am repulsed that professionals such as myself would choose to abuse this. I am torn apart on so many levels, Fi. All of my life I have remained impervious to these certain truths; student abuse and Peter's sexuality. It wasn't as if Peter played with dolls or preferred pink to blue; to the contrary, Peter was good at sport and often beat me in long-distance running. But there were times when Peter would sit too close to his male friends on the sofa; opting to sit next to Sebastian rather than Sharon, even though she was totally gorgeous with enormous breasts and known to give blow jobs. I remember vividly how Peter would smile at Sebastian. Sebastian was fat with small oblong red-rimmed glasses and he was very unpopular at school. There was nothing redeemable about Sebastian; he wasn't funny, sporty, intelligent, sympathetic, clean or kind but Peter seemed to adore him. Whenever there was a Saturday free from clubs, Dad used to ask us if we wanted to invite someone over. Peter always invited Sebastian and I knew that if Sebastian were to come over then his sister would follow along and soon be on the sofa too. So being the red-blooded heterosexual that I obviously am, I would always wait to hear what the outcome of Peter's invite to Sebastian would be before I asked a mate of mine to come over.

At first I thought that Peter was being clever, inviting Sebastian so that he could get a 'turn' with Sharon but as it transpired he had no interest in her. Sharon was sixteen years old and was somewhat of a legend at our school. Sebastian was a prime candidate for bullying but because Sharon was so worldly and generous with it, a goddess in our eyes, everyone laid off of Sebastian. That doesn't mean to say people befriended him as they didn't; they just left him alone.

I would like to meet her again, Fi, for no other reason than to ask her whether her sexual favours were given to try and protect her brother, lending him an armour in the same sort of way that I thought I was. Now being faced with all of this fresh information it all seems ridiculous. It has taken a day like today for us to find out that Peter has a boyfriend. I want Peter and Justin and you, Fi, to believe me when I say that I don't care about his sexuality but it isn't that simple. Growing up, I did care Fi, I didn't want to consider Peter in any other way than like me; but he was unusual and unnerving at times; I didn't know how to combat this or my fear that others would notice. I feel so ashamed.

fLy: And Raymond bawled deep heavy sobs into Fi's clammy cleavage. As Raymond started to lick his tears that trickled down into her buttock-like bosom I decided that it was definitely time for me to leave.

On my journey back home I started to consider 'sex' in human terms. It defines so many relationships and I am at a loss at times. For Hannah it has taken a very practical seat. She recently told Fi that one of her main incentives to have regular sex with Tristan was from the point of view of weight loss. Apparently active participation in sexual intercourse burns around sixty-nine calories in an average twenty-minute session which means she can have a guilt-free extra glug of milk in her mid-morning tea… yawn.

Tristan on the other hand has changed how he has sex with Hannah. He tends to be behind her, his eyes are much softer. As he pushes into her I can see his mouth moving but there are no discernible words for Hannah to hear. And whereas Tristan used to tug and ruffle Hannah's long hair he now gently parts her hair to expose her neck so that he can kiss the softness of her nape. The fucking has changed to sensual lovemaking but with a dialogue that only he knows, and maybe me if I could get close enough.

To start with I thought this lack of face-to-face fucking was because of Hannah's putrid breath but then I had another thought. Maybe it was because Hannah's face is attached to her thin-lipped mouth and seeing her wrinkles and her smudged black mascara would break the impassioned play that was going through Tristan's mind. God knows Tristan has put his tongue plenty of very unsavoury places so I am not sure it would be her breath that deters him in such carnal athletics; but it could have been.

Hannah was obsessed with how she looked, hence the vomiting and the morning inspection of her bones and her skin. There was a motive that was deeply lodged inside of her psyche and although she had entertained the idea of therapy she never really embraced it. She enjoyed having something to concern herself with; focusing on herself and how she appeared. She had decided in her fucked-up, selfish way that the reason for her unhealthy relationship with food was because she wanted to mould herself into that magazine image of physical perfection; believing her way of life was a choice she had consciously made. In that way when Tristan was unfaithful to her (and she was convinced he would be) then no one would be able to point at her and dismiss Tristan's infidelity as just wanting to look at something thinner to fuck. Nonetheless, up until recently, she had never considered the idea of being replaced by someone substantially younger; someone that didn't need to apply copious amounts of youth balm in order to look youthful because the only youngsters Tristan engaged with were his pupils and Tristan would surely never cross the line and commit adultery with a minor? Tristan had also always been so resolute with her in his beliefs that love was blind; he had, after all, quoted Shakespeare on numerous occasions: "Love looks not with the eyes but with the mind." So what drove Hannah's relentless battle with her appearance? What was the catalyst that made Hannah feel so imperfect; that fuelled her desire to expel the contents of her stomach, erupting like a volcano into the toilet bowl? Was it self-loathing, reinforced by her parents, a need to look as depleted as she felt? And if it was, could a therapist undo the splendid work that Sheila and Stan had done? I contemplate this with a mind less knowing than some humans but nonetheless with a mind that boggles at the futility of it all.

I remember a time when Tristan, in the few early days of them being here, would return home from work asking Hannah what it was she thought he would think about during the day. Hannah would giggle and say that it was probably Shakespeare in tights. Tristan would grab Hannah tightly around her waist and tell her that her cheekiness would result in the ultimate punishment. He would look her straight in the eye and purr, "You know what I like don't you? Your freckles." She would nod and very slowly he would move closer to her face and bite his lower lip. "You know that they enchant me; so much so that when I think of you during the day and I am feeling lonely they make me want to tear the clothes off of you and see if there are freckles hidden in places that I haven't looked before." The giggling would recommence and Hannah would react to this in ways that only a fLy could smell and a hardened cock would benefit.

But now these moments of young love have all but vanished. To begin with, as Tristan's interest started to peter out, I assumed it was the stress associated to not impregnating Hannah. But as the weeks rolled into months I thought that the lack of emotionally intense lovemaking was as a result of how she smelt. I knew she was aware of her breath as she would clean her teeth and scrub her tongue at least four times a day. Why? Well because her breath smelt like sick. I am not sure that it would taste the same but I would speculate that it did. I can't imagine that it was deceptive like parmesan cheese that smells of sick but actually tastes of something salty, or spaghetti bolognese that smells of body odour but tastes of onions and juicy, meaty gravy.

Tristan, one evening after work, asked Hannah if she had been sick and Hannah said that she had been drinking warm white wine with Fi and this Tristan could believe. He had often alluded to the nauseating breath that he would have to endure during parents' evening. They would talk to him post welcoming drink and lean in toward him as they asked questions about their 'gifted' offspring. But it wasn't just the white wine that lent itself so well to vomit-breath, it was the concentrated orange juice that made him cringe when he saw mothers and fathers gulp the non-alcoholic alternative to the wine or lager that was on offer prior to the event. But Hannah would have this smell of sick bowls on her breath regularly, it was a fragrance that was now a part of Hannah and he didn't ask further questions so he became accepting of it, I think.

It was only me that was privy to the real reason why her breath was so intoxicating. It was thanks to her performance in the bathroom; head well inside the toilet bowl using a hairbrush to ram down her throat to entice the sick out of her stomach, up in to her oesophagus and then out through her mouth. Her ability to make herself sick was becoming more and more of a challenge, and more and more ineffectual. When I first met Hannah the vomiting sessions were relatively easy. Once her mind was in the right place the actual vomiting was a doddle; she would come into the bathroom or visit the downstairs loo and just pop her two long fingers into her mouth; within seconds the unwanted matter was out. Then as the regularity increased, a more invasive strategy had to be employed. She would get results, initially, if she used her index finger to tickle her tonsils which would then result in the gloopy, lumpy brown contents of her stomach being deposited in the white porcelain toilet bowl. But as the tonsils became rather well acquainted with her finger she had to use her whole hand; her mouth would open and a thick dribble would varnish her lips as her hand disappeared into the red cavern; a good reason as to why Hannah now keeps her fingernails short. On one or two occasions she scratched her larynx, resulting in a throat infection and then another time she couldn't rid her hand of the highly effluvious miniscule little chunks of sick that stuck under her nails and wedding ring. It seemed an impossible odour for her to neutralise. And after the whole hand down the throat had stopped working Hannah then employed anything that had a long handle – her gag reflex was a thing of the past. Just imagine the fun and the money to be had from a gift like that in those many shifty 'private dance' emporiums. Hannah could have, and still could in fact, capitalise from a talent like that; all those desperate punters! As they say, every cloud has a silver lining.

Joking aside, I need to fill you in on what Hannah would look like after one of her regurgitations. And why should I need to tell you about it? Because this is what I see, smell and live for. Life as it is. For me life is infinitely better with Hannah. She is dynamic; not only do I see what goes in, I see what comes out and I see the pleasure sprint across her face when she succeeds in evicting the last of the calorific residue. Her successful efforts always end in the same way, and I like it when one can foretell the events. After her final heave she will stand up, away from the loo, and look at herself in the mirror. She will not bother to wipe away the thick sputum that coats her chin or the mascara that runs down her face, diluted by the salty tears that trickle from her eyes. Instead she will look at the image that greets her and talk to herself. As she talks with relaxed, exhausted lips, more fluid slips from her lips and falls onto the white enamelled sink that sits below the mirror. She vows to buy mascara that won't run down her face but she never does. The site of herself indulges her. She tells herself that she is the living embodiment of 'disgusting' in all of its guises – piss-soaked knickers from her tumultuous heaving, stinking breath, black smudges strewn across her face, diaphanous bile glazing her lips and chin. In these moments the truthful reflection empowers her and to her, it felt brilliant. I know this because she is happy, just for a brief time, afterwards. And I understand it because for a very short time she was all that she saw; a desperate woman with no need to describe how she felt. She would be upsetting to look at if you cared for her but I didn't; I was merely entertained. However, these moments of glorious smells and self-knowledge were quickly forgotten as she wiped, cleaned, washed, and disinfected her face, hands, wrists, gag utensil and toilet. Soon the aftermath of such an event would start; the stomach cramps would set in as the acidic bile gnawed away but this reassured her. I wondered what Tristan would say if he were ever to witness this. "The empty vessel makes the loudest sound"? I know that he would chastise me for taking Plato out of context but Hannah was empty, and as she became more empty the volume of the chundering became louder. Maybe he would refer to Shakespeare for a more sympathetic quotation; not that I am aware of any.

5

fLy: There was one afternoon puking session post-lunch that was interrupted by a persistent banging on Tristan and Hannah's front door. Hannah and Tristan had endured a Sunday lunch with Sheila and Stan. I don't know why they had been invited; as always Sheila sat and talked and ate whilst Stan said nothing. Prior to lunch he had sat in a chair by the patio window, enjoying the sun that graced us. After lunch he did the same; initially I deduced that he was sitting there because he liked the feeling of warmth from the sun but then I became wise as to why. Outside of our patio doors we have a small but practical area of grass. Our garden has a wooden picket fence that sits in front of an evergreen hedge that shields us from the athletics pitch. There is a small gate that leads out onto the sports fields which ever so occasionally offers a glimpse of activity beyond our boundary. Stan would sit and stare, speechless, looking shiny like a worm. I would wait until the sweat on the back of his neck, just below his hair line, had become more apparent. I would then relocate myself so that should a small globule of fluid roll down and onto the back of the chair I would be there, ready to enjoy. But it wasn't only me that enjoyed the salty efforts that his sweat glands produced. When his brow would furrow and then his upper lip sparkle and tickle, out would pop his tongue to taste these salty, sweet offerings. And what was the prime reason for this briny excretion? The anticipation of seeing very youthful bodies in shorts and vests as they exercised around the track, of course.

Stan didn't wear aftershave and would let the heavenly smell of his oily, flaky, dandruff-ridden scalp permeate the cloth on his shoulders. The whole room would become heavy with his scent, soaking into the carpets and curtains. Sheila seemed immune to this smell as she never commented on it but mid-conversation she would excuse herself and go over to Stan and swipe the dandruff off from his shoulders. The look of distaste would swell in Tristan's eyes as he watched the dermal confetti catch in the sun rays as it tumbled onto our cream-carpeted floor. Stan didn't seem to notice when Sheila would do this as he never seemed to acknowledge her; such was the depth of his dirty imaginings. However, I noticed and made a 'note to self' (as Fi now annoyingly says) as to where my evening's 'amuse-bouche' would be found.

Sheila had her fixations too when she came to our house; the food in the cupboards, the number of tampons in the box in the downstairs loo and the unopened mail that sits on the small table under the hallway mirror. Sheila would wait until Hannah left the kitchen and would go through the cupboards to the left of the sink, pulling the packets forward and checking that there was nothing behind them or the tins. When she would go and wash her hands prior to lunch she would rifle through the cupboard in the downstairs loo, scanning the various bottles of cleaners and loo rolls and would grab the box of tampons as if booty on a pirate's ship. She would count them and then make a note of the number in her black 'day-to-day' diary that she kept in her patent black leather shoulder bag that smelt of lipstick and aloe vera face cream. After leaving the lavatory she would quietly tread to the hallway table and flick through all the letters that lay haphazardly on top of each other. Invariably she would replace them with a shuffle to straighten them and that was how Tristan and Hannah knew that Sheila had been looking through them. It didn't bother either of them but Tristan did ask Hannah to one day try and catch her doing it so as one could ascertain the reason behind her nosing through their mail. Hannah said she would but she liked thinking that her mum was interested in at least one aspect of her life, however menial.

The lunch followed its usual course of inane conversation and overeating on their guests' front. The coffee was served with chocolate minty thins and twenty minutes later Sheila and Stan would be saying their farewells. Tristan clipped the lead onto Wallace and disappeared through the back garden and out across the playing fields, whilst Hannah scurried upstairs to start vomiting before her body really had much time to start digesting then converting and then, worst of all, absorbing the calories. She would look for the foods she had consumed and their colours as she heaved and retched, out of her gaping mouth, taking mental note of those that had yet to be ejected. This little ritual would persist until Hannah could only sick up bile. However, on this particular Sunday, mid-chunder, there was this knocking on the front door as I had mentioned. Hannah opened the bathroom window quietly to gauge who it was that was bothering them. If it had been Fi she could have just wiped off her face and shouted down or if it had been a Jehovah's witness or someone of that ilk she would have just let them carry on knocking but aggravatingly for her it was one of Tristan's students. A pretty one. So Hannah stood back from the window and called down that she would be down very shortly. Hannah had to de-sick herself and reapply a modest amount of make-up in record time before being able to go and attend to the young lady outside.

Hannah, upon opening the door, saw a girl of about sixteen or seventeen years of age. I knew it was Sasha; she looked slightly flushed and there were two strands of her long blonde hair stuck to her sparkly glossed lips.

Sasha: *Sorry, Mrs Stephens, to have interrupted you on a Sunday; it is just that Sir, Mr Stephens, said to drop round my prep when I had finished it today. He gave me a deadline extension which was about to expire.*

Hannah: *No problem at all, honestly. I am sorry but I don't know your name and Tristan, Mr Stephens, didn't tell me he was expecting any of his students today.*

Sasha: *Sorry, Mrs Stephens. My name is Sasha Burnham; I am in Sir's first-year A-level class.*

Hannah: *Well, I would invite you in to wait to see Mr Stephens but he has just gone on his Sunday afternoon walk with his dog so he could be gone a couple of hours.*

Sasha: *Yes, I had meant to be here earlier but the Sunday bus service is so unreliable from where my dad lives; I was at home this weekend. Sir did mention to me that he would be going on a dog walk in case I had wished to join him. It is a real shame that I missed out on that as I love dogs and from the cross-country running class I have really become very fond of the countryside around here.*

Hannah: *Do you live nearby, Sasha?*

Sasha: *Well not too far, but too far to walk, so it meant that I had to get a bus in to deliver my already overdue prep; Dad wasn't able to drop me back. Again I am sorry for bothering you, Mrs Stephens.*

fLy: As Hannah shut the door she muttered under her breath, "Spoilt bitch," but I suspected then that she had a small inkling as to why Tristan had extended Sasha's prep deadline.

Tristan's fantasies had reached a point where reality and fantasy could become a smudged line; he realised that he could construct situations that moulded themselves to the next chapter of his life, rather than wait for Cupid's arrow to strike. He had spent hours and hours just looking at her handwriting; he had spent hours and hours going through various made-up situations at school where Sasha may need to be comforted, helped, held, advised, saved. Tristan had spent many evenings in front of the television next to Hannah, holding her leg but existing in another world. His eyes would be slightly more open, more glazed, as he watched and smiled and reacted to the noises that Hannah was making to the usual 'reality' television shows that she subjected them to. Tristan would profess an interest in them as he said that he would like to stay 'in touch' with popular culture and to see whether there could be a tangible connection to the Masters of Literature. No doubt he was referring to Shakespeare but I think that dear William would have stayed well clear of writing about such mindless bollocks. Or maybe not. Discuss...

As Tristan watched various women stare into the camera and profess their love for the nation and for their parents and for the people in the local supermarket and for the people that they hadn't met but knew supported them in their daily quest to be popular, he disappeared into his world of long, tousled blonde hair and billowy white cotton shirts. Laughter didn't exist in this world; just smiles in varying degrees of sincerity and foreheads taking the lead role. There would be horses, undulating green hills for galloping across, a villain with rotten teeth, a scholar, an ugly person that offers insight through madness, a virgin and finally an unsung, unknown, more mature, selfless saviour. Or maybe his world was one where everyone was dressed in foil to reject and reflect the soulless infiltrations of plastic reality. Or maybe he was just sitting there thinking about her young, springy-to-the-touch body and her young, pink hole.

Once again I have departed from the chain of events. After Hannah had shut the door on Sasha she tried to nonchalantly walk into Tristan's office; she idly flicked through the typed work that Sasha had handed to her. Hannah didn't pay any attention to the work set nor to any of the script. What caught her eye, unsurprisingly, was the heart-shaped, luminous pink Post-it note that Sasha had stuck to the last page of her assignment. "Thank you and Sorry." Sasha's handwriting was fat and squashy, preceded and then followed by a smiley face. As she placed the few pages of work onto the desk Hannah noticed a stack of files to the left of the desk light. The top two files belonged to two different students, Ana Baston and Joshua Mingles, and the next two files belonged to Sasha Burnham. Hannah immediately recalled Burnham Overy Staithe where Tristan had proposed to her.

The first file that belonged to Sasha was full, at first glance, of essays and note-taking; the second file was far more incongruous with only a few pages of A-level printouts, but mainly it consisted of miscellanea. There were typed poems and doodles, printouts of news articles about the Burnham family; there were collages made from magazines, timetables and lists of words, again typed, that had no correlation to each other. None of it really made sense to Hannah nor to me but I knew that this file could fill a glorious, serialised episode of reality TV of heartbreak, fake tears and snot.

When Tristan arrived back home from his dog walk, life for Hannah had returned to normal. Hannah was in the process of washing up from lunch and as usual Wallace came running in to say hello, tail wagging and tongue lolling happily out of his mouth. Hannah huffed and turned to look at Tristan. Unusually, she took an interest in his return.

Hannah: *How was the dog walk? Oh, before I forget, a girl stopped by and dropped off some prep.*
Tristan: *Did I miss Sasha by much?*
Hannah: *I didn't make a note of the time she arrived but maybe you had been gone twenty minutes or so. How was the dog walk?*
Tristan: *That's a shame; I had suggested that she was here a bit earlier so that she could come on the dog walk with me. There are some truly wonderful views that I wanted to show her. Did you put her work in my office?*
Hannah: *No in the dishwasher. How was the dog walk?*
Tristan: *Sorry, yes it was a nice walk. I say that but in retrospect, maybe not. I saw Raymond, fine in itself but he has decided to start*

training for the next 'Ironman' competition. He was on his way back from a fifteen-mile run when I saw him and I think that he had muddied himself up on purpose. He was covered in dirt, thick mud actually, which is quite surprising as the ground is very dry out there; the whole look was startling really. I have not seen him in a leotard before so maybe it was just as well that Sasha wasn't there.

Hannah: *What colour was the leotard?*

Tristan: *Not seen one like it before, but then why would I have? It was khaki and camouflage with a matching rucksack that Raymond had fastened around himself to keep it as motionless as possible as it was filled with bricks. He said that he was getting back home and then grabbing his bike and then straight off for a three-hour cycle ride. Whilst he was chatting to me he kept jogging on the spot and insisted he showed me the padding that was cleverly concealed around his buttocks to ensure that the cycling wouldn't affect his penile artery. I wasn't sure where the padding started and where his testicles began; what a look. So in answer to your question, the walk was good but I spent nearly the entire walk trying to get that vision out of my head. So now I am going to go and do some marking and make sure all is in place for the lessons this week. I have to also to think about the school play. I have been shying away from that of late.*

Hannah: *In that case I will give Fi a call and see if I can pop round for a glass of wine. I will grab a bottle from our fridge if that is ok with you, Tristan, as Fi never has any chilling; there is only one thing worse than not having any white wine in the house, it is having white wine in the house that is warm.*

fLy: As Tristan walked into his office, his stomach knotted, he started to do little tiny farts. He was feeling nervous about seeing Sasha's work; he wanted a note from her but he knew that wouldn't be the case. He was also anxious that Hannah had come face to face with Sasha and what's more that Sasha had seen Hannah. He looked around the room to make sure that all the files appeared to be untouched, he only really cared about the personal file that Sasha had given to Tristan. It was still at the bottom of the pile and he was falsely relieved that Hannah had not read it otherwise she would have been asking questions! He went and hid the questionable file in the cabinet underneath the hanging files that held all of his own coursework ideas, lesson suggestions, and literary-related newspaper articles. Tentatively he opened the assignment that Sasha had delivered.

Tristan: *You are the only pupil, Sasha, that still keeps on giving in work that is not typed but I love it. I love thinking of the pen that was conducted around the page by your beautiful soft hands. I can imagine the musical rhythm in the knuckle of your thumb as the pen marks the words onto this very paper. Oh! Why didn't you get here earlier, Sasha, then I could have taken you for the walk and shown you all the places where one day I would like to hold you and kiss you and enjoy the view. I could have set my impatient desires free and told you how I felt about you; I could have just looked at you without worrying that someone will spot me looking at you for just that second too long. I look at you every time you are in class with me; and that is all I want to do, Sasha. During the day, even when it is outside of our class time, I engineer it so that I get to the luncheon hall at the same time as you, making doubly sure that it is the same time as you so that I can watch you lean over the hot dishes on offer at the canteen and see the heat lamps infuse your face with a golden, angelic glow. Do you know, Sasha Burnham, that I chew my food slowly so that I can prolong the amount of time that I can be legitimately sitting in the dining hall without raising suspicion? I get a rolling, nervous stomach on days when you are late coming into lunch; what if you are ill or have decided to miss lunch? And then when I see you, on those days, the relief races over me like the air rushing into the car when the windows are rolled down. I get aroused when I see you eat your pudding; the way the spoon passes your lips and your mouth closes over it. The way that you pull the spoon slowly*

71

out of your mouth; I can imagine your tongue working overtime to ensure that every sticky bit of Sticky Toffee Pudding is cleaned off of the stainless steel tool. And then there are added visual delights when you manage to let a little of the custard drip on to your chin and you get your finger and wipe it off and then you suck your finger! How I wish to be sitting next to you then so that I could remove the custard from your chin and that it would be my finger you were to suck. I make sure that I get one of the chairs by the large bay window in the staff room in case I can catch a glimpse of you going for your cross-country run. I can sit there until you are on your way back to your house so that I can 'bump' into you as you stride back with cheeks flushed and your breathing ever so slightly heavy. I love seeing you with your long hair pulled back tightly off of your face so that I can see your earlobes and gentle hairline that curves away behind them, exposing an area of skin that I can only imagine is as smooth as silk. I am a mess. I need to start marking the other pupils' work and then I will come back to yours, Sasha. Then I can take as long as I wish in the company of your thoughts and opinions, in the company of your paper and your ink.

fLy: On that note I decide to go and gatecrash Hannah's visit to Fi; by now the formalities and 'How are you?' will be over and the wine will be open.

Fi: *A crisp with your wine? I have some pitta bread and hummus or some delicious parmesan cheese that we can take chunks of, like the Italians? I always prefer having something to eat when I am drinking.*
Hannah: *I am happy with the just the wine, Fi, but I am sure I will have a nibble once they are out. Sounds lovely. How are Justin and Peter? Has Raymond spoken with Peter since the barbecue?*
Fi: *Well no, Hannah, he hasn't and to be honest I am not surprised. Raymond has not been the same since then. I was shocked that Peter didn't have the respect for Raymond to tell him what the situation*

was before turning up with Justin and behaving in such a contrary way. When we met him before he was entertaining, but in a crowd he has proven to be gregarious and entirely 'un-us'. Surely Peter would have known that Justin would have behaved like that in a group; Justin just seemed to be intent on being rather foul-mouthed. Thank goodness the kids didn't hear any of it. Thankfully, Raymond has the 'Ironman Challenge' to focus on to take his mind off of current events. Physical and mental exertion has always been a way of coping for Raymond but this challenge, I fear, may even be too much for a gladiator like Raymond.

Hannah: *Gladiator?*

Fi: *Well it's all thanks to Netflix, I know I mentioned it to you before but there is a plethora of historic broadcasts, not just films, which I never really appreciated. We really have started to enjoy learning more about the bygone era. Raymond has been taking it to heart. He says he has been dreaming vividly about the Roman Empire; he really feels that he can identify with those that were the professional gladiators. Not the gladiators that were the convicted criminals or slaves of course. He truly empathises with the brotherhood of gladiators, the 'Collegia'. It reminded him of the camaraderie he and his friends from Uni had and still have. For example, his friendship with Bruno; he promised Bruno on our wedding day, years ago, that if ever anything were to happen to Bruno, he would take care of his funeral and make sure he had a proper, respectful send-off; spooky as it is, just as the 'Collegia' used to.*

Hannah: *Is Bruno unwell; is he at risk then?*

Fi: *Ok, well when Bruno left University he decided to try and make ends meet financially by becoming a male escort; I am not sure he would want you knowing that actually so do keep it between ourselves. And Raymond felt that in that line of work Bruno could find himself the target of angry husbands or boyfriends. He could find himself ill with disease because of his increased contact with multiple partners and thus exposing himself to sexually transmitted infections; some of which you know are deadly.*

Hannah: *Does Bruno still work as a male escort, even with his IBS issues? Surely that could be a bit of a problem?*

Fi: *Well it and the other issue have sort of curtailed the regularity of work.*

Hannah: *What other issue?*

Fi: *Well sporadic bouts of impotence actually so he had to start being more selective with what his role for the evening would be. There are quite a few ladies that just want the company.*

Hannah: *Impotence? A prostate issue perhaps?*

Fi: *No, both of the doctors that he went to see have said that it is primarily down to cycling.*

Hannah: *Cycling?*

Fi: *Bruno didn't always wear those padded Lycra shorts but even with those, Dr. Goldstein said that there was still risk. But as Raymond says, "Amat Victoria Curam."*

Hannah: *What does that mean?*

Fi: *"Victory favours those who take pains," or something along those lines. So I have had to let Raymond continue with his training for the 'Ironman' competition even though I am not convinced it is the best idea. But Raymond does try to minimise the risk of erectile dysfunction by wearing very supportive, cushioned shorts. But the saddle is where it is, the shape is the shape it is and Raymond, likewise, is the shape he is. So we follow a routine in order to help reduce the risk.*

When Raymond finishes his training he drinks a herbal supplement called 'Tongkat Ali'. Then I give him a very gentle but effective testicle massage, soft but assured. Increasingly I have noticed that the smell of his undercarriage is changing, which I find slightly off-putting but I put it down to the Lycra and the padding heating up as he pedals and making him smell different.

Hannah: *Well apart from promising Bruno that he will take care of his funeral, which I have to say is not a virtue unique to gladiators, and the wanting to get fit, to be at one's physical peak, there must be some other mannerisms or quirks that you can allude to that reinforce this gladiator identity crisis?*

Fi: *There are, Hannah; and I like the fact you are insistent for detail. I am sure that if I were to chat to other friends, like I do with you, which I wouldn't by the way, they would just half-listen and accept, whereas you make me explain and this assures me. I know you listen because you ask questions, you interrogate how I perceive a situation and this reassures me of my convictions. I think once I tell you the following you too will know that Raymond was once a gladiator.*

For a while now, even before watching the history programmes series, he has been suggesting I put some of his sweat into my face creams, along with some of his pre-seminal fluid, as he says it is an aphrodisiac plus an anti-ageing agent. And then lo and behold after watching the gladiator series we find out that little trick was used by the women of those times. And it wasn't just any man's sweat it was only the bodily fluids from the more acclaimed and famous gladiators of that time. You see?

Hannah: *Did he always suggest you do that? Even from the early days when you first met? In fact, come to mention it, I don't think that I actually know how the two of you met or even where?*

Fi: *I have told you before Hannah that we met at Uni; but I think that was about the depth of the detail. I am quite a private person at times and I think it was when you first moved here that we discussed it briefly. Well, we both met studying Economics at Manchester and he asked if he could borrow my notes after one lecture as he had been having difficulty hearing what was being said because he had bad build-up of earwax in both of his ears. I was truly flattered that he had asked me so of course I agreed. After that we used to sit near or next to each other in lectures and would go for coffee in the break together. We started spending increasingly more time in each other's company and then one day he asked if I would like to go for a campfire dinner one evening and that sounded intriguing. It was maybe a week after that I went along to his room on campus. It was a single room, basic but clean and in the centre of the room he had a camping gas stove and some tin plates. As I sat down he put a hat,* which he said he had made, on my head which had corks hanging down from the brim, like those you see the Australians wearing in the Outback. He handed me a steel mug full of red wine and the evening just flew by. We had such a good evening pretending we were out under the stars; he played cowboy music on his CD player whilst we munched and chewed our way through cold pork ribs and hot baked beans. He told me how he really enjoyed physical fitness and the importance of it to focus the mind. He showed me his routine that he did every morning before leaving for class. His legs and his arms were muscular and strong as he heaved and bobbed up and down; he could do thirty press-ups in thirty seconds and sixty-two squats in a minute. After about three hours of chatting I went to leave and he took my hat off — it wasn't for me to keep — but then he put it back on my head as I had hat hair which he said didn't look very nice. So he kissed me through the dangling corks. It wasn't the easiest of kisses I had ever had but it was the best, Hannah. We didn't sleep with each other for another four months or so.

Hannah: *And what was that like, your first time?*

Fi: *This is embarrassing, Hannah! I hope I can recall it all correctly. We had decided it was going to be special, having waited for so long. We had both had some tests done to make sure we were both clear of any STIs and both came back negative — I hadn't told him that I was a virgin but went along with it to show willing. We had been playing with the idea of going away to a hotel, or going camping for our first time, but we decided that it would be best if we just spent a Saturday together in Manchester shopping and then having some lunch and going back to his room. My room had quite a lot of pink in it; duvet, rug, teddies, posters of puppies on the wall and he said that the pinkness and the puppies with their lolling pink tongues made him feel uncomfortable. Anyway his room smelt nice but was very sparse. There was a single wooden chair, his neat and tidy desk which had on it his small stereo player, an alarm clock with built-in timer facility and a mug which had his toothbrush and toothpaste in. Under his desk was a Manchester United rubbish bin which he had* *inherited from his next-door neighbour when she died and to the left of that his camping box. There were no pictures of any sort around his room and his duvet was brown, his pillow pale blue. It was quite a sterile place but Raymond changed that! That afternoon whilst shopping he had bought some fragranced candles and a new CD of 'Whale Song'. He created our own oasis of relaxation and calm in that little room of his; such a talent. He spent about an hour or so doing impressions of several sea creatures: seals, orcas, elephant seals, dolphins and so the whale CD was so fitting. He instructed me to take my clothes off and then I had to undress him but leaving his socks on. He said that he wouldn't take his socks off for intercourse until he was in love with someone.*

Hannah: *He takes his socks off now, I trust?*

Fi: *Oh yes, he does Hannah! In fact, that is how he proposed to me. One evening after a year and a half of dating he told me to take his socks off slowly. As I did there was a handwritten label sewn into the elastic of the sock saying, "You have to say yes, Fi! Marry me?" I was so happy that for the next few days I couldn't concentrate on any of my studies.*

fLy: The conversation then dissolved into wedding dresses, bridesmaids, make-up and flowers so I left and went back home. My options were to go and listen to Tristan talking to a folder or to go and sit with Wallace. I chose the latter.

6

fLy: Wallace was curled up on the sofa, fast asleep. The washing machine and dishwasher were on and their rhythmical whirl and whoosh made me feel soporific and I too dozed off. I am not sure how long I was asleep for but when I awoke Tristan was in the chair that Stan usually occupies when he comes over for Sunday Lunch. He was reading aloud some text from a French play. It had been translated into English and was originally written by Pierre Choderlos de Laclos. Tristan would stop occasionally with his HB pencil and draw diagonal lines through paragraphs of text.

> **Tristan**: *I have decided, Wallace, to create a new sort of existence for myself and combine reality with art. I am going to use this play to start the fire that will reignite my life and begin Sasha's. It will be an innocent beginning with an ending yet to be decided, ha!*

fLy: And with that he carried on editing the text, occasionally smiling and making very quiet "ah yes" utterings.

Hannah arrived home around the same time that Tristan's concentration was wavering. He noticed that Hannah was a little drunk and her breath smelt as it usually did of warm white wine. I, however, thought it was more likely as a result of a tactical chunder on her way home either in Fi's loo or in the bush by the science lab; her breath was slightly too acidic even for the cheapest of white wines. I knew that her calorie conscience would be going mental with all of the parmesan that she gorged on with Fi.

She swaggered over to Tristan and took the play out of his hands.

Hannah: *One of your favourites I see, Tristan. I am not sure whether it is the play you so love or the film version?*

Tristan: *The play of course! I am not a literary philistine; no one in their right mind could ever truthfully say that a film is better than the written word.*

Hannah: *I am not saying which is better; I was commenting on your love for it. And I think in this instance, if you were true to yourself, you do prefer the film.*

Tristan: *What makes you say that?*

Hannah: *Uma Thurman's tits.*

Tristan: *You have a good point!*

Hannah: *I remember you watching and rewinding, watching and rewinding that scene where Uma's boobs are surging up and down. I don't ever recall you turning the pages back and re-reading a section of that play over and over again. And what I do know for sure is that you have never suggested reading Les Liaisons Dangereuse to each other to get us horny. You have only ever suggested watching Dangerous Liaisons to get us in the mood.*

Tristan: *Well do you fancy watching it now?*

Hannah: *So long as I have a glass of wine in one hand I don't mind what I have in the other.*

fLy: So Wallace was nudged off of the sofa and whilst Tristan put the DVD on, Hannah fetched the cold white wine from the fridge and two glasses from the cupboard. The white wine was poured and the film was started. Anyone without insider knowledge would view this scene favourably, two married people sitting down to watch a favourite film feeling slightly concupiscent. But I knew differently. Right from the start, before Hannah had taken off her top and bra, and before she had unbuttoned and unfastened Tristan's trousers to expose his turgid penis, Tristan's thoughts were apparent to a perceptive, clever fLy like me. Tristan watched the film but his eyes were alive as he superimposed two of the characters with himself and Sasha. Sasha would not be the young Uma Thurman but the virtuous Madame de Tourvel played by Michelle Pfeiffer. His regard for Hannah was the same that John Malkovich had for Uma Thurman; something to pass the time with and to enjoy carnally. Tristan's love for the innocent Madame de Tourvel mirrored his for Sasha; but unlike Madame de Tourvel, Sasha was never a 'challenge' presented to him by a domineering super-bitch; he had just fallen for Sasha from the first moment he saw her.

After the film had finished and Tristan and Hannah had fucked, Tristan left Hannah asleep on the sofa and went back into his office. He wanted to know a little about Sasha's background; he knew her father was called Edward but knew nothing about her mother or what they did for a living. He knew he needed only twenty minutes to get his 'Sasha fix' before waking up Hannah and going to bed. He powered up his computer and clicked the Internet icon. In the search field he typed "Edward Burnham".

Unfortunately, there were many results so he clicked onto the images page. There he was, undeniably. He had blonde short hair with the same shaped, green eyes. He clicked onto the image and then on to the 'view page' option. On the company home page there was a 'search' function so Tristan was able to look up 'Edward Burnham'. Edward worked for a pharmaceutical company in the capacity of 'Director'. He had worked there so far for fifteen years. He had a degree from Manchester University in Economics and had spent two years of his life Teaching English as a Foreign Language (TEFL) in Australia. He has an interest in the arts, mainly theatre, and hopes one day to be able to work as an aid worker in China. Tristan felt immediately opposed to him but was unsure as to why. Tristan should be relieved that he and Edward shared so many interests; he should have been pleased that Edward liked the performing arts; something that Tristan could talk about with confidence. Tristan had always wanted to go to Australia, or so he kept telling Hannah and Raymond, so here was something else that could bridge any awkward silences should there be any. There would be, at least, this common ground to break the ice when he and Edward first met. But it wouldn't be the first time, would it? It was parents' evening soon but it wasn't in that sphere that Tristan was thinking about.

But what about parents' evening? In two weeks' time there was a real possibility that Edward would be there; if not Edward then maybe Sasha's mother? Tristan hadn't even considered this. Usually Tristan would focus on talking to the mother on parents' evenings as they were the ones that tended to be more involved on a daily or weekly basis. The dads would make the usual attentive noises but Tristan certainly didn't want to make sweeping generalisations when it came to Sasha's parents. He wanted them both to feel how interested and concerned and caring he was for their Sasha; a Sasha that he too wanted to call his own. How does someone go from being called Mr Stephens to Tristan, Son even, without awkwardness? As he chews over the detail Hannah is starting to wake up, groaning slightly, so I flew out to the sitting room to watch her.

Hannah has been lying down on her side, her right cheek pressed up against the arm of the sofa. As she sits up, she gets the cuff of her jumper and wipes her face. She removes a sticky white lace of saliva from her lips that has small, spindly tendrils attaching her to the upholstery. Her breath is smelling of rotten bananas and salty cheese biscuits for some reason and her mascara has coagulated, gluing her right eyelids together. To me, Hannah smelt delicious but as Hannah arose and took herself to look at herself in the mirror in the downstairs toilet she made an "augh" noise. The skin around her face was getting looser, and the lines on her forehead like train tracks. The creases from her lips to her nose reminded me of open gutters and the so-called 'laughter lines' that forked from her eyes permanently echoed her miserable pre-vomit scowls. Her hair was getting thinner, and as she pawed her left hand through her hair another bunch of strands came free. The skin behind her jawbone, below her ear, was getting itchy now as well as being flaky. She opened the drawer under the white basin to find a salve of some sort. Rifling through the wooden tray she found tooth floss, cotton wool, some plasters and a tube of anti-fungal cream that Tristan had used for his athlete's foot a few months ago. A similar cream, if not the same, was used for nappy rash so she thought it must be safe to use on her skin. Hannah thickly applied the cream and very soon the itching had died down.

The following day Tristan was back in class and the day was quite dull. Hannah was at home throwing up and Tristan was preaching the various virtues of differing texts to differing age groups. I decided to venture into the staff room to see if Raymond was in there or the much-awaited Maths teacher had arrived, who was coming in as maternity cover for Tabitha Franklin.

It is here that I want to give you some background colour on Miss Franklin but in truth there is not much to tell about her apart from the fact that she is forty-five years old and has a long pointy nose. Her eyes are set quite far apart and her eyelid skin seems too thin but stretchy; there always seems to be extra. She has always been overweight and her pregnancy makes one worried as to whether to congratulate her, offer her a seat, or to just ignore the whole size situation in case she is just that little bit extra overweight... No one knows who the father of the child is but it is rumoured by those in the caretakers' shed that Judd was the culprit. He too has a long pointy nose but his eyelids are of normal flesh apportion. In fact, Judd is very similar in looks, posture and character to the rake that he uses religiously on a daily basis. That baby may have lost out in the looks and personality department I fear.

As I enter the staff room I feel an instant warmth; this room is always a little bit too hot and today the air is a potent concoction of differing exhaled breaths. In the mix I can detect tea, cigarettes, coffee, tuna, garlic, carious teeth, minty toothpaste, and whisky. I decide to stay a while longer even though Raymond and the new teacher are absent. It is quite wonderful in here today, the smell is totally hypnotic and the low purring of conversation puts me into a somnolent mood. I am slightly stirred by one of the younger male teachers and a colleague of equal years I should think, as they move their chairs over towards me. I am on the picture rail above the old Etonian four-column radiator so I stay where I am as I am confident they won't see me up here and try to squash me. They are talking in guarded tones so immediately my gossip antennae are aroused and I listen intently to their conversation.

Man with hair gel: *Burnham.*

Man without hair gel: *I overheard Anderson saying that she was stunning but I have yet to see her. Her subjects are more arts-based so her classes tend to be the other side of the school for most of the time.*

Man with hair gel: *Why don't we skip having lunch in here and one day go to the dining hall? You can point her out to me at lunch.*

Man without hair gel: *Does she have many admirers do you think?*

Man with hair gel: *Plenty but there is one in particular. I won't mention names but let's have a wager and see if you notice it too.*

Raymond: *I see you two boys over here by yourselves! Come on, share the news.*

Man with hair gel: *Raymond, nothing gets past you. Must be your army training.*

Raymond: *Self-taught – never been in the army. I just employ their rules of discipline and surveillance. Everyone can do it and it* *has proven to be very useful to me over the years. But avoiding the question doesn't work with me. Now lads, what's the scoop?*

Man without hair gel: It seems there is a girl called Sasha Burnham that is making many heads turn and chins wag, ours included, and there is one head which is particularly turned. I have been given the task to find out whose head it is. Any ideas?

Raymond: *I can tell you now, it's not mine, boys.*

fLy: With that in comes the Head of Teaching, Mr Fallbuoy, and all of the staff stop talking as the new maternity cover teacher follows him in. She is formally introduced as a Miss Letty Swallow. She is suitably pallid-looking, probably damp to touch; so I take my leave after ten minutes of Mr Fallbuoy's depthless waffle with the hope to locate Sasha. As I fLy out of the staff room, the long, oak-panelled corridor seems exceptionally busy and there is quite a strong draft whistling through it. I think the door at the end of the corridor has been wedged open, which is unusual. The wind is making it difficult for me to navigate my way to find out what the situation is, and so once again I have to settle and watch. I am able to find temporary lodging behind one of the ornate carved wooden gargoyles that protrude from the corner where the wall meets the ceiling. Below me I recognise quite a few of the faces from sitting in on Tristan's lessons and I feel very much like I am at a zoo but without the glorious trappings of animal shit to go and feast on. The girls make little huddles and the boys make little huddles and they all move up the corridor as if on a giant travellator. As they reach the dining room at the end they fragment off in one of three directions; to the hot food area, the cold food area or directly to the tables to reserve places for their friends. From where I am perched I can just see the lonely shoes of Tristan; his ankles are crossed and his grey flecked trousers are hitched up to reveal his dog paw print black and brown socks. They were last year's Christmas present from Wallace. So I know it is him even though I cannot see the upper torso. In the melee of students that just passed I did not espy Sasha so maybe she is on a run or just merely late. But as I decide to chance fLying again I see that it is Sasha that is keeping the door open. She is sitting on the floor leaning back into the large wood and glass panelled door. I slowly traverse towards her but my progress is rather slow. The man with the hair gel appears from the staff room and strides purposefully to the door.

> **Man with hair gel**: *Sasha? Why are you sitting on the floor and letting all the cold air in? Aren't there other places you could sit?*
> **Sasha**: *Yes, Sir; sorry I just didn't feel well and had to sit down immediately. I think Ana went to tell Mr Stephens. He is always on duty in the lunch hall early on a Monday. I didn't think it would be a good idea to disturb anyone in the staff room.*
> **Man with hair gel**: *That was a very wise idea as we were being introduced to the temporary maternity cover member of staff today. Ok well let's get you up and when Mr Stephens is here, I will take my leave.*

fLy: Tristan makes his way down the corridor, desperate to run but maintaining his purposeful walk; his eyes are wide trying to filter in as much detail on the situation as he walks toward the damsel in not too much distress.

> **Tristan**: *Sasha?*
> **Man with hair gel**: *In your capable hands, Mr Stephens, I have to go now as I am late for a meeting regarding next year's syllabus.*
> **Tristan**: *Sasha, are you strong enough to walk back to my classroom? I don't think it would be a good idea to take you back to your boarding house as I saw most of your year group at luncheon. I would rather that for the next thirty minutes or so you will be supervised.*
> **Sasha**: *I could go up to the second floor Sanitorium and sit with Nurse Katy.*

Tristan: *You could but if you are feeling light-headed the last thing you need to do is go climbing stairs. If you start to feel poorly again I will go and fetch Nurse from the San instead, ok?*

fLy: As Tristan walked he lent slightly forward to try and hide his turgid member. All he was doing was holding her arm but the mere touch of her made him tingle; the only way he could try and convey his supposed concern was by means of wrinkling his forehead, his foppish greying hair making a frayed curtain over his brow. If only I could hear what was going through his mind. How many Shakespeare quotations would be racing through his grey, lovestruck cerebellum? He guided the unstable Sasha into his classroom and pulled a chair out next to his and gestured to her to sit down. Granted Sasha was slightly pale but girls have 'pale' days but I am really very sure that Tristan would be treating her the same regardless of her pallor; one cannot pass up an opportunity to hold close what one craves.

Tristan: *I'll get us both some water and then we can reassess how you feel afterwards.*

fLy: As the excited man left the classroom he said under his breath, "I have a desire to hold my acquaintance with thee." The Bard, he had to be referred to in such times of such anticipation, for Tristan at least. I accompany him and have to fly quite fast to keep up with Tristan as he runs to the school kitchen to grab and fill two pint glasses; clever – the larger the volume of water, the more time Sasha will be in his sole care. He returns to the class rosy-cheeked and trying to hide the fact that he is slightly out of breath. He passes her the pint of water and advises her to sip the water and not to gulp it down. Tristan pulls his chair a few inches closer to Sasha and for a few moments there is an obvious silence. Sasha breaks it by thanking him for looking after her and Tristan beams as he dismisses it as 'nothing'. They make idle, aimless chat about Sasha settling in at school and her roommate Ana before the conversation moves toward something more compelling.

Tristan*: Are both of your parents coming to the parents' evening next week, Sasha?*

Sasha*: Yes, they are, Sir. Usually only Mum makes the effort but this time round Dad is coming too, under duress though as it is my birthday that same day. My mum phoned school to ask for permission for me to be excused from Evening Meal; that way Mum, Dad and I could all go out for a celebration dinner after the parents' evening. So whatever you do, make sure you don't upset them, Sir!*

Tristan*: Sasha, I am really impressed by your work and you seem to have really approached the coursework in a very mature and intelligent way. You will not have to be worried about what I will be telling your parents. Now, on a more personal note, how old will you be? I hope that you will be saving me a piece of cake, assuming you're not too old for cake?*

Sasha*: I think cake is the only thing birthdays are good for, Sir! I can't say that I enjoy them otherwise. Historically my parents always seem to save an almighty argument for my 'special' day which starts as I unwrap the presents that my father has bought for me. My mum will tut at him and Dad finds it infuriating. From relatively nowhere the fighting starts. Don't get me wrong, there is no physical violence but their words are vicious. I sit and listen and wonder where this malevolence is harboured for the rest of the year. Maybe they argue whilst I am away at school; maybe that is why they have sent me to boarding school since I was thirteen; dressed it up as a commuting issue or something like that anyway. Should be interesting at the restaurant, not for me but for the other lucky diners! Maybe you will be in luck, Sir, and it may have already started by the time they get to your 'Teacher Station' at the parents' evening. Well, as I say, it is a first that they have attended a parents' evening together; no I need to correct that statement as it infers that Dad may have been to one independently of Mum,* *but he just hasn't. Not enough networking possibilities presenting themselves at such events.*

Tristan: *What do your parents do for a living, Sasha?*

Sasha: *Well, Dad works for a pharmaceutical company, he heads up the global business development side and Mum works for a family during the week, taking the kids to school and doing after-school pick-up I suppose; a bit of cooking and cleaning but nothing too stressful. She could have done that with me but I suppose she wasn't going to get paid for doing that. I sound really cynical, I wish I didn't, it doesn't help, it just makes me feel bad. I think Mum made a mistake stopping her proper job when she had me and she begrudges Dad's success, I think so anyway; God knows I have thought about it often enough.*

When Granny was alive she would say to Mum that the best job in the world was being a mother and I think when Granny died so did Mum's belief that it really was. I went to boarding school and Mum started looking for work. I remember her first job back was at the firm she used to work at but she said that everyone had forgotten her and no one wanted to help her back up the career ladder. She didn't want to have to move company and start again at the bottom and she really didn't like how computerised and inhuman it had all become. There were so many systems now in place to replace the 'personal touch' and everything had to be recorded; phone calls, meetings, hitting sales targets and having to get on with everyone. So she left and told me that if I wanted to I could become a day girl at school as she would have the time and energy to take me to school, collect me, shop for me, cook for me. But I was happyish being a boarder at school and I saw how badly bullied the day girls were so I said that I was fine as I was. So that was how it was left. And then when it came to doing my A levels I had to change school regardless of my state of happiness and so I continued in the same vein of being a boarder. I wish I had at least tried being a day girl at some point when my mum offered it; I really missed out I think.

Tristan: *Your mum did too, Sasha; and your dad.*

Sasha: *I don't think Dad would have noticed other than the change in school fees. He was never around when I was growing up anyway. He was always away on business and at weekends he just succumbed to his tiredness and spent much of the time on the sofa with a mango juice and Sky Sports. But Mum was good; she taught me to cycle, took me swimming, did my homework with me, taught me how to sew, how to change a fuse, check the tyre pressures on a car, lots of things really. I can't even think of one thing that Dad did. He never read to me when he came home from work when I was little; he would say goodnight though and give me a kiss. But Granny would be the one that read to me whilst dear Daddy drank his Winter Whisky Cocktail, whatever that was, and ate his crisps downstairs listening to the radio.*

Tristan: *Did Granny live with you?*

Sasha: *No, but all she wanted was to spend time with me.*

fLy: And as she said that, Sasha crossed her legs and I noticed, as did Tristan, that she hitched up her skirt so that it was further up her thighs, showing more of her legs and just making it possible to catch a glimpse of her stocking tops. That was intentional, I knew it, and I think Tristan did too because his mouth within seconds dried and he had a big glug of water. The game was on; Tristan's interest was not one-sided and I think this glimmer of light would make his days more intense and his thoughts more difficult to separate away from Sasha.

Tristan: *I am sure your dad missed you too, Sasha; it is just that sometimes everyday routine stains our eyes and masks the art, beauty and passions that exists in it. The familiarity of it all strangles the ability to see the wonderment in our everyday life. Trust me, Sasha, no one could ever…*

Sasha: *Ever what?*

Tristan: *Well, I am sure that if I were a father then I would cherish any time with my child but I also know that one's own behaviour plays foreign at times, unrecognisable even with hindsight.*

Sasha: *You don't have any children?*

Tristan: *No, not yet; one day hopefully… anyway, are you getting hungry, you must be? I could walk you back to the canteen; you do appear much brighter now; and hopefully we could both grab a bite to eat before the kitchen closes?*

Sasha: *I am hungry, Sir, I wasn't sure if it was my stomach or yours that I heard rumble! But before we go anywhere though, Sir, I am really thankful for you taking your time with me today; chatting with me. I think that is what I miss the most about being a boarder. Having someone older and wiser to discuss things with or to help when things may be a bit muddled.*

fLy: Sasha looked at him, straight in the eye and after one long second she smiled; her intense gaze made Tristan blush. As they made their way to the canteen they walked in my opinion too closely to each other. I left them to their lunch as I was not only peckish myself but I was starting to get fatigued and I had started to wonder how Hannah was.

7

fLy: When I returned home, after having feasted on a rather bloody, mushed-up bit of furry road kill, Hannah was ironing in front of the television watching some programme about 'The Menopause'. As she finished ironing a shirt she would take a few glugs of cold white wine and then move onto the next. I had not witnessed her do this before but thought that it could be a good way to encourage more 'homemakers' to engage in some of the more static activities this role involves. "Drink wine and iron," would be my advertising campaign should I ever be employed to push the merits of housework.

I was annoyed that I hadn't noticed this before and considered that maybe I was off my game. I am sure that Wallace would know, but then he doesn't have the same interest for detail that I do; he is just happy in his dog's life.

I sat and watched Hannah as she finished the bottle of wine and the ironing as all other forms of entertainment that day were sadly lacking. I didn't fancy flying back to find Sasha or my other interests there as the school day had pretty much finished and soon Tristan would be heading home to start his marking. But as soon as I had resolved myself to another night of just existing there was a knock at the front door. It was the man with hair gel!

He wanted to speak with Tristan about the school play because Mr Fallbuoy had put him in charge of budgeting for the props, scripts, wardrobe and the like. He was very keen to start work on it this evening as his girlfriend was out which meant he could really concentrate on the task in hand. As the 'Man with hair gel' talked, Hannah held onto the door frame and shifted her weight from leg to leg as if agitated. Hannah invited the 'Man with hair gel' in which was quite unusual but then this, I think, was one of the first times she still had a bottle of wine whirling round her veins by 6pm. 'Man with hair gel' accepted her offer and came in. He happily accepted a glass of red wine, not white, whilst he waited for Tristan.

Hannah ushered 'Man with hair gel' on to the sofa and handed him the remote control. She teetered off to the kitchen and opened a bottle of Tristan's special red wine and excused herself. The Hannah I knew then re-emerged. Up the stairs she leapt and promptly stuck the handle of the toilet brush down her throat. The thought of what the toilet brush cleaned plus the stench of bleach assisted Hannah with clearing out the alcoholic contents of her stomach so that she would be able to drink more wine without worrying about the calories. She frantically searched to find her blackcurrant throat lozenges that she had recently started to use to mask the smell of sick on her breath but had no luck so she just sloshed her mouth out with some minty toothpaste. It didn't work too well but there was a definite change in her aural bouquet.

She applied some pale pink lipstick, bronzing blush to help camouflage the redness around her eyes from her efforts during vomiting and went back downstairs to the guileless form that sat supping his red wine and watching *Reality Shows: Fact or Fiction* on television. There was a definite atmosphere in the room, a tension that I couldn't quite fathom. Hannah grabbed herself a fresh glass of white wine from the fridge and then sat in 'Stan's' chair facing the 'Man with the hair gel' who was still on the sofa. I knew he felt uneasy as his hands started to stick, just a little bit, to the glass and his lips stuck, just a little bit, together as he spoke to her about the day at school. He told Hannah about Miss Letty Swallow and shared with her a brief resume of Miss Swallow's career to date that he had heard from Mr Fallbuoy. Hannah appeared to be listening to him but I could tell that she was attracted to the 'Man with hair gel' and his conversation was secondary. Her body language was the first sign; she pushed the sleeves of her jumper up to her elbows so that her small wrists could be seen with their little blue veins pumping blood at a faster rate and she started to play with her hair; flicking it and twirling it. Hannah then moved from where she was sitting to next to him on the sofa, explaining that she would find it easier to rest her glass on the little coffee table that was positioned near to him. The 'Man with the hair gel' didn't try and move along to make more space for Hannah he just slowly looked at her as she sat down. I could tell that he was assessing her. This sort of flirtation was new territory for me. On one angle there was Tristan's emotional fantasy with Sasha; she was the embodiment of his heroine Hermione; and then there was Hannah's reaction to seeing someone she fancied and then there was 'Man with hair gel's' way of acting upon his instincts in a far more animalistic or obvious way.

With Tristan, I can figure out what is going on very easily; he verbalises nearly all of his emotions and feelings. He will either talk to Wallace on a dog walk (me in tow), talk to himself in the mirror or will talk to the files in his office but Hannah only really talks to Fi. Would Hannah talk to Fi about this member of staff in the way that I hoped she would? And is Hannah really interested in the Man with the hair gel (who turned out to be called Jean) or is she just a bit pissed and feeling horny?

Their proper conversation commenced with Hannah asking about Jean's relationship with his girlfriend; you know, whether he lived with her or not; how long they had been seeing each other, that sort of thing. It turns out that they had been going out for four years but then they split up due to an indiscretion on his part (which involved a Russian pole dancer) and two years later they managed to put the past behind them and started again. They were not engaged as they weren't the marrying types. I wonder what those types are?

I was momentarily distracted when the front door opened and Tristan came in; neither of them seemed to hear and carried on talking, such was their level of interest in each other. Tristan came in and said hello to them both and Jean complimented Tristan on having such a wonderful wife as she had made him feel totally welcome whilst waiting to see Tristan. He then asked Tristan if Sasha was feeling better and with that Hannah's expression changed from gloating to goading. Tristan answered Jean as they walked toward the office and Hannah, to her annoyance, could not quite decipher the response; her eyes narrowed as she tried to hear what was being said. I zoomed into the office before the door was shut and made myself comfortable at the top of the curtains. It was dusty up there but the view and the acoustics made it all worthwhile, and besides, dust can be full of tiny, tiny bits of human debris: tasty.

Their dialogue was very straightforward and no further mention of Sasha was made. They discussed the up-and-coming production and all was very civil. But as Jean left he made a comment that Tristan didn't verbally respond to but mulled over whilst shaving in the morning. Tristan kept repeating that his interest in Sasha was not because she was a younger version of Hannah but because she was the one that made him 'feel' again. Sasha made him breathe differently and at no stage did Hannah ever do this to him. Sasha made Tristan feel as if every sensation had a silver zing to it; and everything that he saw of beauty he wanted to show to Sasha; Sasha was not a younger version of Hannah at all.

When Hannah traipsed over to Fi's the next day at mid-morning, I followed. I knew that Fi would be the obvious person that Hannah would confide in – let's face it, there isn't anyone else that Hannah socialises with or talks to, bless dear Hannah and her cotton socks, and I was intrigued to know what her screwy brain was thinking.

Hannah: *I am so pleased to have a friend like you, Fi. I don't know many that would put off their swim session to have a coffee and a chat with me.*

Fi: *You have always been there for me, Hannah, especially with Raymond's Trans-Personality issues, so this is the least I can do. You said on the phone that you were concerned about something. What is it?*

Hannah: *Well, last night someone came round to chat to Tristan about budgets for the school play; possibly the same person that you had mentioned. Tristan wasn't home yet from work and so I invited him in because I knew that the school play was going to become something of a focus for Tristan. In fact, he had already started looking at scripts. I had seen this same man before in the staff canteen and at the various socialising evenings but I had never really noticed him. However, when he was at our front door I couldn't believe how I was affected by him. I invited him in but then I went upstairs to put on make-up and I wanted to look nice, to look sexy for him. This isn't how I usually behave. When I reappeared downstairs he was watching television and I felt as if this was 'us', my life sitting there. That he was the man I was meant to be seeing in my sitting room. We chatted for a brief while about his relationship and the interlude with the Russian pole dancer and for those minutes I felt alive again. The conversation was nothing but the feeling in the room made my arm hairs stand on edge and my pants smudge with cream.*

Fi: *That is disgusting, Hannah. I don't need to know that.*

Hannah: *That's exactly it, Fi; I need to tell someone. This is so uncommon for me; but you are the only person I could possibly say this to. This isn't window shopping; this is me being controlled by something far stronger than just acknowledging that someone looks* 'hot'. The thought of him just consumes me. I am thinking of having some sort of mid-term party at our house just so that I can invite him and have a reason to be near him or to speak with him.

Fi: *Who is this teacher?*

Hannah: *Jean Lempriere, I think; well pretty sure anyway.*

Fi: *Jean Lempriere is head of the languages department, the one I had mentioned, and has become somewhat of a friend. In fact, Jean is coming here this weekend; he is having a day of tuition from Raymond. They are going off cycling in the morning and then Raymond is going to do some sort of fitness course with Jean. After they have finished their 'boot camp', as Raymond likes to refer to it, Jean's girlfriend is coming over for a spot of late lunch so maybe you and Tristan could join us? That way you can see Jean in his real life, with his real girlfriend and hopefully can put to rest this fixation, close that dangerous box called 'Curiosity'. I am only suggesting this, Hannah, as I know that obsessions can be dangerous and this way you will be able to evaluate your inner turmoil and realign your sexual energy with Tristan.*

Hannah: *Where on earth did all my "sexual energy" come from? For the first time in months, maybe years, I have been lit up by someone. This is the most alive I have ever felt; and it isn't down to the conversation, or the fact that he listened to me, as is the usual pitiful explanation given by a married woman about to go and fuck someone else. I feel a constant heat between my legs, a gentle buzzing, when I just think of him.*

Fi: *This is all too much, Hannah. I don't think I can have this conversation, Hannah, with so much detail. I get too flustered, too embarrassed, as I feel that this is too private, too much of a sensitive topic.*

Hannah: *Why sensitive topic, Fi? Are things ok between you and Raymond?*

Fi: *Well I feel anxious, really anxious, Hannah. Raymond and I are going through an extraordinary period at the moment of role-playing which I get very excited about in the sorts of ways that you* *have just mentioned and this is difficult for me to accept; to feel so turned on. For example, last night he called me 'Boudica' and put a wig on me. He had bought it off of the Internet and it arrived yesterday morning. I thought that it was another pair of padded cycling shorts as the packet was so bulgy but it wasn't. Raymond made me sit down with him as he opened the package. He did not tell me what was in it but told me that it was for me. As he tore open the protective plastic bag there was this long, red-haired, curly, luscious sort of wig which cascaded down over his lap. Raymond was so deft in getting all the waves and ringlets in the right places and opened it up over the biscuit barrel so that the crown would be comfortable for me to wear. It was like a dream come true, Hannah. All my life I have wanted long hair with reckless curls and burning colour and there it was in our kitchen. Raymond had also purchased a special type of comb with which to style the wig. He was taking so much care as his fingers snaked through the synthetic fibres. I was mesmerised by him. I felt like a voyeur sitting in my kitchen, observing someone so involved in their work. All along I had this sensation of excitement as I knew that I would be wearing that very wig later on and that Raymond would be admiring me in that wig. I could imagine his thick eyebrows furrowed with intensity as he would regard me in the same way that he looked at the wig then on the biscuit barrel.*

Later that evening, as we finished our brown rice and mackerel dinner, Raymond ordered me upstairs. He has started doing this thing; when the kids are in bed he puts on a deeper voice and calls me 'Centurion'; and so I marched up the stairs and panicked. I didn't have the right sort of clothes to complement the wig or to mimic the clothes of Boudica so I improvised and I just wore my black bikini and a pair of Raymond's pale brown socks. I don't have any sandals as you know because Raymond thinks that toeless shoes are not practical. So I pulled the socks up to my knee, and sliced rips into them to try and mimic a roman type of sandal, I suppose. As Raymond entered our bedroom his tone softened and as soon as he saw me, he said he saw 'Boudica'. He dictated, or rather instructed me around the bedroom and put me in all sorts of different positions. I asked him which position he liked best but he said his state of arousal was because he was instructing Boudica how to take his hardened Hasta; that by the way, Hannah, is a spear the gladiators would use to thrust with. As a gladiator, he had no rank per se, so the concept of a mere celebrated fighter imposing his will to someone as brave and recognised as Boudica was total eroticism! I have to say that I did like wearing the wig and seeing Raymond's delighted face in the mirror on occasion. I felt empowered, Hannah. I liked being able to fulfil a fantasy of Raymond's. Does Tristan ever talk to you about fantasies; yours or his?

Hannah: *No not really, Fi. I think there is some work to be done on our relationship as it currently stands. When I see him I feel uncomfortable, as if I am a fraud. I no longer wish to make him happy, I don't care about his work and his stage productions and I don't like most of his mannerisms. I don't really respect him anymore and I am far more likely to come to you if I was in trouble or just fancied a chat than bother him with it all. We seem to exist together but when I look at him I see a human; a bog-standard, no-bells, no-whistles human. He is reliable and pleasant-looking but he will never save the day or make the room rock with laughter. He is 2D and it makes me feel old and I am fed up of old. I am fed up of his stupid dog and his horrible stripy, overly long scarf that hangs on the peg in the hall. I am fed up of him talking to me about sodding Shakespeare and certain sonnets which keep him brimming with interest and plumbing a depth of intensity each time he reads them. I am fed up remembering how we used to be; he was the same but I was different! He always talked about Shakespeare even then and I thought that was fascinating but it's not; it is dull and even though Tristan thinks that it is amazing I don't! I couldn't care less that text can evolve in the same way as visual art. He gets high telling me about how his classes love Shakespeare and that they too marvel at the philosophy and insight that Shakespeare offers to the reader or* *the listener or the watcher. But just like the much maligned text, I have evolved too. I'm not the same but I don't think that Tristan has even noticed and the only thing I don't want him or anyone to notice is my ceaseless ageing. I used to look at Mum sitting in front of her dressing table mirror when I was really quite young and wonder why she spent so long putting on make-up. I would think her ridiculous for taking so much time and spending so much money on foundations and eyelash curlers. I didn't understand why she would be happy to let Dad and I see her with her gelatinous mask on but no one else. Even going to the supermarket warranted her putting on a full face of make-up; and I think that I am turning into that person, whom I would look at with such disdain. Oh fuck all of this; I know it is early, Fi, but have you a glass of wine going spare?*

fLy: Fi very kindly put a warm bottle of white wine on the table with a glass of ice and as Fi drunk her warm water with lemon in it, Hannah drunk her warm wine and ice cubes in it. Fi reminisced about her mum who sounded as frumpy as Fi, and Hannah just drank. After twenty minutes Hannah left, taking the half a bottle of wine with her. She made her way home for some late lunch and a comforting chunder.

However, as soon as Hannah was home she went into Tristan's office. Wallace ran in beside her and as she took her place in front of the computer, Wallace curled up over her feet. Hannah opened the control settings to have a look at the Internet search history. There were quite a few requests for information on 'Edward Burnham'. I knew that the surname was ringing a bell in Hannah's head but she couldn't immediately place it. So Hannah double-clicked on one of the searches and up popped a large image of 'Edward Burnham'. The blonde hair and sharp green eyes immediately made Hannah realise why Tristan was so interested in him. There was the father of the girl whom had come round that Sunday and that Tristan had cared for when she was feeling poorly. Hannah closed down the computer and went into the kitchen. She put the bottle of wine in the freezer and took herself upstairs. Thirty minutes later she re-emerged; she was breathing quite hard and her breath smelt of freshly grated parmesan cheese. Without really looking at the freezer, or the bottle or the glass; she managed to pour herself a good measure of the now ice-cold white wine. In two gulps the glass was empty and within two seconds it was refilled. With a stony expression Hannah walked over to the house phone and dialled Fi. When Fi answered she told Fi that she thought it was a great idea if she and Tristan were to join them for their late lunch this weekend with Jean 'plus one'. Not long after the bottle was finished, Hannah bounded upstairs to go and look in her wardrobe for what to wear to Fi's get-together. Her countenance had now definitely shifted; the glare in her eye was now rippling with anticipation.

It was actually good fun watching Hannah try on so many different outfits, some of which I had never seen before. It was refreshing to see her practising her smile; talking to the mirror at the imaginary person that was complimenting her on her figure. I could feel the buzz of excitement when she settled on an outfit and then put on her make-up and stilettos so that the whole ensemble was assembled. And hand it to Hannah, she looked vibrant and oddly she looked happy.

When Tristan arrived home later that day, Hannah had put her outfit aside in her wardrobe, including the underwear that she would be wearing, and told Tristan about the plans that she had made with Fi. Tristan was ecstatic when he realised he would be able to monopolise Jean for a whole afternoon. He was very pleased that Hannah had been so thoughtful to co-ordinate this with Fi and Raymond. He rarely sees Jean at school and he never really has the opportunity to spend any quality time with Jean. During school hours Tristan would have to rely on the odd free lesson or lunch break to get chatting about the play and as yet this had not happened. He was, in Hannah's mind, disproportionately excited as he reached for a bottle of chilled Prosecco and poured them both a glass of the slightly sharp fizz. Hannah didn't care what his euphoria was about as all she could focus on or think about was seeing Jean again. And as the bottle of cheap plonk dwindled toward empty, Tristan became amorous. Very slowly he took her by the hand and led her upstairs. Hannah could feel Jean's hand guiding her up the stairs and Tristan no doubt was guiding Sasha's. Neither of them spoke audibly during their impassioned session of lovemaking but both were mouthing the names of their heart-throbs covertly; their eyes truly were sparkling throughout and momentarily I felt quite sad for them both. Thankfully, that pathetic pang soon passed as I watched Hannah climb out of bed and espied the little plops of cum drip out of her onto the synthetic tendrils of carpet as she walked to the bathroom for her post-poke-piss.

Fi and Hannah spoke a few times on the phone and plans were put in place for the late lunch on Sunday. As usual Wallace was invited and as we all left for Fi's house, Tristan grabbed two scripts with which to occupy Jean and himself after lunch. Hannah was in her preordained outfit but was not feeling as confident as she thought she would. Tristan made no comment about how she looked and I could sense that this slightly rattled her; so Hannah asked Tristan if he thought she looked nice. He said that he thought that she might get cold legs but in retrospect the fact that they would be inside for most of the time made him change his mind; she looked fine but maybe a little too glamorous for a casual lunch. As they waited for Fi or Raymond to open the front door, Hannah looked at the cars parked in the small driveway that curled around the front of their house. It was mainly tarmac with a smattering of pale yellow small stone that made a noise like a pepper grinder when driven over. There were three cars parked, one which she and I recognised to be Raymond's, complete with rear-mounted bicycle racks; but the other two she and I were unsure of. My attention was diverted to the door as it was opened; inside a tall Japanese lady welcomed us all in and shouted to Fi to see if the dog could come in. But it was too late to await a response as Wallace had already run inside and up the staircase toward the children's bedroom; he was a smart dog.

Tristan introduced himself and Hannah as the lady beckoned us toward the room where they were all sitting. Hannah suddenly excused herself from following and darted into the small toilet to check herself once more before presenting herself into the room where Jean and his girlfriend would be sitting. Rather than follow Tristan, I decided to go with Hannah as I was curious as to why she disappeared now as she had already been to the loo several times before coming out. Once inside the green wallpapered closet, Hannah put the lid of the loo down and stood on it. By doing this she could get a good enough reflection of what she looked like in the mirror that hung over the old, large white china sink and she noticed for the first time that the skin on her legs looked like that of a plucked chicken. Her skin was taking on a bluish tinge, pimply too. The high-heeled black patent shoes that she had chosen to wear to elongate her legs, had made her feet look as if she may well have chicken talons stuffed into the pointed toes. She stepped off of the loo and walked over to the same mirror. She looked at her face's reflection and then leaned forward as if to get an even closer look. With that she quickly left the toilet and slammed the door, such was her haste. I kept up with her as she walked and then ran back home. As she opened our front door, she finally started to cry and went upstairs to her bed. She lay beneath the covers until she was woken by Tristan's front door key turning in the lock about five hours later. During that time Fi had come round to the house and left a note for her through the letterbox to see if she was ok; Tristan had tried calling her but he was too consumed with the play to let Hannah's bizarre behaviour bother him too much. Even when he arrived home he just went straight into his office and started typing, not giving Hannah a second thought.

Hannah, I think, felt quite alone as she regarded herself in the mirror; her eyes no longer had that sparkle that they had when she was on her way to Fi's and her mouth had resumed its usual languor. She put on her slippers and grey tracksuit and made her way downstairs to the fridge where a fresh, new bottle of white wine loyally awaited her.

When Tristan emerged from the office he made his way over to Hannah and gave her a kiss on the forehead. He leant forward to grab the bottle of wine that was rested against her feet but it was empty so he opened up a bottle of red wine and poured himself a glass.

Tristan: *You know Jean is Head of Languages at school?*
Hannah: *Fi told me actually.*
Tristan: *It all seems as if it were meant to be, Hannah; this choice of play that I made; Jean being French and Jean heading up the budgeting for the play. It's really odd but beautiful in a way. Obviously we will be doing the play in English but there is a connection that this historic French literature, this art, has made with today's reality. It is as if there was a message, as yet hidden, for me to reveal; a beauty to be nurtured perhaps.*

fLy: I could see what he was doing and I wondered too if Hannah was also smelling the same familiar odour of bullshit. Had he already started to deceive himself; to cajole himself into an act of adultery by decorating its immorality with the heavily burdened brush of fate?

Hannah: *Does Jean like the play?*
Tristan: *He has heard of it but never seen it so I suggested that he stop by tomorrow and borrow the DVD so that he could get a feel for it. I said that you would be in most of the day. I could, of course, take it into work and leave it for Jean in his pigeonhole but I am trying to keep the play slightly under wraps from the other members*

of staff; until at least it has been seen by the drama group. Would that be ok with you, Hannah?

fLy: In the morning Hannah phoned Fi to explain her absence from the late lunch and told Fi that she had come to her senses before she had a made a fool of herself in front of Jean or any of the friends there. Fi told Hannah she had not missed anything really; it was a rather disjointed affair with Tristan dominating Jean's time on the sofa whilst Raymond was compiling spreadsheets of fitness goals and aims for Jean over the next few weeks. Apparently Fi, Bruno, Bruno's friend and Jean's partner sat at the kitchen table desperately creating conversation for the sake of it. She couldn't even recall what the topics of discussion were. But she did say that she was pleased that Hannah had come to her senses about Jean and that it was just as well as Jean had not enquired about Hannah's absence and his girlfriend was really nice. With that Hannah finished the phone call with a marked rapidity and made her way towards the fridge. As she reached inside of it I knew that there was one of two things she would choose to imbibe; Chardonnay or Diet Coke. I couldn't be bothered to find out which so I decided to make my way to the staff room for mid-morning break to see if Tristan, Jean or Raymond were there.

8

fLy: On my short journey toward the main area of the school, I have to pass the English Room where Tristan teaches and so I happened to glance toward it. To my surprise I saw Sasha and Tristan both sitting at Tristan's desk. I immediately changed course and flew around all of the windows to see if there was a way in. All of the windows were closed and the door firmly in its frame. I would have to sit and watch, to observe rather than to hear, through the glass window. I made one last reconnoitre of the windows to make double sure that there was no way that I could get in. There wasn't so I patiently spied on them both through the glass. Very soon I realised that this exercise was not fruitless; their body language was very much in evidence. There was only one book on Tristan's desk and it was a text book; it wasn't prep or foolscap. In one hand Sasha had the yellow highlighter and in the other she had a yellow and black striped HB pencil. She looked as if she were reading to him and as she did he just stared as if studying the shape of her ear. Sasha would look up and rather than divert his eyes immediately down toward the page he would carry on looking at her. To begin with she would appear to be uncomfortable and move or adjust her seat but after the third time, she held his gaze and then would look down and continue reading. Occasionally he would point at a section and she would scribble something in the margin of the text; but most of the time she would be reading and he seemingly taking the part of all the other roles.

It was evident that she was practising for a specific part in the school play. However, having seen the film several times and overheard Tristan's mutterings, I knew that there was only one part that Tristan had in mind for Sasha and that was the part of Madame de Tourvel. As the dialogue progressed so did my want to be inside the room, on the other side of the glass. All I wanted to do was feel the electricity that would have been bouncing around that classroom; I felt desperate, like a moth trying in vain to get to the light. The energy that poured from Tristan's eyes would have powered the wind farms that blight the coastline of Norfolk and the heightened breathing that Sasha's shoulders exhibited left me in no doubt that the room would have smelt of pheromones and glistening pussy. Agreed, the chosen play is charged with sex and the pursuit of it but this was more than just an empathetic appreciation of good writing. Looking through the window I could see that Tristan's fantasies were now, to a point, looking more plausible. Place your bets please…

The end of break was signalled by a loud bell and Sasha and Tristan stood up simultaneously; the phrase 'saved by the bell' was probably never truer. As the door opened to Tristan's classroom I had to make a choice of whether to dive into the room to inhale and enjoy the smell of the air, to detect if I had been correct in my earlier assumptions, or to follow Sasha and Tristan. I chose the former and flew into the room just as the door shut. At first the smell reminded me of warm plastic and stale breath but as I flew closer to the chair that Sasha had been sitting on, there was the unmistakable odour of damp cotton and, ever so slightly, of freshly ground black pepper. On the desk I could smell the sweat from Tristan's hands and from under the desk I could smell the merest hint of sweat from the skin just behind the testicles. It is a perfume which is very similar to that of the oily, watery globes that sit on the cheap Sunday roast as it sits under the Carvery's heat lamps; 'joint juice'. There was enough evidence of sexual excitement here to satisfy my olfactic curiosity so I positioned myself near to the door, ready to escape when the next consignment of human minds entered the room.

As the children, young adults and teachers marched past the windows on their way to various classes I was aware that if Tristan and Sasha wished to keep their affection for each other secret then there would have to be a change of location. Around three sides of this classroom there were windows which offered nothing in the way of privacy as they were bare of curtains and the room was a bland, honest square; there were no cupboards or hidden corners in which to disappear.

A better room for them would be Mr Harbinger's room which sat above part of the main school stage and dressing room. It was on the first floor and far darker than Tristan's; even on the sunnier days the shadows from the clock tower would mean that Mr Harbinger would have to have the lights on. It had not been decorated or updated in years; the carpet was brown and was made in a similar way to a coir doormat; flecks of skin and shafts of hair would sit upon the minute plastic fronds that reached up with their tiny height into the room and the curtains that flanked all of the windows were orange in colour with a red and brown dart that ran through them. That room was certainly not conducive to romance but judging by earlier tensions, room décor would be irrelevant.

Once I am out, I make a perfunctory visit to the staff room and upon spying Miss Letty Swallow I make an about-turn back home.

As I approach my front door I am delighted to see Jean entering our house and accelerate so that I can go in via the front door rather than entering through my usual point of entry and exit. Jean is wearing the usual 'teacher' outfit of caramel-coloured chinos, white shirt and blue tie. Hannah, on the other hand, has obviously spent all morning getting ready. I realise that, in having watched Tristan with Sasha, I have forfeited seeing Hannah's wardrobe raid; her desperately looking for something to wear on the off chance that at any minute of the day Jean would be dropping by to collect the DVD.

She had plumped for some very tight-fitting jeans and a white shirt that could be mistaken for one of Tristan's which she had tied in a knot at the front, just above her belly button. She had painted her toes and fingernails a fresh cherry red and had tied her hair in a loose ponytail. Her make-up was very simple-looking but clever as it had given her a healthy glow. She invited Jean in for a coffee which he accepted and rather than go and sit on the sofa like before he followed her to the kitchen and stood with one hand on the counter and the other with his thumb looped into his front trouser pocket. He looked very relaxed and his mannerisms concurred.

Jean: *So tell me, Hannah, where were you yesterday? Raymond told me that you would be coming along to the late lunch but I didn't see you. You are delightfully thin, Hannah, but not so thin that I can't see you so I know you definitely weren't there! I think I would be able to spot you in the most crowded of rooms.*

Hannah: *I didn't think anyone noticed; least of all you, Jean. From what Tristan tells me, you and he spent the afternoon talking about Les Liaisons Dangereuse.*

Jean: *You are avoiding answering my question, Hannah.*

Hannah: *I did come along but only briefly. I had to come back home as I felt awkward. I had probably worn the wrong clothes or just knew that I would be better off letting you and Tristan talk; he is very excited about this year's drama production and I would only have been a distraction.*

Jean: *The only reason I agreed to being involved in this play Hannah was to get distracted, to get a little closer to Mrs Stephens.*

Hannah: *You mean to me?*

Jean: *Yes, you Hannah, not Tristan's mother.*

Hannah: *But until the other day you had never even seen me let alone met me!*

Jean: *I hadn't met you, Hannah, but I have seen you. I see you going to the sports centre in your tight black Lycra looking elegantly fragile.*

Hannah: *Why? Why me? You are in a school surrounded by younger women, plump with youth and energy!*

Jean: *Because you have what they don't.*

Hannah: *And that is?*

Jean: *My attention.*

fLy: You have to agree that was a knock-out reply that left no room for Hannah to interject. She was visibly delighted with his response and as Jean left with the DVD Hannah closed the front door and ran over to Wallace. She held his face in her hands begging him not to say a word to Tristan. What a pathetic act of childish excitement. I wasn't sure what to expect next but should have known that a glass of wine was on the cards. She opened the bottle that had been chilling in the fridge and she poured herself a large glass which she gulped down. Hannah then recharged her now empty vessel and thought to call Fi. But something stopped her from doing so and instead she went over to the stacked CDs and found one by Madonna. She pressed 'play' after she had selected track eight and turned the volume up high. In the middle of the sitting room she danced like she was having some sort of epileptic fit. She had, at first, her arms out to her sides and span round and round; her face wore an effulgent smile that made her look half-deranged and half-drunk. Her eyes sparkled as her starry gaze looked into the distance. As she spun she started to giggle and the dancing became even more energetic, with periods of sprinting on the spot and creating shapes with her liberated hands and arms. As the music pumped, Hannah continued laughing and dancing. I sat with Wallace, both of us bewildered and baffled.

Later on Tristan came in and didn't pay any attention to his wife and called Wallace to go for his walk. As they left I opted to follow as I had had enough of watching Hannah; there is only so much gurning and twisting and twerking one can watch without getting bored. But there was something about Tristan that evening that seemed charged. As usual he grabbed his long striped scarf and wound it round his neck and large Adam's apple; a strand of grey hair that was on the scarf caught on his teeth. I don't think that I have mentioned his unusual teeth before because they are not protruding or so obvious that all one does is try not to keep looking at them whilst talking to the person. They are straight and fairly white, not stained, but they would get in the way of his lips at times and he would have to use his forefinger to reposition them. When Tristan was making love to Hannah or when he was in his office contemplating his production of *Les Liaisons Dangereuses*, his lips would get slightly stuck to his front two teeth. And as we left the house that evening, he kept pushing his tongue up under his top lip to release the sticking flesh. He was noticeably excited and I hoped that Wallace, and I, would be privy to the reason why on this walk.

As we made our way across the athletics track, Tristan started to sing. He had a good voice, I think, well better than Hannah's at any rate. He started to sing one of the songs by The Police called 'Don't Stand So Close To Me' and the rendition lasted until we were out of the school grounds and onto public land.

Tristan: *So, Wallace, help me. Here I am, a man that loves all that is true and honest. I love Hannah but yet I would give it all away if I could be with Sasha for the rest of my years. Today, Jean Lempriere told me that Dan Winkwood was going to ask Sasha to his brother's eighteenth birthday party that was on Saturday. I felt that my path to Sasha's heart was threatened and I had to speak* *with Sasha. After her English lesson I asked her to stay behind. I had her file and her coursework out in front of me to offer some sort of cover and as she pulled up a chair to my desk I wanted to hold her and reassure her. I wanted to tell her that her work was top-grade and that she would excel in her exams without my lessons or extra tuition. But instead I revelled in this power I had over her; her ignorance of her academic potential made her easy to manipulate. She had red cheeks and kept looking at her files in front of me. I wanted to hold her face in my hands and kiss her; she was so vulnerable and bereft of confidence. But then I saw my chance. I knew that she took her studies very seriously so I offered her extra English lessons in order to guarantee a basis of understanding of the literary techniques that the examiners would be looking for. Dan's invite was for this Saturday so I suggested that we start as soon as possible with extra tuition; and that I was able to accommodate her on Saturday. She accepted, Wallace! I asked her if she had made any plans that evening with her parents and she told me that she had been invited to a party.*

Sasha told me that she had spoken to her mother about the party as she would not be at home for Saturday evening and would go straight back to school on the Sunday. Her mother apparently thought that was a much better idea than to risk someone driving her home at such a late hour and one thing was for sure was that Sasha's mum would not be collecting her. I hadn't realised that Sasha was intending to stay at the Winkwood's house. I felt shaky as the realisation of what this would or could entail for Sasha, for us. She could end up having sex with someone and then feel obliged to go out with them. But then it dawned on me that her mum was happy with this set-up. This, I suddenly saw, could work in our favour. I can see that if Sasha and I were to reach a point in our relationship where she was to stay away from school or home one weekend her mum would be relaxed with the idea; so long as Sasha said she was staying with friends and not her English teacher! This terrible dishonesty stains my conscience, the idea of extra lessons and the lying to her

111

mother about Sasha's whereabouts once we become an item truly bothers me. But I know that after a little while I will explain to her mother and father and they will understand my motive for being so deceitful; but only once I have their trust and maybe even their blessing. But at this point in time I had to intervene, I had to take this first step, Wallace, toward being in Sasha's life in a more concrete way. I know that there is a mutual attraction there; but I have to be very sensitive to her age and her naivety. I have to protect her from the likes of the Winkwood Family and I want to protect her for life. And what do I know about the Winkwood Family that pushes me to this judgement? Well if the truth be known, not much, but I can't risk Sasha being sexually involved with someone that doesn't understand or grasp the enormity of her beauty and brilliance. She is like the sunshine that streams in through the window, she is the energy that keeps my blood pumping, she has the intelligence that can evaluate and justify the works of Shakespeare; the embodiment of his greatest of heroines. If I were a work of literary greatness it would be her mind that I would want to scrutinise and appreciate me. In her there are the windows of fresh air and life that makes one see the beauty of basic grass and glory in the smell of roses. Without her the world is a far lesser place. She was created and then born into this world; and I will never know if her mother and father realised just what they had made. A triumph of looks and mind that can never be summarised into text or photographs. And would anyone see this apart from me? How could a boy of seventeen or eighteen, nineteen or twenty ever understand her? I do, but only because I have read and learnt and felt the enormity of tragedy. I have lived to breathe the works of Shakespeare and now I have the capacity to embrace all that is Sasha. I have to be her Romeo because I know that she is my Juliet; she is my Hermione and I her Leontes. But this time round we will be together and I will love her, every inch of her, gently and softly without tragic end. I have to be clever though, Wallace; I can't frighten her with my intensity of feelings. She has no idea of what power she has over me or others so it is probably *best that I pursue her under this veil of education. Very slowly I will make her realise that we have been brought together for reasons far more important than exams, education and grades.*

Oh, Wallace, if only I could fast-forward my life to when I am with her. If only I could know what she was thinking or doing. I would be a fly on the wall and watch her in private doing the things that I would never get to see otherwise. To be able to see her asleep, her lips slightly parted inhaling and exhaling, her hair cast about her pillow like petals surrounding a beautiful flower, her eyelashes resting gently on each other; oh, what total bliss, Wallace!

fLy: And that gave me the idea to go and see what she was up to in her dormitory. If I could have, I would have thanked Tristan, but I couldn't so I just had to buzz off!

I had been a few times to her dormitory before but I was never sure of when was best to go. Much of the time I had spent going there was fruitless. The girls were either doing prep, asleep or reading brainless, glossy magazines with covers of bright yellow and pink and royal blue. It was time that I revisited that boarding house and became more intimate with Sasha and her companions. I could get the very insight that Tristan craved; after all I am fLy.

I went via home because I wanted to check on Hannah. I was curious to see if she had restarted spinning around the sitting room to Madonna but when I arrived she was upstairs making herself sick. So I waited outside the bathroom and then followed her back downstairs. She opened another bottle of white wine and chose another CD. Before pressing play she went to the cupboard below the sink and pulled out four white jasmine-scented pillar candles and lit them. All of the main electric lights she turned off and then she pressed 'play'. To my delight Michael Jackson was the music of choice and to her delight she poured herself a large glass of wine. She resumed her dancing, out of time and seemingly out of her head. I had no idea she was so fond of dancing nor aware that she was so painfully dreadful at it. I left her to it and made my way into school and toward the girls' boarding house.

I waited, again, by the main front door of Sasha's boarding house hoping that the door would open soon. I knew that there would be another, less time-consuming way to get in but I didn't want to waste time finding an entry and then to be stuck. I didn't have to wait long as Richard Dellaway from Learn'2'Drive arrived to take Minty Golbriath out for her millionth driving lesson. Richard Dellaway (his name is emblazoned on the side panels of the Honda Jazz car) buzzed the door entry system and introduced himself through the small speaker by the door. The door buzzed open and as Minty came out all nervous and teary, I took the opportunity to enter. The house smelt of toast and butter and the television was on in the Common Room. So I headed that way. Much like the boys' boarding houses, the television would be on and no one would be watching, but unlike the boys' boarding houses there was a small selection of various styles of knickers drying on the radiators that encircled the room. Tempted, I flew over to them to see if there was anything of interest to me still staining their gusset but all of them smelt of washing powder. I made my way up the shallow flight of stairs to the first room. There were two girls in their beds, reading magazines, and so I left. This was the story for the further six rooms I visited, but then I found her. To be honest, when I first peered in to the room I didn't realise it was Sasha's room. There were photographs Sellotaped to the cream-painted walls and all of them were of dogs or horses or groups of girls with huge smiles squashed into the 4" by 6" paper rectangles. There was no music playing and the only sound was of a ticking clock and the rhythmical rubbing of flesh. As I flew into the room, there behind the door on the floor, was Ana. Knowing that Ana and Sasha were good friends I decided to carefully position myself on the top of the brown curtains. Even if my hunch was wrong about this being Sasha's room I decided to stay so that I could enjoy the spectacle of Ana meticulously massaging what smelt like aloe and beeswax into her skin. Ana was naked and her legs shone in the light of the room; as she finished her arms and shoulders they radiated with the same glistening glow of her lower torso. Her skin looked like satin. She squeezed another palmful of cream from the white plastic tube on to her hand and she started to firmly apply her salve to her spongy breasts. Her nipples became hard as she massaged them, working round the dome like shapes. Her nipples were quite large but her areola that surrounded the fleshy pastilles were brown and expansive and quite shocking to me as I had not seen boobs such as these, each with a dark plum tattooed disc that covered much of the ample milky white skin that wrapped each mammary. She then moved her hand toward her stomach, rubbing her stretch marks with possibly too much vigour. By the time she had stood up to moisturise her globe-like bum cheeks, Sasha arrived. As Sasha entered the room she came over to the window; I thought that she had spotted me and would try to swat me dead, but instead she drew the curtains. She then turned and went to sit on her bed not commenting on the state of Ana's undress or the fact the curtains had been open. Quietly Sasha opened a file and started to write whilst Ana finished saturating her young skin with parabens and perfume. Ana screwed the top back onto her near-empty tube of cream and nonchalantly asked what Sasha was doing.

Sasha: *I'm doing extra work. I think that I am going to fail my English paper.*
Ana: *But you are brilliant at English! What are you on about?*
Sasha: *Well, Mr Stephens says that I am falling behind. He has suggested extra English lessons starting this Saturday. But I don't mind; I really like him, in fact I have a crush on him. I rather like the thought of spending some extra time with him, and just him.*
Ana: *Eugh! Why him? Of all the teachers, Sasha! If you had*

115

said Mr Lempriere I would have agreed, he is so much sexier and younger! But Mr Stephens! He is such a creep!

Sasha*: I like him. I like his eyes. I like the way he talks; the sound of his voice. I dream about him sometimes. I have had some really erotic dreams about being with him in a classroom and when I see him it is like I am back in one of my dreams.*

Ana*: I had no idea you had a crush on him, Sasha. I should have guessed it would be someone a bit weird. How much of a crush do you have on him? I mean what if he were to make a pass at you; what would you do?*

Sasha*: He would never do that, Ana. I met his wife when I had to drop some late prep off to him at his house. Have you seen her? He wouldn't want me, she is thin and beautiful and most of the first fifteen rugby team fancy her. They see her in the gym on the running machine when they are on squad training and all of them say that they have had a wank thinking about her. But if, let's say, he were to come onto me, then yes, I would.*

Ana*: What? All the way?*

Sasha*: I don't know but my dreams are so explicit, it would be hard to imagine that I would say no.*

Ana*: I know this is wrong on so many levels, Sasha, but I think he does like you, you must know that, Sasha. I mean I watch him in English lessons and the way that he looks at you when he thinks no one else is looking at him.*

Sasha*: Really? Like when?*

Ana*: Well of recent when we all had to watch part of that documentary on Henry James. Do you remember he went and stood at the back of the classroom? Well I would occasionally look back at him to see if he had picked up the remote control, indicating that we were near the end of watching that painful male presenter lisp into the camera about poor Edith Wharton and her enforced exclusion from dealing with 'the' letters. Every time I looked at him, he was looking at you and only you, as if transfixed.*

Sasha*: You are reading too much into it; we have all done that,*

Ana! You seem to spend every lesson focusing on something other than the whiteboard or the teacher; a million miles away.

Ana: *But it is not the first time this has happened. I haven't mentioned it in the past because I didn't realise you fancied him. And what about the school play, Sasha? You told me today that he has cast you as Madame de Tourvel and Josh as Valmont. I mean every time we are in class reading a play he always asks Josh to read the part that is opposite you. And inevitably, he interjects and suggests that Josh reads it differently so that he ends up reading it himself so that Josh can supposedly learn.*

Sasha: *He's the bloody drama teacher, Ana, and I can't question why he has decided to cast Josh as Valmont. In class he has to step in because Josh's reading is so monotone and dull, what's he supposed to do?*

Ana: *So why did Mr Stephens cast him as Valmont? It is a huge role in the play and you couldn't get someone less dynamic than Josh. Why didn't Mr Stephens put Charlie in that lead role? Charlie is brilliant. He can act really well and has a stage presence, his voice is clear and he can do accents. It doesn't make sense. Have a think, Sasha. Why would he put Josh in that role? I am pretty sure I know why Mr Stephens chose Josh and it was because he didn't want you to fall for your co-star, 'Valmont'.*

Sasha: *That is ridiculous, Ana. How long have you spent working all of this out?*

Ana: *I have only just started thinking about it but it makes sense.*

Sasha: Sounds to me that you should spend more time thinking about Charlie I didn't realise that you had a soft spot for him. Isn't he a bit too blonde and a bit on the chubby, zit-ridden side for your liking?

Ana: *He is but that is just it. He has something about him that I think is intriguing and that is why he should be Valmont. He would be perfect; not too good-looking, but good-looking enough to attract the bored ladies of the French court and when he is in a room he seems to stand out. Why don't you suggest it to Mr Stephens; or at* *least ask him why he picked Josh for the role of Valmont; you could ask him on Saturday when you have your extra English tuition.*

fLy: Sasha walked over to the window, pulled the curtain back slightly and peered out for a few minutes and then returned to her bed and took up her file again and started taking more notes. Ana then resumed her position on the floor and brought her knees up to her chest. She reached up to her bedside table and retrieved a small pencil case. Inside were a selection of nail files, clippers, clear nail varnish and tweezers. She pulled out the nail clippers and then spent an age cutting her toenails and then varnishing them. The ritual was quite boring and once again there was nothing there for me to enjoy so I left. I visited the shower room and the laundry room on my way out so that I could familiarise myself with the layout of the girls' boarding house and to see if there were any air vents that I could use for entry in future. I was hoping that I would have reason to be visiting again soon.

9

fLy: When I arrived back home the light in the office was on and the curtains drawn. Hannah was no longer dancing but preparing dinner. It was some sort of vegetable stir fry; they ate meat infrequently now as Hannah had read that it made cellulite worse and your metabolism slow down. The atmosphere in the kitchen was far calmer now; the candles had now been extinguished and the stereo was off but Hannah still looked very happy as she supped on her wine and flipped the beansprouts in the wok. I noticed that the small dining table that used to sit in the kitchen had been moved into the sitting room in front of the double patio doors. It had been laid with placemats, cutlery, condiments and glasses; it looked rather romantic and I felt rather confused. Tristan came out of his office after Hannah had called that dinner was ready and he commented on how pleasant the table looked. Tristan sat down as Hannah walked over to the table holding the two plates of food, steam rising from them. Before Hannah sat down she went back to the kitchen and produced the wine from the fridge and as she walked over she started talking to Tristan.

Hannah: *Jean came round today.*
Tristan: *Jean?*

Hannah: *Yes, Jean, as in Mr Lempriere.*

Tristan: *Ah yes; of course, to collect the DVD. Did he stay and have a coffee or tea?*

Hannah: *Yes, he did, he stayed only briefly though. He had a coffee, I am not even sure if he finished it. But I did give him the DVD but he didn't say when he would watch it or return it. I am surprised that you didn't see him this afternoon to check as to whether he had been round to collect it; I would have thought it would be high up on your list of priorities.*

Tristan: *I did see him actually. He told me that Dan Winkwood's brother was having an eighteenth birthday party this Saturday and that most of the girls had been invited to go along; which is a shame as I had already suggested to Sasha Burnham, you know the girl that dropped her prep off the other weekend, have some extra English lessons on a Saturday, early evening. I have been meaning to chat about it with you for a couple of weeks now; her English is starting to drop in standard and having met her parents, her father in particular, I just wanted to make sure that her grades will not be letting her or her parents down. Would that be all right with you?*

Hannah: *How long will the lessons go on for? Will you be paid for this?*

Tristan: *I can't really charge her for it as I should be able to have all of my students at a level that maximises their potential without having to have extra tuition. All of the pupils here are only accepted after rigorous testing to ensure that we have the 'cream of the crop' so for one of my pupils to get less than excellent grades would reflect harshly on me. There will be some sessions where I could walk Wallace at the same time as much of our syllabus is about the understanding of a text so we could discuss this outside of the classroom environment; that might actually really work, you know to be outside of the 'classroom'. Don't get me wrong though, the classroom is a necessity when practising for the actual written exam. I know from first-hand experience that often students know their stuff but don't know how to answer the question in the way* *the examination board expects. I have many practice papers which I can utilise to ensure Sasha grasps this. She is a bright girl so I can't imagine that more than four or five extra lessons will be necessary.*

Hannah: *You do what you think is best for Sasha and more importantly for you. I would not like to think that Mr Fallbuoy has anything but praise for you and the work you do. You are very diligent and I think that it is admirable of you to go the extra mile with Sasha. I mean, even the work you do with the school drama productions is exceptional. Isn't Sasha in that too?*

Tristan: *Yes, she is playing the role that Michelle Pfeiffer played in the film, Madame de Tourvel. A challenging role for any young girl but one that I hope she can execute convincingly.*

Hannah: *I too have been thinking about the play Tristan, and all the time that you will have to plough into it. You will really need the support of the other staff members with regard rehearsals but in particular with the budget. This idea to do Les Liaisons Dangereuse is great but it will be an extravagant play to put on and to do it on a tight budget will be difficult. You wouldn't want the costumes to be anything other than grand so maybe it would be advantageous to become better or rather closer friends with Jean? He is still in charge of the budgeting, isn't he? Maybe it would be a good idea to first ask Jean and his partner, Fi and Raymond over for dinner and then if that goes well to make it more regular but with just Jean and his partner? What do you think? I think it would just help cement your relationship with Jean because there are bound to be times in the next few weeks when you will need to lean on him. You don't want to be putting a play on to all of those parents that was less than convincing and it would be a shame if the set or the costumes were to blame.*

Tristan: *You know, Hannah, you have amazed me this evening. I am very lucky that you are so aware and so supportive of me. I think that is a first-class idea. I will mention it to Raymond and Jean tomorrow in the staff room but I will tell them to contact you directly to organise dates and times.*

Hannah: *Do that but make sure you give Jean my number as he doesn't have it.*

fLy: I was in awe; Tristan had cleverly spun the extra English lessons to Hannah and Hannah had managed to take the first step toward legitimately being in Jean's company without doubt of reason. After they had finished their meal, Tristan, as usual, cleared away the plates and did the washing up; Hannah meanwhile took herself to bed. When Tristan joined her twenty minutes later they made love, each of them splendidly happy in their contrived deceitfulness.

The following morning was different for both of them; they both bristled with energy as they pranced about their bedroom, smiling at each other, putting on their outfits for the day. Hannah dressed in her black gym clothes and Tristan put on the newer of his two dark brown suits.

Hannah: *What time do you think you will have finished your extra lesson with Sasha on Saturday? 7.30ish?*
Tristan: *I would hope so, yes.*
Hannah: *Well that would work well because if Jean and Raymond are able to come over for dinner then that timing would be perfect. I do hope that they can come. I never thought I would say this but I am so pleased that you are doing this play and with such enthusiasm; I am looking forward to the dinner and to the play.*
Tristan: *I'll grab them today. Thanks again, Hannah.*

fLy: And with that dollop of cordiality Tristan kissed Hannah on the forehead and left. Hannah once again started to spin around and finished her glass of water before she, too, exited the homestead to go and sweat with other like-minded people in the school's gymnasium. I rarely go with her on these outings but in this mood Hannah is difficult to ignore and she really is quite magnetic. Hannah left the house saying goodbye to Wallace and even promised him a walk when she arrived home later. It didn't take long, maybe a couple of minutes, to get to the gym but for the entire journey Hannah had been humming 'Like a Virgin' and it was starting to drive me crazy such was her drone but luckily Hannah stopped as soon as we took our first step through the double glass doors of the gym. Hannah briefly looked at the cork noticeboard that covered the length of the left-hand side of the entrance lobby. I am not sure Hannah was actually interested in anything that she was reading but the Language Building faces it so maybe she was hoping that Jean would be peering out of his classroom window watching the gym lobby to snatch a glimpse of her 'fragile' form. After a few minutes Hannah continued her journey down the four steps and then veered left into the changing room. On the far wall was her private locker (another staff perk) and from it she produced her MP3 player and her indoor workout trainers. She looked at herself for one last time before exiting and within seconds she was inside the actual exercise room and on the first of the gruelling workout machines.

The room was square with a rubbery light blue floor. It was the type of flooring that looked as if there had been a huge mountain of rubber paste plopped into the centre of the room and then rolled out to cover the floor and halfway up the walls. Once rolled I can imagine someone sprinkling brown and white plastic shards all over it as if a cake, and then re-rolling. There were inch-thick dark blue exercise mats arranged around the room, near the weights and in front of one of the walls of mirrors. These were the sorts of mats that showed sweaty, wet, bare feet marks when you walked on them. The room had a particular, maybe unique smell about it (I have not been to other gymnasiums, you see, with which to compare); a highly odorous mixture of damp, sugary sweet asshole and peppery cheddar cheese. I really liked it in here and could well understand why Hannah visited so often. I am resolute that I will come again...

First off, I had to find somewhere to position myself so that

I would not be in anyone's way so I went and sat on the top of the mirror that ensconced the wall that faced the aerobic exercise machines; the other mirror faced the weightlifting apparatus and the view there was mostly of over-muscular teenagers straining as if about to do a really hard tiny turd. The place I nestled was rather comfortable as the bevelled edge of the mirror that touched the plastered wall made an excellent viewing platform. I could very clearly see all of the faces and bodies of the people inside the gym, mainly thanks to the mirrors, and I was close enough to Hannah to hear if she started to talk, or God help us, sing to herself. Hannah pounded away on the running machine and then she moved onto the step machine. The last piece of equipment she employed was the rowing machine and as her arms pulled back I noticed several of the boys starting to sit up and watch, slowing down with their repetitions with the weights or revolutions whilst pedalling. I looked at Hannah and her focus on herself in the mirror was intense and consuming, her eyes drilling holes into her reflection. The vigour of her workout was exhilarating and I could see the interest of the boys growing as she came to the end of her workout. As she stood up I noticed the seat of the rowing machine, wet with sweat, with perfect impressions of her arse glistening in the glow of the gym's strip lighting. It was very similar to potato printing with paint, instead of potatoes her arse and instead of poster paint, her sweat. And after she had left the gym to go back into the changing rooms, Dan Winkwood ran over to that very piece of apparatus and licked the seat. There was a roar of laughter from the other boys. I wondered how often he did that; maybe he was a fly in his past life.

I made my way out of the gym; Hannah would be returning home and then having a shower, all of which I have seen before and I wanted to make sure I was in the staff room for morning break.

10

fLy: When I arrived at the staff room and not to my surprise, it was still stuffy and still smelt sublime. The chairs were all randomly placed in and around the room, maybe three or four at each of the three tables. There were a couple of teachers already drinking their coffees and flicking through documents and two others were sucking the ends of biros. Soon the atmosphere changed as more staff came in and the still air soon became stirred as the chatter increased. Jean and Raymond walked in together, both holding mugs emblazoned with the school motif and Raymond gesticulated to a group of chairs that sat under the ledge where I had perched. As soon as they had sat down, in trotted Tristan.

Tristan: *Just who I wanted to see, what luck!*
Raymond: *All ok, Tristan?*
Tristan: *Couldn't be better, Raymond. Hannah had a wonderful idea of asking you both and your better halves for dinner this Saturday if it would work for you both.*
Raymond: *Well that is rather short notice, Tristan, but I think we are free; it would be lovely to come over and unwind and share a couple of beers. You free, Jean?*

Jean: *I think we are, Raymond, but I would have to ask Kaori if she is. Should I let you know, Tristan, or your lovely wife?*

Tristan: *Let me give you Hannah's number, Jean, and then you can chat to her directly. I would love to see you on Saturday; I have a prior engagement until about 7.30 but would love to be opening a couple of bottles with you by 7.35, what do you think?*

Jean: *I can't say for sure but as soon as I know I will let your wife know.*

Tristan: *Hand me your phone, Jean, and I can save her number down for you. Raymond will you just double check with Fi and call Hannah just to confirm?*

Jean: *What are you up to prior to our dinner, Tristan?*

Tristan: *One of the girls has asked me to give her a few extra English lessons before the exam season comes into full flight; she just needs the confidence I think.*

Jean: *Which girl? Is she a pupil here?*

Tristan: *Yes, she is; I don't teach external pupils. I know some of the staff here do that but I don't really have the time, especially now with the school play approaching. You are still keen to do the budgeting for the play, Jean?*

Jean: *I have a meeting with Mr Fallbuoy on Monday afternoon to discuss with him what I think the estimated costs will be so if we are able to meet up on Saturday then maybe we could set aside twenty minutes or so to just crunch some numbers. I watched the DVD last night actually and I think you and I have our work cut out to cost this accurately.*

fLy: I stayed on to see if Jean and Raymond discussed Saturday further but instead Jean asked if he had Hannah's number too. Raymond checked his phone and then showed it to Jean.

Morning break was always over quickly and Jean didn't go back towards the language block but instead walked out to the green oceans of lawns that tumbled down over towards the girls' boarding house. Jean selected a number and walked in small circles. He then stood still as he spoke.

Jean: *I can't refuse. I will be there. On my own.*

fLy: Jean then put the phone in his pocket and strode back to the languages block. Once again Jean's turn of phrase, or rather his confidence, impressed me. I could imagine that Hannah was consumed with euphoria and I was keen to catch her still revelling in delight. I hurried back toward home but instead saw Hannah on her way to Fi's house so I changed course and went in pursuit.

Fi was standing at the front door with her default flaccid, farty expression on her face but her eyes (with eye bogey) were wide open, as if staring. Hannah didn't say a thing to Fi as she walked through the door and into the hall. Often there were school children or Fi's own children within hearing distance and I am sure Hannah wanted to keep her dialogue for Fi's ears only.

Hannah: *Fi, it's happening again. Do you remember when I told you about my concerns about Tristan and the possibility of him liking someone else? Well you told me not to overreact and that we were all guilty of window shopping? Well there is someone that I am thinking about, more than I should, but the worrying part or the exciting part is that I think that person likes me too. In fact, now I think about it, could it be a cruel game at my expense?*
Fi: *Is it the same person, or someone new?*
Hannah: *That part is the irrelevant bit of it all. Here I am today energised like an eighteen-year-old when this time last month I felt nearer sixty. All of a sudden I feel as if my life has just started; it has taken something like this to make me realise how dead I felt to the world before. I can't believe how I feel; the attention I get when I am near them and the effortless compliments they say about me is unfathomable or would have been a few months back. Fi, I feel so unbelievably attractive. I think I would actually go out in a lace bra*

and hot pants and not feel like mutton dressed as lamb, such is the confidence that has been given me.

Fi: *Hang on, Hannah. You said that you had that same buzzy feeling when Jean talked to you but you dismissed that twenty-four hours later; and understandably so. Is it Bruno?*

Hannah: *I can't say, Fi; I will tell you when the time is right but at the moment I need to know what to do in this situation rather than receive advice based on who that other person is and how it might impact the dynamics of our friendship. Pretend you are an Agony Aunt in a magazine; respond to me as if I had written to you anonymously.*

Fi: *But I can't respond to you anonymously because I know Tristan and I know how much he loves you. My advice can't be anything but biased.*

Hannah: *Then I should just go. I am so confused but for the first time in years I have something to think about other than the size of my waist or the calories I have eaten today and how I will burn them off.*

Fi: *Is that really all you think about, Hannah? There is nothing of you.*

Hannah: *I don't want to talk to you about my weight issue because that is not why I have come round. I want to feel liberated from this guilt of feeling so fantastically alive; the guilt of realising that the promise of this potential extra-marital affair is making me happy. Last night for example I made a stir fry for dinner, nothing special in that, but I moved the table to the patio doors and laid it. I made an effort, a small effort and Tristan reacted positively to it. And why did I do that? The only reason I can think of is because I was already trying to balance out the pain that I may put Tristan through if he were to find out I had been unfaithful to him. Or did I do it because I can have the affair and justify it by saying it makes me a better wife?*

If the shoe was on the other foot and Tristan started showing me more attention, would I delve into the reason why or would I just think that he was happier at work and was feeling better; less tired? And in that case hasn't the affair made Tristan happier and me happier as a result?

Fi: *But you don't think like that, Hannah. You have been worried about Tristan's fidelity for a while and what's more your marriage is a lie; or at least the wedding nuptials are worthless. Have you had a conversation in the past where you both have said that if an affair was to happen it would be acceptable in certain cases?*

Hannah: *We did once have a chat about it but only as a result of his married friend Andy from University having a one-night stand whilst away on a trip to Venice with the boys. Tristan said that Andy's marriage had been devoid of sex for four months and that every man needs to have sex. If the wife wasn't giving him any sex, then Andy has just fulfilled his basic male need. The sex to Andy was meaningless, utterly meaningless, and to confess to it would give it a gravitas that it didn't warrant. I did see his point, Fi, but then I asked him why a wank would not have sufficed. Tristan said that it is in the male genetic make-up to hunt, to chase and to breed; and the hunt and the chase were a necessary part of the whole exercise. Now maybe for me, bored and childless at home, I need to be the one being chased, being hunted, and this is what is programmed in my genetic make-up. So if I was to err and to give in, to be caught, could I also excuse the whole thing as part of my basic need?*

Fi: *Well, I think this is nonsense. For Tristan to condone Andy's behaviour goes against Tristan's ethos. He often refers to and recites from Romeo and Juliet as being the ultimate piece of literary work; you know he always gets round to asking everyone their top five works of literary fiction. Inevitably the conversation concludes with Tristan telling us his top five. The top four as we know are Shakespeare and the fifth being one of the books by Pat Barker, Regeneration, I think.*

Tristan will say the same thing, every time, about how Romeo and Juliet is the definitive work of fiction because it so succinctly demonstrates that we are no longer cavemen and women because love and the quest to conquer it is a stronger force than survival. So for

him and you to say there are basic needs to be filled for men and women, then we return to cavemen status. A one-night stand still breaks the contract of marriage; but a long-term affair destroys all.
Hannah: *So if Raymond were to tell you he had been unfaithful what would you do?*
Fi: *Divorce him.*
Hannah: *But if you never found out?*
Fi: *At least one other person would know and eventually I would know. Maybe not immediately but I would. And would I leave him then? Yes, the trust would be gone. I remember once my mum, of all people, said that affairs were like cocaine. Having had neither I have no idea what she means but I assume addiction plays a part and I am not sure that it is possible to have just one affair and forever remain absentinent from being attracted to the thrill of it. Maybe that, Hannah, is the problem. I wonder if Tristan's friend, Andy, has ever strayed again, each time it happens the thrill increases but the need to find reason, justification or excuse diminishes.*

Goodness, I remember when I had our first-born, I couldn't have sex for nine months. We did try, admittedly, after four weeks, but I was just too sore and still had piles. We then tried again after three months. It was a disaster. Before we had children, Raymond used to like to suckle at my breasts, but this time when he started to nudge my breasts with his nose they started squirting milk uncontrollably over his face and shoulders and the romance evaporated so we didn't try for quite a while after. I know I have taken a hard line with what I would do but actually I wonder what I would do now if I found out that Raymond had been with someone else during that time on one of his excursions? Would I actually demand a divorce or could I qualify it and accept it? I have never really, deeply thought about it, but I will do. I would have to consider the fact that he is a wonderful dad and soulmate and of recent, a remarkable lover too. Have I told you that we have been exploring Raymond's Roman links more thoroughly?
Hannah: *No, you haven't.*

Fi: *Well, Raymond found an article on the Internet to do with Eunuchs and anal sex.*

Hannah: *Stop there, Fi. I don't want to know the rest of what you are about to tell me; not now anyway. Maybe with a glass of wine later. What I really need now though is your help and advice and to talk about this very real dilemma, you know you are the only friend or person I could ever have this chat with? If it wasn't for you I would be bottling up my angst about Sasha and the 'thing' Tristan has for her, making myself so sick with stress. But you give me an outlet. I still contemplate how long it will be until 'a thing' turns into our marriage's downfall but the question of "what do I do?" isn't such a terrifying one because I could ask you.*

Fi: *Well, what I can tell you is that two wrongs only ever make a right in the mathematical sphere, not in life. Don't go entertaining the idea of adultery on the back of an assumption that he will be at the same game.*

Hannah: *And if I was to say to you that before this other mystery person came into my life I was completely unhappy, then what?*

Fi: *Then you should be examining why you are unhappy. It is not the relationship that is unhappy; goodness we have seen the two of you together and you are happy, not bouncing off the ceiling but you make a good team. If you are unhappy then work out the 'you' in this, not the 'us' part first.*

Hannah: *So whilst I am at home working out why I am unhappy, Tristan is fantasising or actually fucking someone else, yes?*

Fi: *I don't know, Hannah. In fairness I have never had these types of conversations in the past and I am, and always have been, pretty straightforward and sheltered. I look at things from my side of the fence and all I see is that you respect people and treat them in a way you wish to be treated. But as of this evening I will be asking Raymond his opinion on affairs, or rather meaningless sex, to sate a need, and if his reasoning reads along the same lines as Andy's then I will be astonished but equally so more informed of man's attitude toward extramarital sex.*

fLy: So with that Fi stood up and offered Hannah a glass of wine, chilled this time and Hannah accepted. For a little while, maybe only for two or three minutes, there was silence before Hannah asked Fi about Eunuchs and anal sex. Before Fi could start explaining the guts of the matter, one of her children came in to ask Fi to help with their maths homework. Hannah said her goodbyes and left. Shame.

I flew slowly back home; Hannah seemed to rush off and I assumed that she would be crying. I suppose she was hoping that Fi would be wet and warm and fuzzy and airy headed and tell Hannah to go for it and to put herself and her happiness first. But surprisingly, Fi wasn't. The problem with asking anyone advice is that they give it and even if we don't like the advice given, we have heard it; and that would play on my conscience, I think. But maybe it wouldn't; I am fLy after all.

11

fLy: When I returned home Hannah was on the phone asking about 'bum hole bleaching'. I flew over to the kitchen worktop to see what had inspired this line of enquiry and there, open on the granite worktop, was an article in a magazine about different beauty procedures to fight the signs of ageing. There in finest gloss were the puckered images of 'before' and 'after' on show. Whilst drinking in the pictures I listened, like a drunk would listen to the sound of booze being poured into a glass, to the conversation that Hannah was having with this fully qualified beautician called Chelsea. On hearing Hannah repeat the cocktail of chemicals that would be applied to the opening of her back passage, I was delirious. The main ingredient to this secret formula was bleach and I have to say that I love the smell of bleach; not too strong though but that coupled with the smell of arsehole has to tick my number one favourite smells of all time. Apparently, there would be a one-off consultation, then a first application visit and this would all be included in the advertised fee. A rigorous daily routine had to be followed using another sort of secret formula cream that needed to be applied twice a day and also needed to be purchased at an extra cost. Her bum would be babe-tastic within twenty days and Chelsea would be arriving first thing in the morning with her kit to get this magic in motion; I was ecstatic.

When Chelsea arrived the following morning, Hannah had been preparing herself, I suppose on advice given to her on the previous day. She had taken herself off to the shops very early and came home brandishing a cheap DIY waxing kit. After Tristan had left for school she lay on her back with her legs up against the wall, a torch shining into her nether regions so that she could see her hairy task in hand. She carefully placed the wax strip over her anus and with tight-lipped determination she ripped off the 'warmed in the microwave' small plastic rectangle. Upon close inspection, Hannah could see very few hairs stuck into the sticky caramel-coloured ribbon with many hairs still standing resolutely around her bum hole. So she opted for the razor, not recommended but far less painful, and gave herself a very clean shave (I am sure the makers of Gillette would be proud).

By the time Hannah had finished and had gone downstairs, the doorbell rang. Chelsea introduced herself; she was the perfect representation of her profession. She stood there, white clogs engulfing her feet that were resolutely together, her crisp white beautician overalls that were reminiscent to a Karategi. She had beaming white, square teeth, evenly applied satsuma-coloured tan, long synthetic eyelashes slathered with black mascara, fake diamond studs in her small earlobes and long blonde, very straight hair tied in a loose, low ponytail. She smelt of peppermint oil and tobacco and was about three inches shorter than Hannah and maybe two stone in weight heavier. Before she opened her box of tricks she asked Hannah to sign several documents that would remove any responsibility from her or her company if Hannah's asshole was to become infected, irritated or unusable. After Hannah had signed all of the documents she offered Chelsea a mug of herbal tea which she gratefully accepted. Chelsea then started to describe to Hannah how best to position herself in order to gain maximum benefit from the introductory application. With great deliberation they decided that bum up and cheeks splayed would be the most beneficial way to proceed and decided that bending over the back of the sofa would be the very way to ensure this. As Hannah stripped off her clothes, Chelsea told her that she could keep her upper garments on. As Hannah bent over the sofa, naked from the waist down, Chelsea waffled on about their superior product and freshness as opposed to the creams one could buy on the Internet for an eighth of the price. Chelsea then instructed Hannah to use both hands to pull her bottom cheeks well apart as if she were opening a large handbag, looking for a lipstick at the bottom of it. Hannah reddened; the position she had assumed over the sofa may have offered Chelsea the optimal exposure of the area but the angle at which she had folded herself over it made it increasingly constrictive for Hannah's ribcage to inhale and exhale. Chelsea produced from her toolkit a rather large loofah which she started to use on Hannah's lower pinky-brown parts. Chelsea explained that by gently exfoliating the anus, vagina and surrounding area the bleaching cream would be absorbed more efficiently and have quicker, longer-lasting results. Chelsea carried on talking to Hannah; every time she moved the location and direction of the loofah she informed Hannah as to why and where she was going with it but all Hannah could do was grunt in acknowledgement.

Hannah's hair fell over her dangling head as Chelsea worked as gently as she could, both of them oblivious to the sight of Raymond looking through the patio doors. He stayed for a moment too long; obviously wanting to watch this 'girl on girl' action but then tore himself away racing back through their little garden, through the wooden gate and out onto the athletics fields. I concluded, after only a few minutes, that the exfoliating and initial bleaching session would consist of vacuous female one-sided conversation about minor celebs and beauty products so I took my leave and made my way as fast as I could out to the athletics track. As I made my way over the roof I could see that Raymond

135

had upped his gait and was doing a sort of canter towards his house and as he reached his front door so did I. He rifled through his jacket and then patted his pockets trying to locate his keys; he found them in the back pocket of his khaki chinos and opened the door with urgency.

Raymond: *Fi, are you in? Fi, where are you? Have you a minute to have a chat?*

Fi: *Hello, Marcus Aurelius, I am in the kitchen!*

Raymond: *Oh Fi, I am so worried, concerned and shocked by what I have just seen. I knew there was something about Hannah that I was unsure of. And now I know.*

Fi: *What Raymond? What are you talking about?*

Raymond: *Well I went round to Tristan and Hannah's house as you know to let her know that Saturday dinner would be good for you and me, that we would be able to make it, and for some reason I decided not to go to their front door but to pop in via the back gate; I suppose I assumed that if Hannah was in the sitting room or kitchen I could just catch her attention and maybe save time by talking to her through the window in case she was busy doing chores. As I approached the patio doors I could see a lady with her; a pretty lady, young with bright platinum blonde hair and slightly orange skin. I took a step closer and there was Hannah naked from the waist down bent over the sofa performing a sex act with this girl using a loofah! I turned and left immediately as I didn't want Hannah to spot me or the other girl for that matter.*

Fi: *Are you sure, Raymond?*

Raymond: *I would bet my Mudman G on it!*

Fi: *Well, I should have seen this coming. She was telling me only yesterday that she was bored and she came over to ask me for advice. Do you think Tristan knows?*

Raymond: *I wouldn't have thought so. Should I chat to him about it? You know, man to man?*

Fi: *I think we should stay out of it, Raymond. I think if we* *were very, very close friends of them both or if there were children involved then maybe I would say differently but as it stands I think the only thing we can do is just stand by and be supportive. Oh Raymond, I never thought that Hannah would go lesbian.*

Raymond*: Well, I have thought about it in the past; and I concluded that I could imagine Hannah with another woman. It is just always more shocking when it happens; you know you imagine something and then you see it in real life. I have sometimes wondered whether Hannah had a thing for you; I mean the outfits that she wears when she comes round here for casual barbecues or the like, are sometimes unnecessarily revealing. Did you see what she wore last time, you know the time when she disappeared? I caught a glimpse of her as she came out of the downstairs WC, darting for the front door and I felt uncomfortable.*

Fi*: Don't be silly, Raymond. I am sure that I am just a good friend and that's all to Hannah.*

fLy: But as Fi turned back round to face the cucumber she was slicing for the bowl of salad to her right I noticed Fi raise her eyebrows and she exhaled while doing so. I looked back at Raymond and he had a faraway look in his eye.

Fi*: Do you think we should still go to the dinner on Saturday, Raymond? We could say that we had already asked Bruno over for dinner with his new lady friend? We could actually invite him just as a precaution?*

Raymond*: I think that is a good idea, Fi. You give him a call first and if he can make it then maybe would you give Hannah a call? I think it probably best you deal with it.*

fLy: Fi immediately made the call to Bruno but he was unable to make Saturday as he was working that evening. So Raymond and Fi decided that if they were going to be the strong, supportive friends that they should be at this time of confusion, they should go for dinner and act as normal as possible. But Raymond said that Fi should let him pick her outfit to wear on Saturday; it would be unwise to wear anything that might give off confusing signals to Hannah.

I returned home to see if Chelsea had left yet and was surprised to see her car still outside. As I went in I could hear the sound of overly enthusiastic prattling coming from behind the sitting room door so I decided to rest for a while in the hall. I drifted off to sleep for about four hours or so and when I awoke the sitting room door was open and there was a serene hush that engulfed me. I panicked thinking that I had potentially missed something so I did a reconnoitre of the house and found Hannah upstairs lying very still on her bed with slices of banana on her eyelids. At first I thought she was asleep, definitely not dead as I could smell her breath as it tunnelled out of her nose, but I was wrong. A small alarm sounded on her phone and she carefully took the banana off of her eyes and replaced them with cucumber slices. I now wish I had made the effort to listen to Chelsea; this may have been one of her 'Combat the Creases' suggestions but I have no idea what it is good for; definitely in a glass of Pimms and lemonade once the banana and cucumber have done their duty. Recycle is my mantra.

12

fLy: It took a living age for Saturday to arrive but when it did both Hannah and Tristan woke up earlier than normal. They were both overly cordial and interested in the day ahead, what plans did they each have and would Tristan be walking Wallace in the morning before school chapel or popping home at lunch after lessons had finished to walk him? He wanted to know if she would be going to the gym in the morning as she did during the week or would she be going late afternoon; was there any shopping that needed to be done for the supper party? Hannah outlined her day and then asked Tristan about his extra English lesson. He told her that he had enquired about being able to use his classroom for an hour or so at 6pm but the school janitor would be locking up all the rooms at 4pm after the last of the school sports matches had finished. So he would have to ask Sasha to come to their house. He said that he would only need an hour with Sasha so at 7pm he would be free to help lay the table and get the drinks and nibbles lined up. Hannah asked if he would be using the dining table but Tristan thought that in his office would be best the place to conduct the lesson. That way both Sasha and Tristan could concentrate and Hannah would be undisturbed in her preparations for the evening. Thoughtful, definitely, but which sorts of thoughts were being filled...

Tristan had his shower and left for school, wearing a navy suit with a bright red, diamond-patterned tie and Hannah put on some loose-fitting tracksuit bottoms and made her way to the shops to buy the food for the evening's dinner. Within the hour Hannah had returned home with about six bags of groceries which she put away in various places and loaded the fridge with white wine. Hannah turned on the radio and gave Wallace a back scratch and tummy tickle which he seemed to love.

Hannah looked at her watch and found the magic bum cream in the cupboard that was rarely used above the fridge. She opened up the box and once again reread the instructions. As per instruction she then went upstairs and had a bath and a shave, put on the plastic blue gloves that came with the superior product and applied the cream to her dry, shaven and clean area and rubbed it in with 'careful circular motion'. She inspected herself with the help of a small cosmetic mirror and stood up. She opened her underwear drawer and thumbed through the various items of lingerie to don for the evening. She opted for a matching red lace combo that she had bought when she first met Tristan. She looked at herself in the mirror and smiled; from where I was standing it looked terrible but she must have been happy as she didn't bother to change them.

At around lunchtime Tristan arrived home with about five files under his arm and placed them on the dining table that was back in its usual position in the kitchen. Hannah was peeling potatoes at the sink and he told her he was off to take Wallace for his walk. He suggested that it might be nice for Hannah to join him as it would relax them both prior to the evening's entertaining. She finished peeling her potatoes, left them in a pan of cold water and put on her walking boots and coat. It was most odd seeing them both so congenial with each other. I had to follow as there was nothing at home for me and I wouldn't be able to sleep, not today, and I was glad I did. The conversation between the two of them didn't tantalise me but it was ever so pleasant being around two people making an effort with each other. They chatted, of course, about Shakespeare, whether writing down words with a quill heightened one's sensitivity just by virtue of the medium used or whether he was just gifted in the Godly sense. They chatted about the dinner that was being cooked and why Hannah had thought it was the perfect dish for the evening; she wondered whether she should have bought an alternative in case people wanted something less rich. By the end of the walk Tristan put his arm around Hannah's shoulders and suggested that every Saturday they do this. Hannah didn't respond.

When we reached home both Hannah and Tristan had red cheeks from the cold wind that had started to blow; Wallace was panting after having a good run and a chase around and took himself off to the utility room for a good slurp of water. I followed Tristan as he collected his files, delivering them into the office. I had to take this opportunity to get into the office before Sasha arrived so that there would be no chance of being heard buzzing into the room. Again I nestled up above the curtains and sat patiently. It wasn't long until Sasha was shown into the office. Tristan excused himself briefly and reappeared with two large glasses of water.

I didn't get much of a chance to fully register what Sasha had chosen to wear and had I not escorted Tristan, Hannah and Wallace on their walk, I would have gone to the boarding house to watch Sasha choose her outfit and underwear for the night. With hindsight I should have done that as that would add colour to this story but I didn't. As Tristan sat down, Sasha, noticeably nervous, immediately started to talk.

Sasha: *Thank you, Sir, for taking the time to spend with me this evening. I really appreciate it and especially for saying that you wouldn't be charging either. I haven't told my parents about this actually as I know Dad would be annoyed that he would be having to pay for extra lessons when he is already paying a fortune out for school fees.*

Tristan: *Trust me, Sasha, I am delighted to be able to help and without this extra tuition you would do well in your exams but I know that you have a real talent and it would be a shame to not attain the exam results you are so capable of achieving. I don't want you to doubt your ability or for your confidence to be knocked; you are a very able pupil and one that I will readily help where I can. I have taken the time to chat with your other teachers and they say that you are one of their leading students so maybe it is just my teaching that has let you down slightly.*

Sasha: *You are by far my favourite teacher and I look forward to every English and Drama lesson. I was thrilled when you gave me the role of Madame De Tourvel in the school play. I did wonder though why you cast Joshua as Valmont.*

Tristan: *Upon reflection that may have been an incorrect judgement on my behalf but it really is too late to change. Did you have someone in mind that you think would be a better Valmont?*

Sasha: *I do and so does Ana. We thought that Charlie was a more obvious choice.*

Tristan: *Why? Do you like him?*

Sasha: *Yes, I like him Sir, but not in any way other than friend. Ana likes him though; you know fancies him. I think I like someone else.*

Tristan: *Inevitable when you are surrounded by so many fit young peers.*

Sasha: *They are all so immature, fun to be around, but not what I would be interested in.*

Tristan: *I would have thought that there were plenty of boys for you to take your pick from; you have some really nice guys in your year. There must be a plethora of young male adults queuing up to go out with you.*

Sasha: *No I don't think there are but it wouldn't make any difference to me if there were. Most of the boys say I am aloof but I'm not, it is just that I am attracted to someone else which I can't help. But I wish I could help it and believe me I do try.*

fLy: I could see that Tristan had the question on the tip of his tongue but instead he opened the fawn-coloured file in front of him and handed Sasha a piece of A4 paper covered in typed font. Sasha started reading it and Tristan just looked at her. When Sasha looked up Tristan held her gaze and asked her who it was she was interested in. Sasha didn't answer but instead held his gaze back. There was so much electricity in the air accompanying the total silence in the room. I was afraid to breathe in case I disturbed them.

Sasha: *Maybe it would be best if our next extra-curricular lesson was held in one of the classrooms, maybe Mr Harbinger's as it is very private and quiet and will facilitate us being able to concentrate. I don't think that this evening I will be able to focus on anything; it is quite late and I am exhausted from the week. Do you think that is something you could arrange, Sir?*

Tristan: *I think that would be a much better arrangement and I am sorry that you feel so tired. Maybe we could read through the play, just parts of it so that I won't feel that neither your time nor mine has been wasted? I will confirm with you during the week regarding rooms, Sasha. Would that be ok with you?*

Sasha: *I am totally in your hands.*

fLy: Sasha and Tristan read for about half an hour to each other, discussed clothes that Sasha felt her character would wear and then stood up and exited the office. Sasha went out into the hall and into the sitting room; she politely said goodbye to Hannah and walked purposefully through the front door that Tristan had opened for her. She turned and looked at him and very quietly said, "Sweet dreams". Tristan shut the door and went into the office, sat down and put his head in his hands and cried. After ten minutes or so Hannah knocked and popped her head around the office door

143

Hannah: *Is everything ok, Tristan? I thought that Sasha would be here until seven?*

Tristan: *It has been a long week for her apparently and we just kept hitting a brick wall, she wasn't getting the simplest of subtexts. I suggested that we organise another place to meet and maybe at an earlier time. It is very difficult to concentrate fully outside of one's usual learning environment. So I proposed that we postpone this evening and maybe reorganise. I will have to work out the logistics with school and get back to her. So now I am all yours to help with getting things ready.*

fLy: Hannah showed him various bits of packaging and instructed him when to put them in the oven; it seemed they were having a selection of warm nibbles prior to the main meal which were to be served with drinks. Hannah then excused herself to go and get ready for her guests. At 7.30pm the doorbell rang and both Hannah and Tristan went to answer the door.

Hannah: *Ooh, Fi, a toga and black wellies!*

Fi: *The wellies are clean and nearly brand new so would it be ok to leave them on?*

Hannah: *Of course! Come in. What made you wear Roman costume?*

Raymond: *My idea actually, Hannah. All of Fi's other skirts or dresses don't fully come to her ankle and I thought with the weather being so cold it would be wise to cover up.*

Hannah: *But expose her shoulders? Not that it is isn't delightful seeing Fi's lovely shoulders, but might her top half get a bit chilled, Raymond, on your return home? If you want to borrow a coat when you leave, Fi, just ask, ok?*

fLy: As Raymond and Fi followed Tristan into the sitting room, Hannah went to shut the door but she spotted Jean coming down the small, crazy-paved path to their house. He didn't wave, or say hello, he just smiled at her. As he stepped into the house, he took his rucksack off and put it by the hall table just inside the door. Tristan reappeared and congratulated Jean on his timing. He enquired after the rucksack and Jean explained that he had driven over as he wasn't prepared to pay the extortionate fare the taxi company were quoting and excused himself for taking the liberty of bringing with him his sleeping bag in case he was to have more than one glass of wine and wouldn't be legal to drive home. Tristan offered him the guest room and Hannah eagerly offered to go and make the bed up. As she bounced up the stairs, Jean followed very quietly behind with his rucksack. At the top of the stairs, immediately on the left, was their linen cupboard. It was painted white to match the walls and had a small copper doorknob. The door opened out onto the stairs so Hannah was still unaware of her silent follower as she shuffled through the cotton sheets. She pulled out the spare set of white linen, closed the door and continued on up the hall to the spare bedroom that was also on the left-hand side of the hallway. Jean didn't go into the bedroom but stared at Hannah through the space between the door hinge and frame. Hannah carried on still blissfully unaware of the eyes that were on her. Having made the bed, she turned to come out of the room and then saw Jean. Hannah made a small squeal.

> **Hannah**: *You made me jump, Jean!*
> **Jean**: *I didn't mean to do that. I thought I would bring my rucksack up now rather than later. I have a bottle in here for you.*
> **Hannah**: *That is very kind of you, shall we take it downstairs and put it in the fridge?*
> **Jean**: *It's not that sort of bottle.*

fLy: Jean unzipped his rucksack and produced a brown bottle with frosted glass. The label was white with navy blue italics written on it. He held it out to Hannah and as she went to take it he held her wrist.

145

Jean: *This bottle is for you, Hannah, and only you. It is to be used on your gracefully freckled skin, your arms and legs. This oil has the essential oils of Bergamot and Cinnamon Bark added to it, making your senses heighten and more receptive. If you were to let me I would like to massage it into your shoulders at first and then slowly into your back, making my way down over your arse, your thighs, your calves and heels. I would then very gently turn you over and work my way up over your knees, your concave stomach and finally your delicate breasts. I have thought about you every day, contemplating how I would get you to relax and breathe with me slowly, deeply; to see your eyes shut, your lips smiling, groaning with pleasure. I want you and me to experience this; I want you to feel the intensity of my absolute desire.*

fLy: Hannah seemed to be holding her breath and then gulping during Jean's monologue; it wasn't apparent that he was noticing this detail, focusing instead on what he was saying and ensuring that she wasn't able to utter a word because he had put his finger to her lips. He finished by telling her not to say a word but to think about it when she was alone. Hannah waited for Jean to leave the room and then collapsed onto the freshly made bed. A couple of minutes later, when she had regained her composure, she went downstairs.

The atmosphere was very pleasant, Tristan had put on a CD by Massive Attack and each of the guests had a glass of wine in their hands. Jean, Raymond and Tristan had red wine, whilst Fi had white wine. There was a glass of white wine awaiting Hannah next to the crisps, gherkins, olives, wontons and pizza squares. She picked up her glass and nestled herself next to Fi in the small circle of five adults.

Hannah: *So what have I missed?*
Tristan: *Well, I waited until you were downstairs, Hannah, but I think we should all start the evening with a toast. This is to you,*

Hannah, and to the wonderful idea you had for inviting our friends for dinner.

Hannah: *Long overdue but I agree, a lovely idea. Cheers!*

fLy: And they all took a sip of wine and chinked glasses.

Jean: *Ok, my turn; to relaxation – a much-missed pastime.*

fLy: They all made a noise in agreement and nodded their heads as they brought the glasses up to their mouths.

Raymond: *To honesty and the freedom it gives you!*

fLy: Fi flashed a look toward Raymond, his eyes met hers and narrowed slightly.

Fi: *To health, mental and physical.*

fLy: A flicker of a smile waved over Jean's face.

Hannah: *Ah, now my turn. To having open minds.*

fLy: Those around the table all gulped, smiled, and then the eating commenced. There was the usual compliment about the tasty snacks but Raymond referred back to Hannah's toast. He wanted to know what her 'open mind' comment embraced. Jean intervened by asking how they all felt about infidelity. Before anyone could answer his now seemingly rhetorical question, he started to regale a story. It was one that had been on the rumour mill, apparently, and one that both Tristan and Raymond had not heard about. It involved a girl, who had attended the school up until last year and who had a mother who was by all accounts totally stunning. Her daughter was pretty but didn't have the 'wow' factor. Whereas the mum did. Both Tristan and Raymond were keen to know the name of the student but Jean avoided their questions. He continued by regaling what he had been told by Mr Immersley, since being made redundant. Mr Immersley had a leaving party which was attended by very few people; only three had attended from the school, one of which was Jean. Mr Immersley had drunk far too much and he just started talking, betraying secrets he had been told. One such secret was to do with this daughter and this 'wow factor' mum. The girl in question had held her eighteenth birthday party at her house and her mother and father were both present. The mother and father were well off and had a marquee erected in their ample, manicured garden and there were ice sculptures of the birthday girl. On the lawn the girl's handsome seven-year-old dressage horse grazed. Mr Immersley and his wife felt out of place; they didn't quite gel with the other guests but had been invited to attend as they had been long-standing friends of the birthday girl's mother. Champagne of the finest French variety was being served and many of the friends had drunk too much even before the starters had arrived. Mr Immersley and his wife had wanted to leave at the beginning of the night but because of manners they stayed. Inside the marquee were enlarged photographs of the daughter at various stages of her life and the tables were covered in white cotton floor-length cloths. There were purple covers that snuggled around the eight chairs that encircled each table that carried the burden of place names and large vases of lilies. As the music changed from reggae to dinner jazz, the guests were ushered into the oversized tent by humans that seemed to begrudge their employers. The food was served and there was a continuous traffic of girls, particularly girls, making their way to the loo and coming back to their seats with smudged mascara. By the time pudding was served the more adult group had started to impersonate the younger adults; drunk and loose-tongued. There was a call for quiet as the parents were invited to make a speech. The father stood up and made his toast to his daughter and thanked all those there and then he invited his wife to make a speech, just a few words. The mother teetered as she stood up and said that she had always imagined that at her daughter's eighteenth birthday she would feel a sense of freedom; that from that day forth she would no longer be responsible for the happiness of her daughter. But she felt a sense of shame and guilt; a burden she could not carry any longer. The mother told the entire gathering that she had never been sexually gratified by her husband and that she was so pleased that her daughter's boyfriend had a cock that an elephant would be proud of.

The whole of the tented room was ensconced in burdened silence as the words and their implications made sense. The daughter stood up and threw the vase of flowers at her boyfriend and the mother collapsed onto the table saying that she 'just had to get it off her chest'.

The upshot of it all was that the father stayed with the mother and the daughter dumped the boyfriend. Jean wanted to know whose morals were defensible or admirable; and when was infidelity inexcusable.

There was a huge amount of discussion about who was in the right and who was in the wrong. But then Jean threw another curve ball, as Raymond would say, into the discussion by asking whether infidelity was defined only by the actual physical act or whether infidelity was as dishonest when in the mental. Maybe, he said, it was just a case of having an open mind. I listened to this for a short while but then, unexpectedly, started to reflect on my own situation.

13

fLy: I remember vividly the day when I first saw daylight and the rush of my siblings as they charged toward it. I was born out of dog shit that was deposited into a plastic bag, collected from the grassy green tufts that formed the lawn of the garden. A German Shepherd called Vince was the proud producer of the brown, clay-like curl. Every morning just before breakfast, Vince's owner would gather up the excrement and plop it into a supermarket plastic bag that hung from the wheelbarrow. One day, as the bag was opened to shovel another load of bobbly poo in, my brothers and sisters raced to the opening. I, unlike them, felt a need to stay and find out if Mum would come back. But I don't think she ever did.

After what seemed like an eternity I, too, made my way out of the bag to the light that seemed so welcoming and wholly irresistible. Once out, I waited nearby in case there were any indications of my family coming home but there were none. So I just followed my nose, my 'aristae' and later that afternoon I found a place that I now know is my home.

It took time for me to understand why I was here and on this planet; I questioned why none of my family ever came back to their birth place or why there was a lack of community with the other flies that occasionally stopped by. Now, knowing what I know with human families, actually Tristan's and Hannah's, I have concluded that it is because there is no guilt, pain or love to keep us attached. Flies, on the whole, are selfish little pests with clear consciences and an acute attraction to shit.

Vince's family were very dull in many ways. They were not happy but content to live as they did and their children lost their personality to the computer and its mesmerising rapidly flashing screen. The parents drank red wine and ate microwaved meals and their conversation was stilted. They found a common bond in front of the television; they all sat together and had synchronised reactions to the vacuous realm of reality TV that they religiously watched on a near nightly basis. The atmosphere in the house was one of acceptance and in many ways could be perceived as the perfect modern family unit. And it is here that they so reminded me of my own family; in the same area but without the slightest interest in each other.

I became fond of sitting with Vince by the patio doors; he was a very accommodating fellow. He never seemed bothered by me when I was finding it difficult to nestle into his deep fur just behind his left ear. I used to love the smell of his earwax; luxurious, like white truffle, as it oozed its way out from his vertical canal along the fine hairs that sprouted from it. He had a smell about him that became more seminal as the sun beat down on his head through the glass of those doors. Vince was legendary at sleeping and the stillness of the house, with or without occupants, made the air heavy, inviting the arms of slumber to stay tightly wrapped around one.

It was with Vince, or rather because of Vince, I had my first insight to man's cruelty; to feel love and then to have it taken away for no fathomable reason.

Vince thought the world of his owners. Every time they walked around upstairs, Vince's ear would flinch and flicker until the sound had ceased. Every time one of the family would come into the house he would race to greet them, wagging his tail frantically, absorbing the momentary attention they gave him as if it were the best-tasting morsel on the plate. But when it came to moving house the conversation started as to what to do with Vince. The family were changing jobs, school and house. They were moving to a brand new, just built house and Vince was starting to get old and he was a smelly dog. To me he was perfection; always a ready puddle of drool to sup upon and always a soft place to perch when in need of comfort. But to that family he would make the new carpet smell and decided that to move Vince now and introduce him to a new way of life would be cruel so they had him killed at the vet's the following week. They had to find an excuse to ease their burdened conscience and they found reason enough and fairness in theirs. They told the children about Vince's departure from this world to the next once they had returned from the vet's and in a gesture of electronic sympathy paid for them both to get a virtual pet, "of their choice" to make up for Vince's loss. Even though they had been an easy family to live with, there was no way I was going to hang around these people that ignored the beauty of Vince and his stink, favouring instead, I assume, the smell of man-made chemical-rich room fresheners and newly spun plastic carpet. Shame on you humans!

At least with Tristan and Hannah there was energy in my house; and certainly a more forgiving, more tender love for their four-legged friend. Even though Hannah could be accused of ignoring Wallace at times, she would often give him a cuddle and Tristan would walk him as if escorting a dear friend out for a ramble. They were better people from a very basic point of view and their way of living life became very addictive for me; a bit like 'Reality TV' was for my last family.

I zoned back into the infidelity conversation that was still in progress and found that living in the present was far easier and logical than pondering the past. A very solid reason that fLy mentality is superior to human.

As ever, Tristan was able to recite many quotations from Shakespeare to back a theory that he had regarding love; its literary appeal deeply lodged in its fallibility. Yawn.

Hannah stood up and started to collect the dirty plates and cutlery whilst Jean picked up the condiments from the centre of the table. They both moved in unison towards the kitchen. As Hannah opened the dishwasher, Jean bent down close to her.

Jean: *Hannah, I won't kiss you. I won't make love to you.*

fLy: As Hannah lent down to fill the dishwasher her blouse ballooned open so that Jean and I could see the red lacy bra that she had put on. I wondered, as too did Jean no doubt, if she had knickers on to match. She reacted by turning scarlet and obviously tried to ignore Jean as he tried to catch her eye. She then turned to open the fridge and get the boxed hazelnut meringue roulade out. Jean stood in her way and asked if he could get the plates out so she pointed to a small cupboard door and Jean counted out five small white china dishes and then opened another drawer nearer to the sink for the cutlery.

Raymond: *I have to hand it to Kaori, she has you well trained. Next you will be wearing an apron!*

Jean: *Kaori has taught me many things, Raymond, and being helpful is only the start. She taught me Shiatsu massage about a month ago; it was never a form of massage I had experienced before but now that I have half an idea about it, I have really benefitted from it.*

Raymond: *I have always been a fan of massage and the principal of it, I echo the belief that the Romans had; they embraced all of its many wonderful attributes; it encourages healing and well-being. But in which way would you say that Shiatsu is better than, say, a sports massage?*

Jean: *I am not well versed with many types of massage but I think* *that Shiatsu concentrates on energy spots like acupuncture and sports massage is more vigorous with longer strokes rather than focusing on pressure points.*

fLy: With that Raymond was up from the table and rapidly taking his clothes off as if in a stripping competition. He sat down whilst removing his trousers stating that he wanted to test out the new craft that Jean had declared he knew something about. Having safely removed his trousers and socks, Raymond stood up. Hannah emitted a gasp and Fi promptly blushed. Raymond was standing there, naked bar a close-fitting leather loincloth, from distant memory I think it is called a 'sublicagulum'. Raymond looked at Jean, unabashed by his attire, or lack of it, and awaited instruction as to where to position himself and as Jean pointed to the floor Raymond put his hand inside his leatherette nappy and repositioned his penis. Jean took a small cushion from the sofa and Raymond carefully lowered himself onto the floor, all the time looking at Fi. His muscles were pronounced in his arms, biceps bulging, and his buttocks tight, his hairless legs were contoured with shadows and shine. Fi bristled with pride. As the massage evolved so did Raymond's groaning and the three left at the table were void of conversation. Tristan excused himself to go and get the work he had done that week on the play for Jean to peruse once he had completed his task in hand. Whilst Hannah once again started to further fill the dishwasher, Fi filled the kettle with water for coffee or tea, drowning out momentarily the murmurs and sighs that escaped from Raymond who was totally distracted from his surroundings.

Hannah: *What is with the leather underwear, Fi?*
Fi: *I didn't know he wore them on social occasions, Hannah. It is all to do with him trying to reconnect with his past and cement his everyday life with his gladiator roots, I assume. His obsession with his past I equate with Tristan's passion for Shakespeare.*

Raymond has even started planting laurels in the garden so that we can all have our own headdress; kids included! I was coping with this fixation as it was exhibited mainly in the bedroom and as you know, I found it exciting. But now that it is infiltrating into areas outside of our private space, I am starting to worry. At least with Shakespeare there is an element of respect and admiration. If I was to start telling anyone, bar you of course, they would all think that Raymond was having a mid-life crisis and I was going bananas. I am so embarrassed, not ashamed mind you but I don't understand why he is wanting to expose his leather pants to Jean and Tristan. What will they think? What do you think?

Hannah*: I think he looks rather manly and hopefully the boys will be boys and think nothing of it. Maybe this is an unconscious compliment to us all that Raymond considers us as he would an extended family. Maybe Raymond wants Tristan and Jean to become closer friends and explore his reasons for wearing such a get-up?*

Fi*: I think you are right, Hannah. Bless you for making it all seem so normal and ok. You are right about having an open mind.*

fLy: Hannah made a sort of empathetic 'humpf' noise, looked at Fi, gave her a patronising smile and then went over to Raymond to ask if he wanted tea or coffee; there was no obvious answer to decipher from between the grunts, so she then went to the 'office' and ascertained which beverage Tristan would like. On her return she asked if Jean would like anything and he nodded. Fi had made herself a camomile tea and had poured Hannah another glass of white wine from a fresh bottle. For Raymond, Tristan and Jean, Hannah plucked out some fresh glasses from the cupboard and poured them all a large helping of port. I think she thought, as did I, that it would probably be best if they all finished the evening in a state of mild amnesia.

Tristan re-emerged from the office laden with a wad of A4 paper just as Jean was finishing his massage. Raymond was like a limp rag doll and declared that the massage he had just had was better than any massage he had ever had. He pushed himself up and reached for the sofa, he pulled himself up on to it and then continued to sit slumped with an inane smile on his face, eyes all glazed over. It was a bizarre scene but one which all of the adults seemed to ignore. As Jean repositioned himself back at the table, Tristan handed him the stack of papers which were covered with suggestions made on Post-it notes. Hannah handed out the port and all of them seemed very happy. Tristan reassured Jean that he did not have to look at the play that evening but maybe they could think along the lines of having a huddle later on in the week to discuss his interpretations and proposals for the budgeting of the play.

Without having to ask, Fi collected Raymond's clothes and took them over to where he was seated on the sofa. She helped him get dressed and very slowly his soporific stupor lifted. Raymond returned to the dining table and thanked Jean for 'an experience of a lifetime'. Jean then asked Raymond where he met Fi and then asked the same of Hannah and Tristan; all of which we already know. However, Raymond then asked Jean how he met Kaori.

Jean: *Well I first met Kaori in a bar very near to Covent Garden tube station; she was with an American man who was apparently interviewing her. I used to go to this bar quite frequently on my own as I liked the girl that used to make the cocktails. However, on this particular night, Kheerti was off so I was feeling a little bit lonely. I noticed Kaori upon my arrival, mainly because the man sitting to her left was enormous. There were plenty of empty seats at the tables but I liked to sit on the tall metal stools that encircled the smooth dark wood counter. The bar had hundreds of various bottles, an eclectic mix of spirits and liqueurs from around the world, all nestled in front of a huge gilt-edged mirror. So as I sat on my stool trying to catch the attention of one of the waiters, I could see Kaori's face. I was sat to her immediate right. I wasn't to know at that point that*

Kheerti was absent that evening so my eyes shifted from looking at Kaori to looking for Kheerti. It was quite a busy night at the bar and it took a little while for me to get served. I ended up being served by the stern-looking Russian owner, Igor. I enquired after Kheerti but by the time I had ascertained that Kheerti was not going to be serving me that night, I had already ordered a beer. So I sat at the bar with little else to do but listen to the conversation next to me and study Kaori. From his dialogue with Kaori I deduced that she was a lawyer from Japan and that she was looking for employment in the UK. He assured her that his recruitment company had an excellent track record with finding work placements within the legal field in some top-end companies. As luck would have it as I was finishing my beer, the American had to excuse himself to go to the bathroom and that is when I introduced myself. I gave her my number and she gave me hers; I left the bar and thought nothing of it but of where Kheerti was. The following day Kaori called me saying that she was a stranger in a big city and would I mind meeting up with her. So that night we met in the same bar. As we sat at the bar, on near enough the same seats, I enquired after Kheerti but the petite blonde Polish serving girl told me that she had gone back home. So my focus became Kaori.

Fi*: And do you think that she is your forever focus, Jean?*

Jean*: Of that I am not sure.*

Hannah*: Why the uncertainty?*

Jean*: I am a hopeless romantic and when I sat next to Kaori that initial evening, I was surprised by her elegance and when we had our first evening together I was consumed by her delicate mouth and the innocence that burned through her brown, bewitching eyes. But in truth I never had that 'Eureka' moment that romantics like me hanker for and I think that will be our inevitable downfall. She has echoed much of the same sentiment to me.*

Tristan*: So why stay together when you are not even married and don't have children?*

Jean*: Because we make each other happy; we enjoy a plentiful sex* *life and until she or I meet 'the one' we are more settled with each other than without.*

Hannah: *What about the Russian pole dancer that you had your indiscretion with; did you think she was the one?*

Jean: *No I didn't; I was drunk and horny and Kaori was visiting her parents in Japan and the only reason I was 'found out' was because unbeknownst to me there was a Japanese documentary being filmed in the strip club that I used to visit about how the mainstream 'sex industry' in the UK differed to that in Tokyo. Yana, the pole dancer, had agreed to a 'warts and all' commentary which disclosed that I had met her the night before, had enjoyed a few lap dances but unlike Japanese clubs, I had to pay considerably more for the extra seedy business that she offered at a cheap motel adjoining the strip joint. I think her parents, her father in particular, would not have had too much of an issue with my infidelity given his own personal circumstances and routines, but because it was on prime time Japanese television, he did. Kaori was more forgiving, eventually, but as a result of that folly we had a very open and honest discussion about 'us'. Kaori would ultimately like to go home and live in Japan and I would ultimately like not to. In an odd way our relationship has never been better. We are proper, proper friends and I love her very deeply. You know she and I often say that we are not sure we would have this level of affection for each other had all of that very difficult and public situation not happened with Yana. I am sure, Tristan, you could find a Shakespearean quotation that would be very fitting to this insanity?*

Tristan: *"Though this be madness, yet there is method in 't"*

fLy: Tristan looked pleased with himself as he topped up the men's glasses with more port. Raymond and Fi were holding hands and said their goodbyes; it was time for them to retire for the evening. Hannah rushed out to the hall and retrieved a padded, puffy coat that looked as if made from sausages and gave it to Fi. Fi gratefully put it on and both Fi and Raymond once again bid their farewells; Raymond repeated his congratulatory praise to Jean for his massage. After they had left Tristan asked Jean if he wished to get some sleep or whether he wanted to go over a few pages but Jean opted for the sleep option. All three of them went up the stairs, and all three of them slept soundly.

14

fLy: Wallace was the first to wake that next morning; in truth I was but no one would have known; but it was Wallace that went upstairs to arouse Tristan out of his slumber. Tristan opened his eyes slowly and looked across at Hannah. Hannah's make-up had smeared itself all over the white pillow cases and her mascara had made dirty smudges across her face. Her breathing was heavy, she was near snoring and her breath beautifully bitter. Tristan stood and looked at himself in the mirror, I suppose he was wondering what he would be like to wake up next to. After a couple of seconds regarding himself, he slipped on some shorts and scampered downstairs to Wallace. Tristan found the patio door key under the flower pot on the sill in the kitchen and let Wallace out into their little garden. When Wallace came back in, Tristan sat on the floor with Wallace and gave him a cuddle and then a tummy rub. He told him that he loved him and that no matter what happened in the next few weeks he would do his best to keep seeing him and taking him for walks; possibly with Sasha. He told Wallace that to understand the matters of the heart would take a human mind and that he didn't expect that of him but he was worried about Hannah and needed Wallace's help. To know that Wallace was by her side, should he and Sasha decide to be together, would offer some sort of comfort to him. Wallace could, in theory, offer some sort of companionship and a salve to her heartbreak and pain. He was talking like a madman but then in fairness they all did. After Tristan had unloaded the clean dishes, glasses, knives and forks from the dishwasher he went and returned upstairs. He was greeted by Jean, dressed with his rucksack on his back. Jean asked Tristan to extend his thanks for the lovely evening and hospitality to Hannah but was going to head off back home. He said that he slept very well and had stripped the bed ready for washing. Tristan went back downstairs with Jean.

Tristan: *Thank you for telling us about your story with Kaori. It was an inspirational tale and one which I will remember. Not often does one hear a narrative of such integrity. Please send my best to Kaori and I hope that at our next get-together Kaori will be available to join us; she sounds like an extraordinary lady.*

fLy: As Tristan shut the door he looked at Wallace who was standing by his side. With ponderous eyes, Tristan turned to Wallace and said, "As a master once said, 'Nothing will come of nothing.'"

Tristan went once again upstairs and sat on their bed. He looked at Hannah, still blissfully asleep. He started to whisper to her, almost inaudibly, about how he was caught between two feelings of regret and contentment. On the one hand he felt regret because he would have to tell her that he too never had that 'Eureka' moment with her but contentment because he knew that without him she would be still be with Sheila and Stan living her friendless, terrible life so he felt he had saved her. How he kidded himself! He gently stroked her face and her hair; he gazed at her freckles on her nose and on her chest. She was, he said, very beautiful but not the beautiful that he wanted anymore. He pulled the duvet back slowly and climbed back into bed; pulling the pillow around his head he drifted back to sleep. The house was very quiet and very still. Bored, I left and went to visit Sasha and Ana.

I was fortunate when I arrived at the boarding house because the front door had been left ajar; one thing I had to do before leaving that day was find a way in without having to rely on that boarding house door being open. I made my way through the common room to Ana and Sasha's room. Ana was asleep but Sasha was sitting up in bed reading an enormous book. It was a softback book and the pages were well thumbed. I couldn't quite catch the title of it from where I was so I had to wait patiently. Sasha was turning the pages and smiling; she looked over to Ana and she called her name quietly. When Ana didn't respond after several attempts she took off her knickers and folded them neatly and placed them just under her pillow. She sucked at her index and middle finger on her right hand and it then disappeared under the covers. She held the book in her left hand and the rigorous movement of her right hand resulted in Sasha having to roll onto her left side, steadying the book against the wall. Once again she had to suck her fingers until sufficiently lubricated and once again they disappeared under the duvet. She turned the page twice more before she climaxed and then she lay on her back breathing heavily through her nose. Once the breathing had subsided she took herself for a shower. I happily followed and was rewarded with a visit to the toilet for a pre-shower shite.

There was nothing exceptional about Sasha's body. She had adequate breasts with average-sized pink areola, and a stomach that was flat with a belly button that was oval in shape, purplish in colour and stood slightly proud. Neither on her face nor on her body did she have any acne; her pubic hair was predominantly platinum blonde. Her bottom was nicely curved and her spine was straight. I was slightly disappointed not to have something to marvel at.

After she had spent a good ten minutes in the shower she towel-dried herself rigorously, sprayed herself with moisturiser and then wrapped herself up in her dressing gown and returned to her room. Ana was now awake and lying on her side, her eyes open.

Ana: *How was the English lesson?*

Sasha: *It was fine. Nothing to report at all. I am hoping you have lots of gossip about Dan Winkwood's party. Did I miss much?*

Ana: *Where to start... Well Dan Winkwood was devastated you didn't go to the party. He asked me where you were and I wasn't sure you wanted everyone to know about your extra English lessons so I said that you were meeting up with your mum.*

Sasha: *Couldn't you think of anything better?*

Ana: *No I couldn't; I was pretty impressed I actually thought of covering up your true location. But Dan seemed to get over it in fairness and ended up shagging Lisa in his parent's Range Rover.*

Sasha: *Nice. What about you, Ana?*

Ana: *No joy for me on any front. I tried chatting with Charlie but he seemed preoccupied with talking about football; but then so did about seven other blokes. Dan's brother had separated himself from all of us mere seventeen-year-olds by occupying the annexe above the garage with his mates. All ten of them pretty much arrived together, found Dan's brother and then skulked off together to smoke marijuana and listen to Bob Marley. I ended up standing at the end of the drive as lookout in case either Dan's parents arrived or the police rocked up. It wasn't the best of parties I have ever been to but at least I am able to sit here and string a sentence together this morning which is a first for a very long time. What about you, what did you learn with Mr Stephens?*

Sasha: *Not much at all. We went into a small room in his small house which he calls his 'office'. I think Mrs Stephens is starting to decorate it as a nursery as the curtains were covered with elephants and childlike impressions of sun and plants; not a pattern one would associate with computers, mark cards and files. It was near impossible to concentrate in there as it was so stuffy and Tristan* *kept shuffling in his seat. I felt really out of place there and uncomfortable; the only other room we could have been in was the sitting room but that is open-plan with the kitchen and Hannah was in there preparing for a dinner party. I suggested that our next meeting should be in a classroom to maximise our time together. As much as I like being with Mr Stephens, I didn't enjoy being with him on Saturday evening. The atmosphere seemed so stifled. It was a pointless exercise so I think that if it proves too tricky to get a classroom on the weekends then I will probably suggest that we forego the extra lessons.*

Ana: *Who was the dinner party for?*

Sasha: *Mr Stephens didn't say but as I was leaving I saw Mr Evans and his wife dressed in a toga jogging across the athletics field. Mrs Evans was running as if she was a troll.*

Ana: *Mr Evans! That has jogged a memory. Last night, before Dan and Lisa started getting friendly, I was standing in a small group with her, Abigail and Darcy. Lisa said that she had seen Miss Swallow with Mr Evans snogging passionately. Apparently she had been asked to go and sort out the lost sports kit box in the Cricket Pavilion as a punishment. Once again she had been caught smoking behind the recycle bins and once again they had to find some boring menial job for her to do. Her punishment is always set post prep and as always Lisa carried a torch with her as she is terrified of the dark, and even though the college's low level lighting was on, illuminating the path, she still had her torch on. As she arrived at the pavilion she shone the torch through the window out of habit to look at the stinking pile of muddied whites, socks, boxes and gloves in the large plastic tub that she would have to rifle through. But instead of shining the light into the kitchen and locating the bucket she apparently caught Mr Evans with Miss Swallow, his tongue in her mouth and both of his hands up the front of her avocado argyle-style knitted jumper! And Lisa, being Lisa, waved at them and proceeded to go in. She asked them both how they were as Miss Swallow smoothed down her jumper and Mr Evans smoothed down* *his hair. Miss Swallow and Mr Evans both responded and wished her a good evening then left together. Neither of them offered a reason for being there. I said to Lisa that this could either work for or against her; she will either become top of the class in Economics and Maths or she will come bottom of the class. Either way she has asked us all to make diary entries to say that she told us of what she saw, how shocked she was and how disillusioned she now feels by what she witnessed. That way if she ever feels that she is being victimised as a result of witnessing this episode she can state that she had anticipated such an outcome and had mentioned it to us all. You would never guess both of her parents are lawyers! Sasha, do you do it often?*

Sasha: *What?*

Ana: *Masturbate? I heard you before you went and had a shower.*

Sasha: *Doesn't everyone?*

Ana: *Well, I don't; it doesn't seem right.*

Sasha: *Well it will do. Lie down, then move over and I will start you off by lending you my book and rubbing you. Then you can tell me if it doesn't seem right.*

fLy: I stayed until Ana had climaxed and then I took some time to find a way in and out of the building; access and ease of it is key for me. I wasn't entirely sure where to go then so thought I would take in the fresh air. The weather was dry and the ground was hard. Cars were arriving and leaving and even though it was a Sunday there was still parent traffic. Several students dressed in jeans and jumpers walked to and from the library, cuddling files to their chests or nonchalantly at their sides, the younger children carrying rucksacks of enormous size on their backs. None of the pupils, regardless of age, looked happy; all of them donned a slightly furrowed brow and weighted step. I could see in the distance the cricket pavilion, clad in whitewashed wooden slats and not far behind that the boarding house where Raymond and Fi lived. I pondered upon the benefits of being a Housemaster;

granted, the living quarters and gardens were bigger than the houses that the staff like Tristan had, but the constant drain on one's privacy would soon make that additional space seem more confined.

I decided to move on and visit the cricket pavilion; there was nothing else to do that morning so I thought to use my spare time wisely. Wooden constructions, such as these, were often easy to get into without relying on the doors or windows to be open and this was no exception. I buzzed around the toilets to start with, then the changing rooms, the main tea area and then lastly the small kitchenette. The kitchenette and the changing rooms had recently been cleaned; I could smell the bleach and the spray polish that Delilah and her merry crew of cleaners used. I took note of the small window that sat above the sink and envisaged that it was here that Raymond and Letty had been espied by Lisa having their sweaty embrace. I squatted on the cream Formica work surface and counted the cupboards and drawers. I felt very relaxed so decided to stay for a while; it was an ideal sun trap and so I looked for somewhere to settle down for a while.

I positioned myself on the chrome mixer tap to make the most of this penetrating, sunny warmth. As soon as I had dozed off I felt as if I had been immediately awoken. I had no idea of the exact time it was or how long I had been asleep but the sun was no longer shining in through the glass window but instead was creating shadows on the stoop. My slumber had been stirred by the sound of clunking footsteps on the wooden floorboards, coming this way. They jarred me back to reality and I made my way quickly up above the white fridge freezer. It was Letty that pushed open the kitchen door and started to pace a small circle, nibbling at her fingernails nervously. Roughly ten minutes later there was the sound of more footsteps and through the kitchen door appeared Raymond.

166

Letty: *Thank God you could make it. I have been so worried. Do you think Lisa will say anything to anyone?*

Raymond: *I hope not, Letty. I never counted on this happening. This is like a nightmare for me. You have nothing to lose, but I have everything to lose, my kids, my wife, potentially my job. A bloody nightmare.*

Letty: *What do you mean, I have nothing to lose? I wanted to keep this job long after Tabitha Franklin was back from maternity leave. I like it here, I wouldn't find somewhere else similar and I wouldn't find someone else similar to you either. I have so much to lose too, not the same things as you but to me, still very important. Now there is a zero chance of keeping this job, staying here, or near you if Lisa starts shouting her spoilt mouth off. What do we do? What should I do?*

Raymond: *We just carry on as normal. There is absolutely nothing else we can do. You and I will have to call it a day; we treat Lisa the same tomorrow as we did before all of this happened; and if asked about it we just deny it; laugh it off.*

Letty: *So you and I have to finish? Are you being totally fucking serious? I don't think so. You cannot expect me to switch off my desire for you; not to want you, not to crave you, not to totally need you. I have never met a man with so much magnetism and power. We can carry on, we have to carry on but we will just have to be more covert and elusive. Imagine what it is like for me being around someone like you; I can't suddenly give you up! I am like an addict and you are my heroin but there is no rehab for getting over you.*

Raymond: *I see your point Letty. Give me twenty-four hours to think it all through and then I will chat to you in the staff room at coffee break, nothing secretive, just two colleagues discussing their morning. Ok?*

Letty: *Oh Raymond, you have exhibited to me yet another side to you that is irresistible; even in a personal crisis you really know how to be strong for those around you and keep your head.*

fLy: And with that she went on bended knees and gave him head. As soon as Letty's head started bobbing up and down, Raymond pressed the small side button on his Casio Mudman G watch and focused on the little screen. As he came he pressed the same button again and shook his head from side to side, chiding himself for not matching his 'PB'. Letty stood up and turned toward the sink. Contrary to what one would assume from her surname, Letty spat the opaque, jelly-like matter into the highly polished stainless steel basin.

She turned on the tap and both she and Raymond watched his unwanted sperm get carried away in the small vortex down the plughole. Raymond reached into his pocket and passed Letty a mint to suck. Whilst Letty unwrapped the sweet, he told her that he would exit the pavilion first and that she was to wait for twelve minutes before she left. He instructed her to use this time wisely; some push ups, lunges, on-the-spot jogging and finally some leg stretches. As he left, Letty held her hands tightly with her lips pursed. As soon as she heard the creak and slam of the pavilion door she bent over the counter and started to make a noise like a saw going through soft wood. After many seconds of carrying on this way, she abruptly stood erect and started to jog on the spot with a wide smile covering her lower part of her face; I never realised her mouth was so large!

15

fLy: Back at home, Hannah was sitting with Tristan at the dining table that was still in front of the patio doors. They were each drinking a cup of coffee, chatting. Hannah once again asked Tristan if the home tuition with Sasha had been satisfactory to which Tristan reported that it had been rather unsuccessful. He explained how it was difficult to gain Sasha's complete concentration and felt that the room was possibly to blame. He pointed out that the room was quite small for two people to work in, the desk not being large enough to accommodate multiple open books and that he felt that it would be better to try and see if the College would allow him access to one of the classrooms for the next session. She then asked him what he felt the budget would be for the play, where the main costs lay and whether or not funds would be made available to him. The conversation rolled nicely on and by the end of their coffee both had agreed that the evening before was most enjoyable and a success; neither of them alluded to Raymond's choice of undergarments. Hannah suggested that they pencilled in another evening in two weeks' time inviting the same guests; hopefully Kaori would be free to join them too. As they chatted, Wallace became increasingly insistent so Tristan put on his coat and scarf, found the dog lead and took Wallace out. He had only been gone for about five minutes when Hannah decided to give Fi a call but there was no answer so Hannah left a message on their voicemail to see if she wanted to meet up for a glass of wine around 6pm. She thought that they could try going to the pub for a change of scenery.

I also decided on a change of scenery and journeyed to Raymond and Fi's house. The children were playing in the garden and the kitchen windows were open; wafts of vanilla sponge being baked floated out. I flew on inside expecting to see Fi with an apron tied around her middle but she was not in the kitchen. I navigated my way to the sitting room, the WC, the bathroom, the children's room and then I heard noise emanating from their bedroom. I slipped in through the keyhole. Raymond was massaging Fi, asking her to accurately describe any sensations she was feeling, he really wanted her to experience what he had with Jean as masseur. The phone rang whilst he was conducting his research with Fi but they both ignored it. The phone flicked to voicemail and the little green light flashed as the message was being left. Raymond decided that it was time to stop because there were eight voicemails awaiting their attention and he was concerned that it could be a parent trying to get through to them urgently. Fi sat up and whilst she dressed Raymond pressed the 'play back' button on the answering machine. The first six messages were from different parents informing them of their son's return time that evening and then the seventh message played out.

Raymond: *I was right you know, Fi. Now she is asking you out on a date! Why does she want a change of scenery? I listened very carefully to her last night and at times there were clear indications that she was not only bored but looking for a different sexual scenery too. I forbid you to go and meet her Fi. It is not often that I put my foot down but I cannot let this happen. First my brother is gay and next you are being chased by a lesbian. I feel that homosexuality is* *after me; as if my robust, absolute, unquestionable heterosexuality is being hunted out and to be destroyed.*

Fi: *But Raymond you know that it takes two to tango and she may want a change of scenery because she wants to talk to me openly without the worry that you or the children will overhear her. You agreed that we need to be good friends and to be there for her, to support her, and I think that if I reject this invitation, I could regret this.*

Raymond: *Fi, I stand corrected, you are right. Please don't be back too late this evening and if you feel in any way threatened call me and I will come and get you.*

fLy: I stayed at Raymond's and was pleasantly entertained. Fi produced a splendid crumbly Madeira cake from the oven and Raymond played Garden Jenga with their children. It was a lovely, picture-perfect family affair.

At around 4.30pm Fi had a bath. Raymond helped Fi out of the bath and dried her with a very large orange towel. Fi did not make any comment on this so I assume that this was a regular occurrence. With a dry, matching orange flannel Raymond thoroughly dried under Fi's breasts, suckling on her nipple as he did so. The sight of his large head at her even larger breast would usually have made me feel a little queasy but the normality of this situation to Fi seemed to abate this.

Once in the bedroom Raymond dramatically flung open Fi's wardrobe. He and Fi discussed what Fi should wear. When the doorbell rang just before six, Raymond opened the door to see Hannah dressed in some ripped jeans, patent black stilettos, a thick white woolly jumper and a ponytail that looked as if she had sprouted a tuft of hair out the top of her head. She had pearl pink lipstick on, tinted foundation and thick black mascara. Raymond let out a small gasp and ushered for Hannah to step inside. Hannah rejected the invite, stating that she wanted to head off soon to try and get to the pub before all the regulars arrived.

As soon as she finished her sentence she turned to see Fi teetering toward the door. It was now her turn to let out a small gasp. There Fi was, in the middle of winter, dressed in what essentially was a black boob tube, no tights, red clunky low-heeled shoes, large gold hoop earrings and slut-red lipstick.

> **Hannah**: *Your fancy dress outfit from the 'Vicars and Tarts' party! What made you wear that this evening? We are only going to the pub.*
> *Raymond: My idea again actually, Hannah. Every man will look at her in that pub wanting to get to know her better; and even though Fi loves men and their attention, I know that she will be coming home to me for some good old-fashioned lovemaking. It is not often that Fi gets to go out and abandon Motherhood and there is a necessity at times to dress accordingly; I call it heterosexual freedom.*
> **Hannah**: *But the weather is like it is middle of winter, Raymond. Fi will freeze!*

fLy: Raymond reached behind the door and lifted his long black overcoat off from one of the pegs. He helped Fi put it on.

> **Hannah**: *Now you look like a strippergram, Fi.*

fLy: Fi shrugged her shoulders and kissed goodbye to Raymond. As the two of them dissolved into the distance I couldn't help but feel that one looked like mutton dressed as lamb and the other looked like she would be touting for business.

I followed Raymond back into the sitting room and stayed there whilst he went and put his kids to bed. Raymond soon reappeared holding a box file and placed it on the coffee table. He took out most of the paper and flicked through it until he found the film script he was looking for. He turned on his television, found *Ben Hur* on Netflix and started to read the text aloud as the film played. It was too much for me so I went home.

Unfortunately for me, when I returned home Tristan was watching, again, *Dangerous Liaisons*; I could tell this was going to be a long week.

I waited up until Hannah arrived home to see if she was drunk or chatty but Hannah was neither. She took her make-up off, then her clothes and slipped into bed next to Tristan. He was fast asleep. At least I had Monday's meeting between Raymond and Letty to look forward to, so I mistakenly thought.

I arrived in good time at the staff room and found myself my usual viewing spot and in walked Letty. She was the first member of staff there and so she helped herself to the coffee and biscuits on the long table. Raymond walked in minutes later with Mr Fallbuoy and Tristan. Raymond carried on talking to the two men for the entire coffee break and I could see from Letty's expression that she was displeased. Once again I returned at lunch break to see if they would get an opportunity to chat then but once again I was let down. Raymond arrived on his own, and sat on his own at a small table with two seats but there was no sign of Letty, so I went in search of her and found that she was on lunch duty. Deflated, I returned home to find that Hannah was applying the special age-defying bum-bleaching cream on the sitting room floor. With absolutely no interest in doing anything I decided to sit with Wallace and watch the unspectacular spectacle.

Hannah started to sing or recite, "Round and round the garden like a teddy bear; one step, two step, tickly under there," as her index finger encircled her anal opening making the whole thing even more ridiculous. She then adopted the 'Downward Dog' yoga position on the floor and shuffled up to Wallace; maybe she thought she was being humorous; he didn't really react to her at all. He just lay still with his head rested in between his front paws on the floor, his nose nice and moist, me on his rump and his eyes open but only just.

Hannah: *Oh Wallace, I could do with a friend like you. The only one I know would never betray my confidences. Last night with Fi I wanted to talk to her about Jean, about how he makes me feel sparkly; I feel I am 'back on the map' again, noticed. It was going to be a difficult subject to talk about but one that I thought Fi would be able to listen to again. So after our first drink and halfway through our packet of salt and vinegar crisps I asked her if there was anyone in the pub that she fancied. She went a ghastly grey colour and immediately started talking about the new success she is having with the washing powder that she buys online from an eco-friendly supplier. All I wanted to do was to set up the conversation so that I could discuss Jean. I wanted to have that schoolgirl, first-crush banter and elevate my excitement but instead Fi looked worried and bumbled her words. I realise that maybe she has an inkling as to the situation and she feels awkward entering into such a conversation because Tristan is a friend, as am I. We chatted for a little while about marine life and washing powders and moved onto overfishing and tuna, Chinese medicine and endangered species. At one point two men came over to us and asked to buy us both a drink; we accepted and when they came to sit with us they came to the conclusion we were lesbians and moved away, taking the bag of roasted peanuts with them. Fi looked inconsolable, I should have asked her again if she fancied anyone because her reaction to them walking off seemed to upset her so much, but she was keen to get home as the shoes she was wearing were proving most uncomfortable. I suggested she took them off but Raymond had told her that she was not to remove any of her outfit. He really does have such control over her and I don't understand why she doesn't see how manipulative he is; she never complains about it. It amazes me how relationships work or don't work. Look at me, I am so unhappy in my marriage but on the surface one could think I have it all; a house, an employed husband, sex, health, no money worries, but my marriage to Tristan is nowhere near as settled and happy, adventurous even, as Fi and Raymond's union. Maybe having children is what cements them; I*

174

have watched so many programmes and listened to so many songs where couples have just stuck together because of the kids and possibly the kids and the commitment that come with them is the glue that Fi and Raymond have that Tristan and I don't. This is where Fi could have helped me; does she feel happier in her safe relationship or does she ever wonder what life might have been like if she hadn't have met Raymond when she did. I suppose I could stop taking the pill and see if having a baby would sprinkle a magic spell over us but I couldn't stand being pregnant and the inevitable gushing that my mother would bestow upon us. And I don't think it would refocus Tristan forever, on me. But one thing that Jean's attention has done is reassured me that if Tristan were to bugger off with someone younger than me then I would still be able to find a life without him and I am still attractive. Then again, do I want to explore being someone's mistress? What does Jean want from me? Does he just want sex to gratify his curiosity and lust or does he want a relationship? If he wanted a relationship, then what do we have in common? I don't want to jump from the frying pan into the fire for the sake of it. One thing that has to happen first is my total surety that Tristan has fucked that little rodent, Sasha. What I have to do, Wallace, is organise our next rendezvous or dinner and rather than have it in two weeks on Saturday, change the day to this Saturday. I know that Tristan is going to try and book a classroom with Sasha for her tuition so whilst he is ensconced with her I will suggest that Jean comes to see me. I will ask Kaori too, naturally, but will be surprised if she comes along and, I will extend the invite to Raymond and Fi. Oh, Wallace! Once this bum cream has been absorbed I will call them all and then I can start to think about what to serve for dinner on Saturday. All of a sudden, dear dog, my life has a direction, sad as it is, I feel so excited.

fLy: I waited until all the phone calls were made and unfortunately both Fi and Jean were unable to take Hannah's call so she left them a message on their voicemail. She gave an outline to the reason for her call to Fi but with Jean she simply asked him to call her back. It wasn't long until the phone rang. I moved from Wallace's back and flew closer to Hannah making sure that I was as quiet as possible. When Hannah answered I held my breath and then listened to her as she expressed her disappointment that Fi and Raymond were unable to make it; Raymond had an 'Ironman' pre-competition race event on the Sunday which meant that an alcoholic late night was out of the question. She replaced the phone on the holder but her demeanour did not reflect the level of chagrin that she expressed to Fi. No sooner had she turned her back to the phone than it rang again. She let the phone ring four times before she picked it up. Once again I held my breath and as the male voice emanated from the hand piece so too did the smile on Hannah's face develop. At this point there were no words of detail relating to Saturday; just the gratitude of returning her call. Hannah blushed as she listened to the words that tumbled through the plastic phone. She remained very 'cool' as she invited Jean and Kaori over for dinner and cooler still as she suggested that they both come over at 6pm so that she could enjoy the relaxing experience of one of Jean's massages. As she spoke her smile kept growing and her teeth became more apparent; she was beaming with delight. Hannah insisted that Kaori was welcome and that the acceptance of a massage was little more than that; if Raymond had not been so effusive with his compliments of Jean's ability then the massage would never have been something that she would have wanted. As she spoke her fingers on her left hand curled up into a fist and as she replaced the phone she punched the air with both hands. Just as I have seen before, she rushed over to the stereo and quickly chose a CD. This time it was Cher and she hit the play button and turned up the volume. The first song was 'Believe' and Hannah sang out each and every lyric. After hearing that same song five times, I was worried that I would go to sleep with the whirly gig of "Cause I've had time to think it through. I'm too good for you, ooh, oh… Oh I don't need you anymore, no I don't need you anymore, I don't need you anymore, oh." But that night I didn't have any problems with my sleep; neither did Tristan nor Wallace but Hannah stayed awake for a while trying to masturbate in silence. I went to sleep before she climaxed; if she ever did! As the new, beautiful day greeted us all we all awoke with a smile.

16

fLy: Hannah's exuberance was contagious and all of us went our separate ways with positive energy in abundance; Hannah dressed in her black Lycra and bounced off to the gym; Tristan not being required at morning assembly took Wallace off for a walk and I thought it best to get to the staff quarters to see if I could find an auspicious place in which to eavesdrop on Raymond and Letty's 'private' talk. I arrived very early and thought that I would be there for at least two hours before anything of substance occurred but I was wrong. Letty arrived as all the pupils made their way to morning chapel; I could see them through the bay window that overlooked the lawns. Letty had a mug of coffee, a file and her handbag and placed them all on the table under which I waited. I flew over to the window to observe the members of staff file, one morose face following the other, into the chapel after all of the students had been absorbed into the ancient building. However, Raymond re-emerged after ten minutes holding his stomach. He made his way up the small incline and into the main school building. Within moments he was in the staff room. Letty let out a small cry and raced over to him. She threw her arms around him and declared with utter abandon that he 'had made it'. I wanted to point out to her that he had only travelled 300 metres or so but alas I am fLy and my voice somewhat inconsequential. They snogged passionately and then he told Letty that it was neither the time nor the place for her to let her desire overcome her sense of rationale. Letty started to cry, saying that the last thirty-six hours had been the worst she had ever experienced and wanted to know if there was a tangible way forward; had he thought of a meeting place where she could know his body, if only briefly but on a regular weekly basis. Raymond said that he felt a sense of duty; that to deny her of him would be like starving a child and that he thought that their meetings would be less frequent but more rewarding. He suggested that she was to make herself available on a Sunday; he would leave home under the guise of training for the Ironman competition but instead would employ his tent; they could find mutual satisfaction and happiness under the canvas hidden in the surrounding, forgiving, natural countryside. Letty squealed with joy as she flung her arms around him; she couldn't believe that he had been so clever and she told Raymond that she had always dreamed of making love in a tent. Raymond tapped her back as he embraced her and announced that he knew that he 'made dreams come true'. I followed them both out, thinking that Letty would be the more interesting of the two to follow. As I tracked her she disappeared into the ladies' loo and changed her tampon; by the strong clotting smell of things her menstrual cycle was at its end; Raymond would be pleased.

As I made my way home I thought about Raymond's words; I actually felt happy that Raymond had thought of a plan in order to carry his affair on; if he had drawn a blank then what would I have done? Yes, I have Hannah and Tristan to focus on but Raymond was the only one being totally duplicitous and I found this very engaging. I feared that with my own home life Tristan would be a victim of his own niceness and confess his wanton desire for Sasha to Hannah. I worried that Hannah would say it was ok because she wanted to fuck Jean and the sobbing and the screaming would be just momentary. Whereas with Raymond there would be the absolute need to keep everything a total secret. He had so much to lose, least of all his 'role model' status that he felt he had; ultimately this affair would be his undoing and his pride in being the successful family man and iconic father figure would be lost forever.

Upon reaching home I was met with Tristan shutting the front door and I thought it would be wise to make my way with him. Hannah would more than likely be in the shower and I didn't feel that there was too much to gain from her company. As Tristan walked to school he started to recite a poem by the great Master and I zoned out; I have heard enough Shakespeare to last me a lifetime.

I expected Tristan to go to his usual classroom but instead he carried on his travels up to Mr Harbinger's room. He tentatively knocked on the thickly painted avocado-coloured door and awaited a response. Mr Harbinger uttered "Enter" and Tristan did just that.

Tristan: *Mr Harbinger, I am so sorry to disturb you whilst you have a free period but I wanted to grab you whilst there were no other distractions. I come here today to ask of you a favour of sorts. There is a pupil that I teach that has fallen behind with the curriculum and I endeavoured to coach her, out of hours as it were, at home. Unfortunately, neither she nor I found my home surroundings conducive to full concentration and I wondered if you would be willing to let me use your room on a Saturday evening. I have not formally requested that I have a classroom be made available for my use but will do once I know if you would be happy for me to request this room be at my disposal. I particularly like this room because it remains quite independent of the other classrooms and I am wishing to keep these sessions of extra tuition quiet. The pupil that I am having to give added attention to has issues at home of some scale and I do not wish to incite their scrutiny as to why the further level of help is needed.*

Mr Harbinger: *Mr Stephens, first of all thank you for coming to ask my permission but I would have little say, as you know, in the College's decision as to whether you could use this room. Even though none of the classrooms are 'ours', I know that to utilise another member of staff's teaching quarters is quite unusual. What I am struggling to understand is your motive for putting yourself out. Please explain to me why you have decided to take time out of your weekend, I assume at no cost, to help a pupil and why your classroom does not suffice?*

Tristan: *Nothing other than vanity Mr Harbinger. The pupil you will know, Sasha Burnham, is very intelligent and since she has started here her standard of English Literary comprehension has dropped considerably. I would like to ascertain if it is due to exterior influences or whether it is just my inability to teach her in the way that had been successful with other pupils. As to my choice of rooms, well, you know my classroom is very visible and I do not wish to bring unnecessary attention to the fact that I have possibly fallen short of my professorial ability. Your classroom allows me to educate Sasha without the risk of her peers or mine seeing.*

Mr Harbinger: *Yes, I see your point. I had a similar situation with a year five student last year. If it would make it less obvious, perhaps easier for you, I will request that this room be made available to me until, say 8pm on a Saturday. I will disclose that I am needing the room for lesson planning. I can't see that it will be a problem but we will have to discuss who will be responsible for locking the room and where to leave the key; in my pigeonhole perhaps.*

fLy: Tristan and Mr Harbinger shook hands and Tristan skipped down the flight of stairs back into his classroom. As luck would have it, his first lesson of the day was with Sasha and throughout the class he kept looking at Sasha. Sasha did not register his attention but Ana did. At the end of the class Tristan asked that Ana and Sasha stay behind. He dealt with Ana first, he told her

181

that her work was of a high standard but that whilst he understood the merits of 'spell check' he also would prefer that certain words like 'centre' were spelled using the correct English orthography rather than the American modification. He waited until Ana had left until he started to speak with Sasha.

Tristan: *Sasha, I think you made a fair point on Saturday regarding our time together and getting the maximum from it. There is little point in sacrificing our weekends if there be little to benefit from it. Very kindly, Mr Harbinger has said that we can use his room on Saturday but he has stated that he will register with the college his intent to keep the room from being locked by the caretakers and that it will be my responsibility to secure the room and ensure the key is safely in his pigeonhole by 8pm on Saturday. I know that your friends would all understand as to why you are wishing to keep your extra English lessons contained away from your parents' knowledge but few may appreciate the need for us to use another classroom. So with that in mind it maybe pertinent to keep which room is being utilised as something that only you and I, and Mr Harbinger of course, are aware of.*

fLy: Sasha reached out and held Tristan's hand and assured him that she wouldn't tell a soul and that she was looking forward to an hour of discovery and enlightenment with him on Saturday at 6pm.

As soon as Sasha had left the classroom, Tristan started to recite Shakespeare, whining on, quoting from various plays and then lastly from The Tempest: "Hear my soul speak. Of the very instant that I saw you, Did my heart fly at your service".

As the new set of pasty, puffy-faced students streamed into Tristan's class I took my leave. I didn't know where to go now; both home and the staff room would prove infertile grounds to gain more insightful information and I wasn't sure if Ana and Sasha had lessons or free periods. I had the option to go and see what Fi was up to but I found being around her and her youngest child infuriating. I was at a loss.

I traversed along the corridors that took me to the lunch hall; I roamed around the Maths rooms but nothing seemed out of place; and all the while there was this cauldron of deceit and temptation that was brewing; ready for tasting at the weekend. I found myself flying aimlessly around trying to work out what I would do should Tristan and Hannah go their separate ways. Would I try to find a new life, a new home or would I try to stay with one of them? Which would be more stimulating?

I must have been gliding around for a little while because before too long the end-of-lunch bell began to sound. The wind had started to accumulate some strength so I didn't attempt to go home; instead I went to Sasha and Ana's room. I didn't expect much in way of entertainment, I just wanted some respite from the weather.

What was ever so nice about Sasha's room was the feeling of tranquillity. The other rooms in the house seemed to have their music playing constantly, regardless of whether there was someone in there to listen. The posters on those bedroom walls seemed to be uniformly black and white; muscular men holding white squidgy, fat-encased babies or muscular men smoking. In Ana and Sasha's room there was always peace and natural light; photographs that suggested a life outside of school and people that smiled. There was a lack of order to how they were displayed but the differing characters intrigued me. I wanted to find out more about Ana and Sasha. Was it just this personal touch that made their room seem so much homelier or was it because I had been in here a few times now and had delighted in eavesdropping?

On Sasha's and Ana's desk lay folders; their laptop computers neatly to one side; a pot full of pens on the other. Sasha had an alarm clock made of plastic, carefully balanced on top of the files, which ticked loudly. Ana had a small frame with a black and white picture of herself and two older people huddled together. On the window sill were three bottles of moisturiser of the same brand but of varying sizes and smells. Both Ana and Sasha had the same type of small jewellery boxes that sat next to their lamps on their bedside tables; Ana's box was a dark, fuchsia pink and Sasha's a pale, marshmallow pink. On Sasha's bed sat three soft toys; two of them exhibiting signs of age and one of them, in comparison, fluffy and brown. Ana didn't have any cuddly toys on her bed but instead a knitted woollen cushion in turquoise blue with the words "Sweet Dreams" embroidered on it. Their bed linen was white, as per boarding house requirement rules, but each of them had a coloured fleece blanket folded neatly at the end of the beds.

I nestled into the folds of the curtains to await company of some sort and my eye still surveyed the room. I looked at Sasha's bed with more interest than Ana's and saw that under her pillow, just poking out was the play *Les Liaisons Dangereuse*. I wondered why it was not on her desk.

Ana arrived arm in arm with Sasha, both of them laughing and they turned their desk chairs round to face each other. As they sat down they kept on giggling. Sasha cleared her throat as she reached for her manuscript from under her pillow.

Sasha*: Look I said I could prove it – he wrote it in the margin.*
Ana*: That looks like your handwriting.*
Sasha*: I promise you Josh wrote that.*
Ana*: And you never saw him?*
Sasha*: No! I leant the book to him as he, as usual, lost his copy and so he photocopied the book so that he could at least learn a few lines before rehearsal this week.*
Ana*: I never would have thought he fancied you; Mr Stephens, of course does, but not Josh.*
Sasha*: We have a room booked for Saturday.*
Ana*: You and Josh? Where?*
Sasha*: No not Josh, Mr Stephens. We will be meeting up in Mr Harbinger's room at 6pm.*

Ana: *Did he tell you that today? Why didn't you tell me sooner! What will you do? What if he makes a pass at you?*

Sasha: *My concern is what if he doesn't! I think of nothing else apart from having him and controlling him. I want to see just how easy it is to manipulate a situation using my feminine charms.*

Ana: *But you do like him, properly? Don't you or do you just want to research the human psyche; to screw with a few heads?*

Sasha: *I do like him; God knows I fancy him but I don't want to be married to him or date him. Imagine introducing him to my friends at University; having to discreetly tell them that he was my boyfriend and not my dad! Not when I could be introducing Josh!*

fLy: And they both started to laugh again. It all seemed quite cruel and it surprised me, I am not so sure as to why, to see Sasha being so calculating and derisive of Josh.

17

fLy: Tristan the following day spent most of his time in his classroom; Wednesday was his busiest day. Hannah spent most of the day cleaning our house. She is very thorough but today she even cleaned the cutlery drawer and changed the bed sheets; remaking both their bed and the spare room bed. She decided to take a break and open every file on Tristan's desk; she logged onto the PC and searched the browsing history on the Internet. She opened his desk drawers and leafed through his bank statements. There was nothing that seemed to grab her attention so she picked up his waste paper bin, placed it on the desk and picked out four tightly scrunched white balls. She flattened and straightened out each of them. All four of them had his handwriting declaring that he loved Hannah and would always love her. But one of them had a sentence that was scrubbed out violently. She held the paper up to the light to see if she could decipher the hidden words but it seemed to be in vain. She reloaded the bin with the paper, replaced all as it was, and stormed out of the office. She went straight to the fridge, grabbed a bottle of wine, unscrewed it and poured herself a large glass. She picked up the phone and awaited an answer.

Hannah: *Fi, sorry to bother you and sorry to ask the same question; but do you think that Tristan is having an affair?*

fLy: I couldn't hear what Fi said but Hannah once again apologised. Within ten minutes Fi was standing at the front door, thankfully in her usual attire, eye bogey still intact, holding a bottle of very yellow white wine. Hannah ushered her in but instead of showing her to the sitting room, lead her into the office. She picked up the waste paper bin and showed her the letters. Fi put her arm around Hannah as she replaced the offending articles back into the bin as she had found them. Fi took the bottle of wine with her and put it in the freezer as Hannah went and sat on the sofa.

Fi: *Is there a bottle open?*

Hannah: *Yes, in the fridge; help yourself and then bring the bottle over would you. My glass is in need of a top-up.*

Fi: *Look, Hannah, I know I am stating the obvious but you mustn't read too much into these little notelets. All of them say that he loves you and neither you nor I can make head nor tail of what he scribbled out. The words could have been intimate or just uncomfortable for him to write and maybe he thought it best to say them to you.*

Hannah: *What would you think if it were you that had these suspicions of infidelity and then you found the letters? Maybe I am overreacting?*

Fi: *I honestly can say, hand on heart, that I have never doubted Raymond's loyalty to me but if I did have the same concerns as you and I found the letters then I would be worried. In this environment I think that it must be very difficult for male staff and possibly the female staff to remain totally focused but I suppose that is where I am lucky. Raymond has so much to distract him outside of work that I have never considered he would have the energy let alone the time to start an extramarital affair. What will you do; confront Tristan?*

Hannah: *No, I have to catch him at it; I have to know for sure. So I will have to wait until such an opportunity presents itself. I thought that the affair would be conducted under this roof but it's not to be.*
Fi: *What do you mean, 'under this roof'?*
Hannah: *Well I think that the object of his desire is a pupil at school, I have told you before, it's Sasha. I am pretty sure of it actually. She is seventeen so it is legal in the eyes of the law but he would lose his job, our house, our marriage. She was the one that he had tried to tutor at our house prior to our dinner party.*
Fi: *Serious?*
Hannah: *Very. Does Raymond ever discuss pupils at school? Has he ever voiced any suspicions he may have?*
Fi: *The only times he has ever said anything about pupils and teachers was about a year ago. There were rumours about Mr Harbinger and Rex Miller in year five. Now that would have been illegal; at least if what you are saying about Sasha and Tristan is true, then at least there wouldn't be the added tarring of underage sex.*
Hannah: *Where did they say this all happen with Rex?*
Fi: *Apparently in his classroom but nothing was ever proven. Rex had been quite destructive at school and much was apportioned to his home life. His parents were of same sex and he was bullied by his fellow boarders as a result. Raymond tried on several occasions to discover the main protagonists but Rex was so disliked that Raymond never had much success. It seemed that Rex was a liar and friendless so it was tricky to try and decipher the truth from the fantasy. When Brian and Allan, Rex's parents, confronted Mr Fallbuoy with evidence of letters and gifts from Mr Harbinger, Mr Fallbuoy suggested that Rex attend another school. So six weeks later the matter was just yesterday's news.*
Hannah: *But surely if these liaisons took place in Mr Harbinger's classroom someone would have seen?*
Fi: *No, not really. Mr Harbinger is the only member of staff not to have a ground floor classroom. His is on the first floor above the drama studio.*

Hannah: *So if Tristan were to want a place to conduct his private affairs, Mr Harbinger's classroom would be the ideal location?*
Fi: *Probably.*

fLy: The two of them continued their conversation but it moved onto political spheres that were quite frankly founded upon hearsay rather than actual knowledge. It was a rather dull exchange even as the wine loosened their tongues. The time moved quickly for them, both remarking that they had no idea where the time went as Tristan came in through the front door after another day at school. As Fi left, Hannah grabbed her arm and asked her not to breathe a word to anyone. Fi smiled at her and reassured her that she would be her friend in need, any time of the day. Tristan took off his coat and said his goodbyes to Fi as she headed out of the door. From inside the sitting room Hannah started her interrogation.

Hannah: *Any luck with finding another room for Saturday with Sasha?*
Tristan: *Yes, actually. A bit of luck, Mr Harbinger said that I could take his room. Because his classroom is on the first floor, the caretakers are much more relaxed about leaving him with the responsibility of locking up for the weekend. I suppose there is less of a risk that an intruder would just walk past his room and see the TV or DVD player as they might if I were to have my classroom left unlocked. It is a good room actually. I went up to see it today; plenty of space with no obvious exterior distraction.*
Hannah: *Well that will work out well. Jean and Kaori will be coming over at 6pm prior to dinner; he has offered me a massage in lieu of last week's overnight stay.*
Tristan: *Kaori will be coming? I saw Jean today and he told me that Kaori had gone to Geneva to visit her sister; apparently she is ill. Anyway, the more time I get with Jean one on one the better; I really am so excited about the play, Hannah. But, and it is a big but, there is so much money to spend on it, to achieve the look and*

189

feel that I want that I so desperately hope he will petition for from the Finance Office!

fLy: Tristan excused himself, donned his coat and scarf and went out to walk Wallace, whilst Hannah weighed herself, perused her clothes, showered and then finally prepared dinner. After their meal Tristan and Hannah watched a film, *Shakespeare in Love* I think, and they both sat and reminisced about being in Norfolk all those years ago, recognising Holkham Beach in the scenes of the film. Their nostalgic talk culminated with sex on the sofa.

Thursday and Friday were non-productive days for me, I was feeling under the weather and I knew that Saturday had much in store so I remained in the house. Wallace was company of sorts. On the Thursday, Hannah went food shopping and in the evening after dinner, Tristan trimmed his pubic hair. Friday seemed as uneventful as Thursday; Hannah gave herself an all-over body scrub with what smelt like coconut shells and pistachio nuts crushed into a paste of cream cheese and Tristan spent much of the evening in his office.

On Saturday, Tristan went to school, as per usual, for morning Mass and School Notices and Hannah went to the gym. I was feeling a whole lot brighter so I decided that going to the gym and seeing all of those fit and able bodies would only bolster me. Hannah went on the running machine, listening as always to her MP3 player and the boys there made their usual faces, but this time one of the boys came over to talk to her. Hannah pressed the 'quit' button on the apparatus and took her earphones out of her ears as the black rubber conveyor belt slowed. The boy asked her if she knew how sexy she was and with that the entire gym roared with cheers. Hannah blushed upwards from her big knees to her hairline.

Instead of going home with Hannah after her workout, I took a detour into school. I went to the staff room and was pleased to see Letty and Raymond on their own in deep conversation.

Raymond: *I will leave the tent in here at 4pm. All you have to do is collect it after you return from the hockey match. Tomorrow morning you need to park your car here and then take the tent with you, following the small black plastic ribbons I will tie around the brambles once you have exited the school grounds via the gate by the athletics field. The last plastic ribbon you will see will be white. There will be an area, a clearing nearby, that will facilitate you erecting the tent. I will be close and once I see that you have gone inside I will join you. I will not talk to you, Letty, as I don't wish anyone to recognise my voice but you and I will communicate in ways that we will discover tomorrow.*

fLy: Letty's eyes truly twinkled as Raymond talked to her and she talked in the way I would imagine a sheep would sound, high-pitched and uncertain. She was concerned that she would not be able to assemble the tent correctly and Raymond explained that she had the whole evening in which to practise and to get it right; there really was no reason to panic. Letty asked Raymond if there was anything that she should wear and he told her that she should wear clothes that befitted the activity; army camouflage trousers and jacket would most likely be the wisest choice. Letty nodded, stood up and made her way out; she was a lady with a mission.

Witnessing this exchange, I wondered what outfit Hannah, Sasha and Tristan would be considering for their weekend foray. I flew over to the girl's boarding house to see if there were any clothes laid out on Sasha's bed but having drawn a blank there I returned home. Hannah was in the 'Downward Dog' position in the sitting room drying her bum cream so I shot upstairs to see if there were any clues as to what she would be wearing later on that afternoon. On the bed was a pair of knickers, a G-string, still with the price tag attached to them. They were navy blue and made mainly of lace. There was no bra to match or laid out on the bed beside them. Hannah came upstairs humming the tune to one of Frank Sinatra's overrated hits and went into the bathroom and turned on the hot and cold taps to fill the bath with warm water and scented bubbles. Whilst the bath ran she sat on the bed, picked up her new navy knickers and tore the label off with her teeth. She opened her dressing table drawer, located her brand new razor and took that with the knickers into the bathroom.

The actual bath was more eventful than usual; not only did she shave her legs and armpits but she also shaved all of the hair from her pussy (her bum hole already hair-free) and from the tops of her big toes. When she stepped out of the bath she dried herself thoroughly and applied frugal amounts of 'Genital Glitter Gel' to her undercarriage that smelled like sugared strawberry and bile. Hannah then proceeded to give herself a manicure and a pedicure; her choice of nail colour was pearl which seemed rather fitting; aren't pearls made from digested shit?

She walked, naked into the bedroom and was startled to see Tristan undressing. He explained that his classes had been cancelled because of it being a big day for the College; they had reached the regional finals in Hockey and Football so the PE staff and most of the pupils were required to attend the games and give support meaning he had the afternoon off. He too was going to take a relaxing bath whilst listening to some of his old CDs.

Tristan's bath time was pretty tame; he lay still in the water regarding his cock as it bobbed up in the water; buoyant and looking rather like a raw Cumberland sausage. He played with his penis like a child does with a favourite toy; several times he tugged the foreskin over its end and then pulled it back slowly enjoying how his penis looked as it gorged with blood. He gave his fleshy carrot an afro of white soapy lather and then rinsed it clean and that wasn't the only fun that Tristan could have with it; what a wonderful accessory a cock was!

He emerged from the bathroom after nearly an hour, looking pink, almost newborn in shade, and quickly dressed himself in his faded blue jeans, navy cotton shirt, blazer and white tennis trainers. He applied a fine mist of hairspray and splashed his neck and cheeks with his newly acquired musky aftershave.

As he walked downstairs he looked around him and smiled as Hannah appeared. She was wearing a simple long black V-neck dress. It was obvious that she was not wearing a bra as her nipples distorted the contour of the material. Hannah asked if Tristan had time for a quick glass of wine before he disappeared to teach Sasha. She said that it was such a shame to interrupt their Saturday evening together but she felt it very admirable of Tristan to take his work so seriously; the dedication to his pupils exemplary. He said that he enjoyed his subject so much that it was no hardship for him but did wish that he could stay home to witness the massage from Jean; he hoped that she would enjoy it as much as Raymond did. Both of them drank their wine with spurious affection painted on their faces. Tristan finished his glass before Hannah and went into the office; he picked up various text books, reading books and a pad of blank A4 paper. He walked back into the sitting room to say goodbye and to confirm with Hannah that he would be home just after seven and that dinner would be around 7.45pm. He patted Wallace as he left the room and checked that his pen was in the top inside pocket of his navy waffle wool-knit blazer. I could tell that he was a little nervous because little farts were squeaking out of him as he stepped out of the house and his hand slightly shook as he pulled the front door shut. I stayed with Hannah, but it was a tough choice; and one I had been carefully appraising during the time when Hannah and Tristan were drinking their wine together.

I thought it best to dedicate my time to only one of them so that I could fully comprehend and assess the situation; but then the thought of not witnessing the other event was too much of a trade. So I had to decide who I would watch first; Jean would be more direct with Hannah I think, whilst Tristan would be more hesitant and more susceptible to stagnating. By going to visit Tristan after half an hour I hopefully would be privy to a more engaging exchange between him and Sasha. As I made my way to the sitting room I heard Hannah pour herself another glass of white wine. She then went into the downstairs loo to check on her 'wet labia look' lipstick. The doorbell sounded and Hannah took a deep breath. She opened the door and there stood Jean, again with the same rucksack on his back but this time he was also holding a small yellow tool box that was made of sturdy thick plastic with a black fold-up handle.

Hannah told Jean to come in taking the yellow box from him and then took his bag from his back, placing it on the floor; their eyes were locked into each other's as she did so. She faced him and pushed Jean's coat off of his shoulders. He caught it as it slid down his arms on to his hands and reached around behind her, still staring at her, and hooked it onto the coat peg. She silently moved toward the sitting room, Jean following with his yellow box of tricks. She poured him a glass of chilled white wine; still silence. Wallace aroused himself from his slumber and walked over to Jean, his tail wagging with such enthusiasm that his back and middle appeared to roll. Jean crouched down to Wallace and gave him an equally enthusiastic stroke, telling him that he was beautiful. Hannah cast her eyes toward Jean, her smile radiant. Jean looked up at Hannah and he told her that she was beautiful too. Their eyes locked again as he stood tall and he slowly put his glass to his lips, drinking the straw-coloured liquid. As he swallowed Hannah moved her eyes to see his Adam's apple jump up his throat, it was very pronounced. Jean noticed and told Hannah that at school he was always ribbed about it but that the girls always seemed to be attracted to it in later years.

Jean opened his tool box, took out three scented candles and continued to take out the individual bottles with handwritten labels detailing the oil. Jean asked Hannah to get some clean soft bath towels and then to lay them on the floor between the sofa and the dining table. He closed the curtains whilst Hannah fetched the makeshift bedding. When she returned, Jean had lit the candles and had taken off his bright white T-shirt. His chest was hair-free and his nipples were dark purple. Hannah lay the towels on the floor and waited, very unsure of what to do next. Jean took a CD from his box of tricks and loaded it into the stereo. Once the chiming and the twanging had commenced he motioned for Hannah to come over to him. Her nipples were hard and her arm skin covered in goosebumps; Jean clutched Hannah's dress either side at her waist and Hannah spontaneously lifted her arms as he guided it over her head.

Jean: *You look so magical, so sexy, so raw with energy, Hannah. I am going to sit and look at you. I am going to imagine what it would be like to touch you and to rub my most sensual of oils into your every inch of perfectness. And then when I have contemplated you and appreciated you entirely by vision I will then point for you to lie down. I don't want to speak; I don't want to hear my voice shatter the fragile crystal web that protects this moment.*

fLy: I didn't dare move in case I was discovered and slain for the shattering of the crystal bullshit web. I stayed still, marvelling in disbelief as Hannah, nude except for her navy thong, voluntarily started to caress her breasts and stroke her tummy as if in some hedonistic higher state; groaning in harmony with the clangs of the metallic chimes of the music. Jean pointed to the floor and Hannah lay face down on the towels. Jean put a pillow under her chest and drizzled her with oil. Soon he was kneading her like pizza dough across her shoulders and down her spine. He knelt down with a knee either side of her midriff and massaged her arms with long forceful strokes. He returned to her shoulders, moving his hands down her back and out onto her ribs. Hannah continued to groan and the music continued to resonate. I could see that now, this moment, was my cue to go and check in on the English lesson.

As I flew towards Mr Harbinger's classroom I was suddenly

struck with the fear that I did not know a way into Harbinger's room except through the door. I would have to be very crafty and extremely lucky to find a way in that didn't take an age to find. The windows and curtains were shut so I dived down to the covered walkway and zoomed up the concrete steps to the corridor that led to Mr Harbinger's quarters. The door was shut. I retraced my path and went back to the windows hoping that there would be an air vent that I could get through. The rain started to pour down and I was getting desperate; should I fly back home and not waste any more valuable time or should I wait just in case? I found respite on the window sill underneath the old metal window hinge; I had no idea of how much time was passing but my option to go home now had vanished; the rain was battering it down.

To my total amazement, a shard of light effused from the room and then the window was opened. I saw my chance and flew straight in, I didn't even wait until Tristan's arm was back inside; the risk of being swotted by him was one I was willing to take. Once inside I made my way over to the whiteboard and perched on the metal lip that protrudes from the bottom, in between the green and blue whiteboard pens. I had to be near enough eye level so that I could decipher any small flicker of eyelashes or wrinkle of smile lines.

Sasha: *You think I am mad don't you, Sir? But I have always loved listening to the rain and seeing the droplets of water chase themselves down the window panes. I love how the air smells like damp charcoal, exaggerating the smell of warm dust as the radiator heats up. I love the way it makes me want to curl up, to get closer to someone. I love the way the orange glow from the College's road lamps gets distorted through the watery orbs; the light filtering into the room echoing that of a flame. Would you mind if I turn off the lights in the room, Sir?*
Tristan: *I will do it.*

fLy: And as soon as Tristan extinguished the lights, Sasha started to undress. She sat on the desk, flicked off her shoes and rolled her black tights down over her legs and off over her feet. She then stood up and unzipped her denim skirt so that it fell encircling her feet. Sasha pulled her hooded pink jumper over her head and unfastened her bra.

Sasha: *And the other thing that I love is looking at you and imagining you hard inside of me. I have wanted you for so long, Sir, I have made myself cum just thinking of your tongue inside my mouth, your voice as you tell me what to do and how to behave. I was hoping that I would find an inner strength to not tell you, to let you live your life with your beautiful wife but this evening I have succumbed to the heat in my loins; as Shakespeare wrote "Most dangerous is that temptation that doth goad us onto sin in loving virtue."*

fLy: And that was it; clever Sasha quoted Shakespeare and Tristan raced toward her, grabbing her head in his hands. He mauled her face and grasped at her breasts and pinched at her nipples. He held her hair in one hand as he chewed her neck and thrust his knee between her legs. Sasha started to rub herself up and down his thigh as they both fell to the floor. Tristan scrambled with one hand to undo his trousers and to kick them off whilst with the other hand he held Sasha's wrists together over her head. He bit at her lips and breathed heavily through his nose. Tristan parted her legs wide with his knees; he spat on his fingertips and moistened her so that as he plunged into her neither he nor she would tear. As he pummelled into her, Sasha started to wince, she was getting carpet burn on her shoulder blades so he rolled them both so that she was now on top. With each hand he clenched her buttocks and pulled her back and forth on him, her small breasts barely moving, the movement getting faster. He moved his left hand from her behind to be in front of her pudendum so that his thumb was pressing up on her clitoris as she rocked on him. Both of them started to shudder and moan and cry and say 'yes' and then the whole thing was over. They both stared at each other, Sasha on top of Tristan looking down at him with a small, sweet smile. Tristan combed his fingers through her long hair, his eyes filling with water.

Tristan: *I don't know what to say, Sasha. I can't believe that we just made love! We made love, Sasha, and the electricity coursing through my veins makes me want to shout out loud 'Wow!' But I feel that I should be seeking forgiveness from you. On the surface people would condemn me for apparently abusing the teacher–pupil relationship but I feel that isn't the case. I feel so much more for you than I have for anyone else in my life. In truth I just want to hear you tell me that you feel the same way. That you know that I would never do anything to harm you in any way; I have to tell you that I have never been happier. Each day I awake and I think instantly about you, not just your beauty but your intelligence too. Your presence ensnares me, Sasha; just knowing that I am in the same building as you, in the same canteen, chapel or classroom fills me with this feeling of completeness that I have never known. My love for you acts like a force field around me and nothing seems to unsettle me; at worst I feel happy. Every day I have to stop myself counting down the minutes until you are with me again; stepping in through my classroom's door, file clenched in your perfect hands. I look for information from the way you walk in, to the way you sit down. My ears strain to hear anything that you say to your peers, in case there is news of someone you have a crush on, or that has asked you out. I go from sheer anticipation to angst in the few seconds that it takes you to sit down and for the class to begin. And then when you have opened your file and found a pen, you look up toward me and I breathe again. I never intended this to happen, Sasha; I dreamt of it many times but I never thought this wish of mine be granted.*

Sasha: *I don't want to leave here, Sir, with you feeling the need to apologise. I want to leave here this evening with you knowing that what just happened will happen again and I want it to, again and again. Promise me that as I walk out of here to go and meet up with Dan you will think of a time, soon, when you can organise another extra-curricular lesson.*

Tristan: *Dan?*

fLy: I couldn't spend any more time with them; I had to get home to see if I would be in time to watch Jean with Hannah.

I reached home in record time and within seconds I was back in the sitting room. The candles were still alight but Hannah was now on her back, Jean still astride her. He was leaning forward and applying slight pressure on the outer edges of his hands cupping her breasts whilst his thumbs ringed her nipples. He then let his fingertips delicately glide down her body from her collarbone to her toes, chasing their paths with a warm jet of his breath. He stood up and announced that he had finished and that she had no reason to feel guilt for the pleasure she had experienced. As she arose from the floor, her face was red and her eyes were dazed. She slumped onto the sofa, as had Raymond the previous week. Jean fetched her black dress and slipped it over her head. At that very moment Tristan burst in through the front door, proclaiming his apologies for his lateness, breathless as he entered the sitting room. Jean told him that his timing was perfect and that Hannah was relaxed; his goal had been achieved. Tristan looked at Hannah and smiled; he took his files, books and wodge of A4 paper back in to the office and then carried Jean's rucksack up to the spare room. Whilst he was upstairs Jean asked Hannah how she felt. She said that she couldn't remember ever feeling so happy and that what she had experienced then was far more sensual than anything else she could remember. Jean told her that he had never been so aroused in his entire life; he wanted to do it again and soon.

The rest of the evening went smoothly. The food was delicious according to Jean, and the wine flowed constantly. But it was very clear that Tristan was not feeling in the euphoric state that I had thought he would be in; especially after his momentous interlude with Sasha. He didn't finish his dinner and the wine slowly disappeared from his glass. He excused himself to go and get from his office the various notes and receipts for various purchases he had made so far for the school play for Jean to look at. I went with Tristan as I was sure that there was something wrong.

As Tristan closed the door of the office he leant back against it and slid to the floor. He held his head in his hands, as quiet, but decipherable musings stumbled from his mouth.

Tristan: *There may be in the cup*
A spider steep'd, and one may drink, depart,
And yet partake no venom, for his knowledge
Is not infected: but if one present
The abhorr'd ingredient to his eye, make known
How he hath drunk, he cracks his gorge, his sides,
With violent hefts. I have drunk,
and seen the spider.

fLy: He continued to sit slumped against the door blubbing until Jean came to enquire of his whereabouts. Tristan leapt up and wiped his eyes and returned to the sitting room seemingly more settled. Hannah cleared away the plates and condiments whilst Tristan and Jean went through all of the existing paraphernalia that Tristan had amassed for the play. He had printouts of costumes that they could buy or rent, he had numbers of local people that offered dressmaking services and the costs that this would incur, he had pictures of scenery and his suggestion of how much plywood would be needed for each scene change. He had jotted down people within the School Maintenance Team that had offered to help with building the scenery and he had the 'sign up' volunteer list that had been posted on the School Announcements Board. As he read through the names with Jean, he saw Dan Winkwood's name at the bottom of the list.

Jean: *I would never have put Dan down as someone to offer his time for set building for the school play but I suppose it shouldn't surprise me too much, we all do crazy things when we are smitten.*

Hannah: *Is that Dan Winkwood? On the First XV Rugby team? Tall, dark hair, small tattoo of a rugby ball on his shoulder, good-looking but a bit full of it?*

Jean: *That's the one. How do you know of him?*

Hannah: *I see him in the gym.*

Tristan: *Who is he smitten with?*

Jean: *Sasha Burnham.*

Tristan: *How do you know that?*

Jean: *I was on lunch duty in the school canteen last week. Dan and Lisa came in together and both sat on the table directly behind me. It was the late sitting for lunch so the hall was pretty empty. The conversation between the two started off quite amicably but it soon changed, becoming quite heated. Lisa kept accusing Dan of fancying Sasha; he said they were just friends. If he had left it at that then I think that I would have believed him but the problem was, Tristan, that he continued to deny it. Lisa emptied her custard and apple crumble into his lap and then left the hall. I felt quite sorry for the bloke.*

Hannah: *Tristan, you know Sasha, does she feel the same way about Dan?*

Tristan: *Not that I have heard; I can't say it is something I would discuss with her anyhow. And to be honest it is not really something I want to waste my time talking about now. Can we get back to matters in hand, Jean?*

fLy: My eyes darted over toward Hannah. She didn't know I was watching her. I could see that she was enjoying listening to Jean divulge information about Dan's love interest to Tristan. She knew from Tristan's abrasive reaction that Jean had hit a nerve, further confirming her belief that, like Dan, Tristan carried a big bright burning flame for Sasha Burnham too.

18

fLy: The following morning, I awoke much later than I had intended; I wanted to make sure that I was in the car park to see Letty arrive and follow her as she hunted the strategically tied ribbons. As I left home I went via the athletics track. Lucky that I did as Letty was already making her way out through the gate. As I trailed her, I was downwind and could smell her plastic breath mixing with her salty sweat that drained into her armpits. She counted fourteen small black ribbons before finding the white ribbon by the clearing that was surrounded by gorse and brambles, apple and almond blossom trees. The sun was shining and the natural shine on the long grass was all but a distant glint. There were a few empty crisp packets and scrunched cans of Strongbow cider which marred the otherwise romantic setting. Letty scoured the hedges for further ribbons but upon finding none took to erecting her tent, her pop-up love chamber. Once inside she searched through her rucksack for condoms and wet wipes. She took off her running clothes and put on a scarlet red silk vest and a black lace thong. She brushed her hair and waited. I waited with her, I had no choice, the tent was zipped up so I had to be as careful as possible to not get spotted, swatted or squashed; positioning was key. I found an area right in the corner that seemed to offer the most protection but it meant my field of vision was skewed. But beggars can't be choosers.

Raymond entered the tent with much speed and very quickly was undressed. He too had bought a rucksack with him, his carrying mostly bricks, a bottle of water, a pencil with a pad and a small square of lilac silk. He kept opening and closing his mouth wide at Letty, until she mimicked him. He took the silk square and stuffed it into her mouth. Letty tried to smile but was gagged in the process. Snot came fleeing out of her nose and her eyes started to water, her mascara running down her face. Raymond quickly took the silk out of her mouth and wrote that she was making too much noise. She mouthed sorry and he took the opportunity to pop the lilac silk back in.

Raymond instructed her via a scribble that he really liked her outfit and to get on all fours. Once Letty was 'alla doggy' he started the timer on his Casio Mudman G-shock watch and away they went until Raymond penned the next instruction. He wrote that he wanted her to cock her leg like a dog urinating against a big oak tree. As Letty held her leg up at right angles to the rest of her body, Raymond put both of his hands behind his head, his face twisting, lips curled exposing his white teeth. As he came he tumbled down on top of Letty and she folded like a deckchair. For a few minutes Raymond lay motionless over her, squashing Letty. Letty's face was puce as she struggled to breathe, the silk still trapped in her mouth. With great effort she grabbed the pencil and scrawled, "Get off of me. I can't breathe." Raymond, quick to realise the issue at hand yanked the silk free from her mouth and rolled off of her. Letty took a huge breath and kissed Raymond; a sound very similar to that which Wallace makes when thirstily gulping from his water bowl. Letty took the pencil again, "Not sure what to do next." And Raymond responded, "You have had a good workout so just chillax." And with that Raymond changed back into his running gear, grabbed his pencil, pad, lilac silk and water bottle and briskly unzipped the tent. I took my chance and escaped; I had no idea how long I would be stuck in there if I didn't. Raymond was in close pursuit and for a few seconds I considered seeing where he would be going but I decided against it. Instead I stayed close by so that I could survey the tent and its contents.

I had only been in the cover of the tree for a short while when I heard a very operatic voice emanating from inside of the tent. Letty was doing a full rendition of 'The Sound of Music' without backing harmony whilst she changed back into her sporting attire. In fairness it was quite a dreadful sound. As she emerged she started singing 'Maria' but soon realised she had forgotten the lyrics so as she collapsed the tent and meticulously rolled it back up into the small bag, she sang, in less operatic tones, a version of 'Que Sera, Sera'. She was either being prophetic or pathetic; both suited the situation.

My next port of call was to be the girls' boarding house to see how Sasha was. The curtains were still drawn in their room and both girls were awake and giggling. I was sorry to have missed the start of the conversation but it was easy to grasp the topic in hand.

Sasha: *Neither of them did.*

Ana: *What do you mean? Neither? Did you have sex with Mr Stephens too? Oh yuck! What will you do if Dan finds out or Mr Stephens?*

Sasha: *Well Dan won't say a word or Lisa will cut his balls off and Mr Stephens won't say a word because his wife will cut his balls off and you're my best friend so you won't say a word either.*

Ana: *Who was better?*

Sasha: *Mr Stephens, hands down. Dan kept touching the end of his nose with his tongue as he fumbled around trying to get his dick in and once it was he just went in and out, in and out until he shot his load. He is certainly not the love impresario that Lisa would have one believe. Whereas Mr Stephens was something else.*

fLy: Sasha then delivered a move-by-move account of the evening's entertainment with Tristan and I left midway through the narrative; I was feeling tired and I needed to rest.

When I reached home Tristan and Hannah were having a late lunch together. Hannah was interrogating Tristan on the merits of the play thus far and whether he had any regrets attempting to put on such a big-budget production. Without awaiting his answers, she carried on with her questioning but this time wanted his answers.

Hannah: *Will you be seeing Sasha again?*

Tristan: *If you mean for extra English coaching then, yes I will. Progress was definitely made yesterday evening and it seems to work well with Jean coming round. You seem to get on well with him and until the play is in its final week of rehearsal it will have to be this way. I appreciate his feedback, input and advice, I really appreciate the effort you are putting into the play's success. I can, of course, try and schedule meeting him during school hours but just knowing that we have an evening to discuss the play takes the time pressure off. Did you get the feeling that Jean would be happy to come round again? Maybe one evening this week would work well for him so that he can have his weekends with Kaori? Would you be happy for me to ask him?*

Hannah: *I have to admit that his massages, if offered, would be hard to resist. By all means ask him, you can coordinate with him and then just let me know.*

fLy: Tristan said that he would make enquiries the following day both with Jean, Sasha and room availability. The conversation seemed to be very stilted and Hannah's manner was slightly barbed.

Sunday evolved, Wallace was taken for a walk by Hannah and Tristan so I didn't bother going too; Tristan wouldn't be confiding anything to Wallace and I felt that some downtime for me would be beneficial as I could see this coming week was to be one where timings and locations were to be pivotal; I needed to have a good store of energy.

Once again I strategically settled myself in the staff room on Monday morning and felt it best to wait there until I had at least some information from one of my lines of enquiry. I was keen to see Ms Swallow interact with Mr Evans and I was requiring feedback from Mr Lempriere regarding an evening with Mr Stephens and Co. I was curious as to whether Mr Stephens would request Mr Harbinger's room via the usual college system or whether he would once again visit him in private.

I didn't have to wait long until Letty came in. She was helping herself to coffee and bourbon biscuits when Mr Harbinger arrived. They both chatted amicably, sitting in the chairs by the bay window. There was an extraordinary sky that morning; dark, angry indigo with violent strips of fluorescent white light torn through it. The light that streamed into the staff room was very bright, but not with the sunny shards that highlight the dust in the air but rather more with a surgical luminosity that causes one to pay attention. The smell of the warm coffee and milk somewhat neutralised the atmosphere, returning the room to being a meeting place rather than a scene set in a thriller movie.

Jean arrived and nodded over toward Letty and Mr Harbinger and slowly made himself a tea, letting his teabag steep for longer than required. To his relief Tristan came in and the two of them came over to their 'usual' table. Jean said that he would be happy to come over to Tristan's house during the week but as ever would prefer to be able to stay over. They agreed that Wednesdays would be a good time to have regular meetings.

The end of morning break was sounded by the bell and Jean left with Letty; Tristan stole the moment to chat with Mr Harbinger. I decided that I would go with Jean. Rather than go to his class he took a detour to my house. He checked his watch and I knew that he was hoping to catch Hannah before she left home to go to the gym. As he fastened his pace toward our house he checked his breath in his hand, grabbed a piece of gum from his pocket and chewed it. Before ringing my doorbell, he discharged the minty clump from his mouth in to the bushes like a bullet from a barrel.

Hannah: *What are you doing here, Jean? I was just off to the gym.*

fLy: Jean didn't respond and just gently pushed her back from the front door into her hall. He started to undress as he walked toward the sitting room. Hannah followed him visibly perplexed. Jean went into the kitchen and grabbed the olive oil from behind the hob and put it on the floor where they had shared their last encounter. With all of his clothes removed and folded he went over to the patio windows and closed the floor-length curtains. He returned to Hannah who had taken on the appearance of a statue and he took off her clothes, except for her thong and led her to the olive oil bottle. Hannah knelt, looked at Jean's Cumberland sausage of a penis and then continued to lie down. Her breathing was slow but even.

Jean stood above Hannah as she lay face down into the carpet. From a small height, he let the olive oil drizzle down onto Hannah's back. It covered each knob of vertebrae like a trickle of golden syrup and finished in a little pool in the small of her back. With her hands out flat in front of her on the floor, he smoothed the oil out over her skin and massaged her once again, kneading her, pushing his fists into her flesh then firmly moving his hands out over her shoulders, along her arms and threaded his fingers through hers. As he pushed down on her she felt the tip of his erect penis trace along her lumbar. The tiny hairs on her arms struggled to bristle against its coating of oil but her face flushed scarlet as she recognised the touch that brushed against her spine. Jean moved his hands back up her arms, back over her shoulder blades and pushed his thumbs hard either side of her vertebral column, kneading her buttocks with clenched fist.

Hannah groaned as he parted her legs; once again using his thumbs to massage the skin high up on the inside of her thighs. He meticulously rubbed and stroked her legs, down to her toes; every inch of her skin generously basted. Looking at her now she closely resembled a plucked chicken, ready for roasting; all that was required was a whole lemon and a bunch of fresh sage to shove up her cavity. It was obvious that Jean and I had one thing in common; we both love a good Sunday roast.

After only a couple of minutes Hannah rolled over and turned her head to look at Jean. He was standing totally still to her right side. He told her that she was totally magnificent. He dressed and he left.

Hannah sat up, her eyes filled with water and she cried and kept crying. I was stumped; I couldn't work out why. Within ten minutes Hannah too had dressed but her tears kept falling. She opened the fridge and poured herself a glass of white wine and went over to the phone and rapidly dialled Fi. She asked if Fi could come over and soon afterwards old farty flaccid face arrived, near galloping through the gate in Hannah's back garden. Hannah swung the patio doors open and in came Fi, very out of breath.

Fi: *I came as fast as I could; what on earth is wrong?*
Hannah: *I let someone give me a massage and I had an orgasm.*
Fi: *Where were you have massaged, what part of you?*
Hannah: *My whole body, Fi.*
Fi: *Did you have sex?*
Hannah: *No.*
Fi: *Did you kiss or perform any foreplay on each other?*
Hannah: *No.*
Fi: *So it was just a massage? Like the one Raymond had?*
Hannah: *Just like the one Raymond had.*
Fi: *Well I give up trying to understand where the issue is Hannah.*

fLy: And with that Hannah stopped blubbing, dried her eyes, smiled and asked Fi if she had ever told her that she loved her and spontaneously gave Fi a cuddle. Fi, confused jumped backward and made her excuses and flew out of the patio doors and out through the gate but not before looking back at Hannah and flashing her one of her farty flaccid smiles.

I left Hannah with her wine and her inner buzz, and took chase hoping to catch Fi. I caught up with her as she crossed the athletics pitch and accompanied her all the way back to her front door, waiting patiently for her hands to stop shaking so that she could put the key into her front door and unlock it. Fi ran up her stairs and into Raymond's study. She turned on the computer, clicked on the Internet icon and punched into the search field "What are the signs of lesbian?" After twenty minutes or so of scanning through documents and gossip magazine articles she turned the computer off. As she left the study, Fi noticed Raymond's rucksack unzipped. There, popping out the top of a reporter's notepad, was Francis's comforter. She reached down and picked up the notepad. The lilac silk was trapped in between some pages and upon opening it she saw the scribbled conversation. She shut the pad, replacing the lilac silk in the pages and took the items downstairs into the kitchen and placed them onto the large wooden table. Surprisingly, Fi seemed visibly unconcerned.

Returning home, I saw Hannah make her way into the gymnasium and I wondered whether to follow her as I had nothing else to do, or whether to return to the staff room. Neither seemed very appealing as I was sure that Letty and Raymond would have planned their next reunion by now. I also considered going to the girls' boarding house to see if Sasha was in her dormitory. But my mind was made up for me; I saw Dan sitting on the steps of the music block with his arm around Lisa. I went straight over as fast as I could, slowing as I approached them.

Lisa: *Ana told me, why would she lie about it?*

Dan: *I am not saying she lied to you. I did go out with her and Sasha on Saturday night. Sasha asked me to organise it; Ana has liked Charlie for a long time, apparently, and I know that Charlie likes Ana. Seeing as Charlie is my best friend and Ana is hers it made sense for the four of us to go out. The only reason I lied and said that it was just Charlie and me going out was because I had promised Charlie not to say a word. You know how sensitive he is; he thought it was a set-up and he didn't want his undoubted humiliation to become common knowledge. I am at a loss for words, Lisa; I can't even tell you if Charlie and Ana got it on; we were together all of the time. I don't even know why she told you about the evening. We all promised that we wouldn't say a thing to anyone, we were all worried it would get misconstrued, as it has done!*

Lisa: *So nothing happened between you and Sasha?*

Dan: *I am not answering that. You either trust me or you don't.*

fLy: Bored by the lack of spit-fuelled words and confession I moved on. I thought about going home but knew that I would never forgive myself if I missed seeing Raymond's reaction to the pad and silk on the kitchen table so I decided to hedge my bets and go back and wait at Fi's house. I had the time, if needed to spend the next few hours finding an alternative way in; having to wait for their front door to open was always an inconvenience in any situation.

19

fLy: It didn't take me too long to locate the airbricks; a much easier task with houses built before 1930 but quite often they have been blocked up to stop the spiders and drafts coming in. The airbrick I discovered gave me direct access into the pantry that was positioned at the back of Fi's kitchen. The best thing with this little room for me was that, even though a little bit colder than the rest of the house, I would remain undiscovered in the folds of the potato sack and could relax until Raymond came home. I would be able to hear him come in through the front door, and then navigate my way through the keyhole into the kitchen.

I waited longer than I had thought I would as the temperature had fallen outside as the sun had gone down; I was starting to feel chilled. The smell of Fi's cooking tempted me to go into the kitchen but I thought it pertinent to just await Raymond's arrival; however, because Fi had the radio on I was not able to hear what she was doing; I only had my sense of smell as my guide. From all the varying aromas and flavours that had started to emanate it was obvious that she was still adding ingredients to what smelt like a lamb stew. Luckily it didn't take long for the pantry door to open and I was taken by surprise as I was swiftly lifted and taken into the kitchen as Fi grabbed the potato sack. I had to be supremely careful, as she put the bag on the kitchen counter, to slip out unnoticed. Once I had repositioned myself on the cooker hood I stayed alert.

I looked to see if Fi had moved the pad and lilac silk but it lay in the same place as before; very prominently in the centre of the kitchen table. The front door duly opened and shut with a slam and Raymond came into the kitchen having already hung up his coat. He enquired how Fi was and they gave each other a kiss and a brief cuddle. He filled a glass with water, asked how Francis and Lesley were and turned to sit at the table.

Fi: *Oh yes Raymond, before I forget, look at what I found in your rucksack?*

Raymond: *Found in my rucksack?*

Fi: *I was in the study, on the Internet doing some research, and as I went to leave I saw your rucksack open. Francis's lilac silk was in it, just poking out from your pad. I am not sure what it was doing in your rucksack Raymond or what the scrawls in the notepad mean.*

Raymond: *Well, none of it should be questionable, Fi. For weeks now we have been saying that Francis is getting too old now for a comforter. So I decided that I would just take it and see if he missed it as much as we thought he would. I think it fair to say that he hasn't even mentioned it. Pretty successful plan wouldn't you say?*

Fi: *And the pad, the writing is not all yours, some of it is different?*

Raymond: *That was just a fitness idea that Nathan came up with.*

Fi: *Nathan?*

Raymond: *Yes, nice chap, deaf but incredibly fit. What's for dinner, it smells great and I am famished?*

fLy: I stayed where I was until dinner had been served and made my way out inconspicuously through the keyhole, then through the airbrick in the pantry and went home. I flew quite slowly, reflecting on the day and the ease with which Dan and Raymond had lied to their 'loved' ones. In retrospect both of them should be commended for their ability to deceive their partners; quite admirable really. Accomplished liars have their merits; thinking on the spot and convincingly imparting the untruths; a talent that can be deployed successfully in many of life's arenas; two that spring to mind, law and politics, maybe.

At home I found Hannah pacing around the living room and glaring regularly at her watch. I had no idea how long she had been circulating the kitchen and living room area but after about ten or fifteen minutes she declared that she had to go and find 'the bastard'. She threw on her three-quarter-length fawn woollen coat and marched out of the front door. I had obviously missed something, a phone call or a meeting, and as I followed her I was in the dark. She walked quickly into school and located the staircase that lead to Mr Harbinger's classroom. There at the end of the corridor the door to the classroom was shut. The neon strip lighting that illuminated the passageway reflected off of the gloss avocado paint. She took off her slip-on ankle boots and tiptoed toward the door; unlike most of the classroom doors it had no glass panel; just solid wood so she could not just peer in. She knelt down to look through the keyhole, trying to see what was happening on the other side but the key was in the lock on the inside. It appeared that this was fruitless so she sat down and pressed her ear to the door; holding her breath in case the sound of her exhaling and inhaling gave her position away. I had to be very vigilant too as I also did not want to give my position away. My choices were to go back outside and peep in through a window and risk missing the door opening or to stay where I was. I opted for the latter and stayed where I was just on top of the door frame looking down at the back of Hannah's head. Once again she started looking at her watch and occasionally she would itch the skin behind her right ear, her left ear moulding itself into the glossy paint. Silence, for the time, was our only company but the fact the lights were on suggested that there had been or would soon be other forms of interest gracing us. Still the lack of noise continued and Hannah replaced her boots, stood up and quickly ran back down the corridor, down the stairs and out toward her house. I was again trailing her but as she made direction for home I took the chance to fLy up to the windows of Mr Harbinger's room. As I peered in I was surprised to see Letty and Raymond.

Raymond was standing tall with his khaki, multi-pocketed trousers around his ankles, his leatherette panties pushed to one side allowing his member enough freedom to hammer into Letty. He had one hand on her buttock and the other he had held out in front of him so that he could keep checking his watch. Occasionally Raymond would pull a face as if he was straining to curl out one of his almighty turds. Luckily for Raymond, Letty could not see Raymond's face as she was bent over the back of one of the classroom plastic chairs, her dress flicked up over her back. She was wearing a dark green suspender belt, no knickers, flesh-coloured stockings and black patent high heels. Her cheeks were scarlet as Letty, once again, had to incorporate the silk lilac square in her mouth, breathe and remain silent. As Raymond's momentum increased Letty's mastication accelerated. She looked remarkably bovine. With every thrust her thighs wibble-wobbled and her eyes shut and then reopened like a puppet coming to life.

My mind was spinning; first I had no idea where Tristan was; second I was clueless as to the meeting up of Letty and Raymond, and third I was not sure of the arrangements that had been made by Tristan with regard to Jean. I felt aggrieved with Raymond; when he arrived at his house for dinner he made no mention of having to go out again and I was annoyed I had missed the reason he gave for having to go out and get a quickie in with Letty. There was so much happening that my judgement of where to be and when had become confused and possibly even dulled. Even now I was not sure whether to stay and find out more from Raymond and Letty, or to go to the girls' boarding house and see if Sasha was in or whether to go home and just wait with Hannah for Tristan's arrival.

It then dawned on me that as Hannah was on the rampage, she wouldn't be going home until she had located Tristan's whereabouts. I zoomed in the direction that I had seen Hannah taking, originally thinking that she was going home. I took a slight detour and went to Tristan's classroom. Inside were Hannah and Tristan, the volume of Hannah's voice loud enough to reverberate through the glass. Tristan's eyes were wide and his lips were pursed together; not even trying to intervene to try and stem the flow of anger that cascaded from Hannah. Once again I was on the outside and the words, even though loud, were indistinguishable. I was incensed that I had missed out on discovering what had been the catalyst to Hannah's indignation. As she stormed out of the classroom I decided to stay with her and followed her back home. As she stabbed her key into the front door her enraged ranting commenced. She kicked open the front door, hung up her coat and started to shout at poor Wallace.

Hannah: *You see, even you, Wallace, his beloved Wallace is taking a back seat. Maybe I should have thrown that at him; maybe he would have cared if I said that you are at home all day and lonely. Maybe he would have apologised and said that he should have called to let you know that he would be finishing off some work before coming home. What are we? And since when did he have to finish work? He's a teacher for God's sake; not some high-flying financier or lawyer. You know he smelt of perfume, and not mine either. I know he has been with her. All I have to do is catch him with her and then... and then what? And then what?*

fLy: With that she fell crumpled onto the floor and cried, heaving into Wallace. His face remained the same but he leant into her as she snotted into his coat, her tears flooding out of her, her manic words muffled by his thick coat. Eventually the tears stopped and she walked to the kitchen and pulled a short length of kitchen tissue from the roll that sat stoically by the sink and blew her nose, wiped her eyes and spat into the white absorbent paper. As if on autopilot she walked to the fridge, pulled out a bottle of white wine and poured herself a large glass, which she guzzled within seconds. She helped herself to another glass and went over to the phone. Hannah dialled a number and then replaced the handset. With a saddened face and heavy limbs, she took herself up the stairs to bed. Quietly she applied her bum bleaching cream, assumed the downward dog position whilst it dried, sniffed throughout the procedure and eventually went to bed.

Tristan came home roughly an hour later; he found Hannah fast asleep and so decided to have a glass of red wine. He sat with Wallace, gently stroking him; Wallace lovingly looked up at Tristan.

Tristan: *I really am in love, Wallace. My hands are tied. In an ideal world I would tell Hannah but I can't. Sasha is about to take some exams which will affect her University career and I cannot expect her to make any rash decision about our future but I cannot deceive Hannah the way I am. I never loved Hannah; not the way I do Sasha. All I ever wanted to was to rescue Hannah from her abominable parents and now I find myself needing to rescue myself from this stale and lifeless existence that I am in. With Sasha I have regained my heartbeat, sometimes I can hear it in my breath, and I am trying to find the words to explain this to Hannah in a way that she could understand, even empathise with. You see none of this is her fault; she is beautiful and she is tender but she is not Sasha. As the Master so succinctly wrote, "The fault, dear Brutus, is not in our stars, But in ourselves, that we are underlings."*

20

fLy: As Hannah approached the gymnasium the following day, Jean ran from the language block calling her name. Hannah stopped to hear what it was that Jean so desperately needed to tell her. He told her that he had organised with Tristan another meeting to discuss the play together at our house that evening and that Tristan would be engaged with the actual play rehearsals straight after school had finished. Tristan anticipated being with them shortly after 7.30pm. It would mean that Jean and Hannah could have potentially two hours together and he asked if Hannah would be willing to spend that time with him. Hannah agreed but inquired as to what he wanted to do in those two hours. Jean told her that Tristan had enlightened him to the night prior and that he had asked him to give her another relaxing massage as Tristan felt that Hannah was like a coiled, uptight spring. Hannah smiled as she accepted his offer and agreed that she would benefit hugely from his efforts.

Jean arrived that evening at 5.30pm. Hannah had spent a good hour in the bath shaving and then moisturising herself prior to his arrival. She was wearing very little make-up and her black long dress. As Jean hooked his coat on to the peg in our hall, Hannah faced him and removed her dress. This time she was naked; no navy blue thong just her hair-free body greeted Jean. Jean put his hands around her middle, turned her so that he was walking behind her into the sitting room. He guided her to the sofa and insisted she was not to lie down but to remain standing up. Jean sat on the sofa and turned Hannah to face him. She looked down at him as his eyes seemed to trace every inch of her. He unzipped his trousers and pushed them down over his bum. Both Hannah and myself instantly saw the bulge in his trousers push through the opening in his boxer shorts. Jean pulled Hannah toward him and he breathed out, heavily, onto her shaven mound, making sure his lips did not connect with her smooth, hairless flesh. He again turned her around so that he could look at her flabby arse and she voluntarily bent down to exhibit her now near-white bum hole. Once again he breathed out, but this time blowing cool air directly onto her arsehole. Hannah asked him what he wanted to do and he didn't respond. Instead he went over to their stereo, located the CD he wanted to listen to and told her to dance. As Madonna's 'Justify My Love' spewed out of the speakers so Hannah started to move. Her arms flailed in the air as if she was floating to the ground from a great height before running her hands up through her thinning hair and grinding her hips down and round. As the song came to a thankful end, Jean motioned to her to lie down. Rather than massage her, he just traced every inch of her body with his fingertips; no pressure applied, and her flesh pimpled with the electricity. And so it went on; for hours... BORING!

At eight o'clock Hannah dressed herself and made her excuses as she once again left the house; Tristan was late, again, for no given reason and she felt it extraordinary that he would be late to see Jean; love interest or not. Jean said he was happy to wait at our house and helped himself to a glass of white wine. From past experience I knew that I should go with Hannah even though I was really feeling exhausted. We repeated the events from the night before; straining at Mr Harbinger's door and getting nowhere and then returning home, after checking on Tristan's classroom of course.

When we did get back home Tristan was already there which took us both by surprise. Tristan was already midway through making his apologies to Jean and upon seeing Hannah recommenced his tale of lost keys and the big wooden trunk where the costumes were stored.

Jean: *My goodness, Tristan, I didn't think that story would ever end; especially second time round whilst telling Hannah. So much unnecessary detail. I think if your mate Shakespeare was here he would be shouting, "He doth protest too much." I probably have taken that quotation totally out of context but I know that a simple apology would have worked for me. I have had a very engaging time with your lovely wife and I am sure that Hannah was as equally entertained.*

fLy: Tristan was purple with shame, annoyed by his amateur storytelling.

Tristan: *I wasn't to know that you were here on your own, Jean. I would have given up the search much earlier had I known Hannah had gone out. I over-explained myself as a result of my seemingly bad manners. Hannah, where did you go?*
Hannah: *I came to find you, Tristan. It would be unheard of that you had forgotten a meeting with Jean so I thought that something must have happened and I was worried. Nothing more than that.*

fLy: The atmosphere for the next twenty minutes was spiky but after Hannah had poured half a bottle of white wine down her throat she started to laugh and to flirt with both men. Before the men had finished deliberating where the ever-mounting cost of production could be cut, Hannah said goodnight to Tristan, Jean and Wallace and took herself off to bed. I found the budgeting discussion futile and so I followed Hannah upstairs.

Once upstairs and in the bathroom, she hurled up her dinner and white wine, washed her face, cleaned her teeth, blew her nose (small remnants of sick and snot soaked the tissue – yumtastic), and applied a thick layer of white cream to the loose skin that covered her skeleton. She took a small handheld mirror and squatted over it to assess the paleness of her undercarriage and smiled. I was intrigued as to what Hannah would do next as her eyes seemed to glisten, to sparkle. It was an expression most out of character.

Hannah walked quickly to her wardrobe, opened the door and proceeded to pull out her underwear drawer. From underneath all of her various colours of knickers and bras she found a Polaroid camera. From the same drawer she managed to locate the photo printing paper and loaded the white pad of zinc paper into the camera. She then shut the bedroom door and turned off the main light to their bedroom. With the bedside light still on she positioned herself naked over the camera lens, hovering about two feet above. Once her feet were firmly rooted to the spot she leant carefully over and turned off the small bedside light; darkness and sound swamped the room. I heard her joints slightly crack as she balanced herself in such a way to press the button on the upper front of the camera. With an illuminating burst of flash and a quiet whirr of the mechanical motor a picture emanated from the camera. Hannah turned the small light back on and once again smiled at the image she regarded. If only we had all known the image of a bleached bum hole would have made Hannah smile we could have put a few strategically placed pictures around the house!

Hannah returned the camera to her drawer and slid the single photo alongside her neatly folded T-shirts that lay on the shelf above. I knew that I wouldn't have to wait long to find out what she would do with the picture and in the morning after Tristan had left the house to go to school my preconceptions were affirmed.

As soon as the front door closed, Hannah jumped out of bed,

threw on her white bathrobe and unearthed the photo. She looked at it again, smiled (again the bum shot achieved the unimaginable) and went downstairs to Tristan's office. She opened the top drawer of the desk and located the packet of new white A4 envelopes. After removing one from the cellophane she put the picture inside. She removed the protective tape and sealed the envelope, pressing down the lip to ensure it was properly closed. She took a 2B pencil and wrote "Mr J Lempriere." She replaced the packet of envelopes, shut the drawer and returned upstairs. Her morning routine then commenced as it always did resulting in her being dressed in her gym outfit.

Before going downstairs, she retrieved the envelope with its precious load, tucked it under her arm and made her way out to the gym. Her first stop was the Language block. As Hannah approached she saw a girl of about sixteen years old, quick footing her way into the double glass doors. Hannah accosted her, asking her to drop the letter into Mr Lempriere's pigeonhole. The girl smiled, and obligingly took the oversized envelope. Hannah slowly jogged back toward the gymnasium and I made the decision to follow Lisa…

Lisa pushed the envelope inside her A4 lever-arch file that was already stuffed with loose paper and topic sheets and made her way hurriedly into the class. I chased her into the classroom and stopped above the door frame. This was my first time in the language block and my first time in one of Jean's lessons. I was impressed by the skill of the man as I observed the faces of the class. Each and every pupil watched him and responded to him as he asked questions, laughing as he read from a book in French. I cannot speak French, nor do I understand it, so my only avenue of entertainment was to assess how he engaged the students.

At the end of the lesson, all of the potential scholars filed out in silence from the classroom. Lisa didn't stay behind to deliver the letter. I stayed with her as she flanked Dan out of the building. Once outside she asked Dan if he had a moment. Dan, duty-bound, stood still whilst their peers disappeared in varying directions. Lisa told him that she was sorry for not trusting him with Sasha; excusing her interrogation as an act of jealousy which most girls would suffer if their boyfriend was the most coveted boy in their entire year. Dan took the compliment well, neither blushing nor sweeping it aside but instead asked her if she was going to be able to get out after school for a walk at 5pm before evening prep commenced. Lisa coyly accepted and they agreed to meet by the cricket pavilion.

I took my leave and knew where I was to be at 5pm; I could rest till then. I went back home and awaited Hannah's return. It was another sunny day and the sun that streamed in through the patio doors was a magnet to both myself and Wallace. Wallace was a fine friend to have; his breathing when in deep slumber was possibly the best noise to listen to, lulling me into a heavy sleep.

I was awoken later on that afternoon by Hannah shouting at the phone to "ring" but as we all know a watched pot never boils or something like that anyway. She opened a bottle of wine and put 'Justify My Love' by Madonna on. She sat on the sofa, legs apart, head thrown back, and masturbated. Rather than watch that display, I focused on the digital clock above the oven. As soon as it registered 16.45 I was off. Wallace was still asleep; God that dog can sleep!

I was at the cricket pavilion in plenty of time but I was not bored, I liked watching the sun and the clouds. They are the perfect couple; each of them brilliant on their own but magnificent together. I enjoy the sun and the blue skies but neither have an individual interest to me. But, the sun ensconced in clouds creates pictures, storyboards that are interpreted by everyone for hundreds of miles. They see that same, ever-changing canvas.

I carried on watching the sky, appreciating that maybe the sun and clouds were perfect companions because the contrasted each other so well; everyone needs the contrary to realise the harmony;

everyone has to suffer pain to enjoy the pain-free and without a point of comparison there is no true understanding of life.

> **Lisa**: *I have 'permission' to go inside if you want to, Dan.*
> **Dan**: *Caught smoking again.*
> **Lisa**: *Of course. You would think by now I would have found somewhere else to smoke!*
> **Dan**: *Or maybe you enjoy sorting out the lost property bin; your penance is your salvation?*
> **Lisa**: *Or maybe I enjoy what the cricket pavilion offers to us; a little bit of privacy and shelter. This time I have a genuine surprise for you.*

fLy: The notion of having to endure Dan and Lisa having sex bored me. There is no art in teenage proddings. The entertainment is short-lived and his gelatinous secretions would be tied up in rubber sheaths; so nothing tempting for me to stay and taste. So I left, whatever the surprise was going to be would be mundane by my reckoning.

As I coursed my way home I saw Hannah running, head to toe in black, toward school. Naturally I followed and naturally she found her way, with me in tow, to Mr Harbinger's classroom. Once again Hannah sat on the floor with her ear pressed to the door. There was sound, some grunting and some yelping. Hannah's breathing changed to forceful exhalations of sick- and wine-smelling breath; it was delicious! There was a piercing shriek and a low-sounding moan which concluded with Hannah jumping up, turning the knob and forcing her way, screaming, in through the unlocked door. Hannah was immediately silenced as the vision registered. She turned instantaneously and ran. She ran so fast that I could truly see the benefits the workouts in the gymnasium had given her. Hannah did not go home but instead directly to Raymond and Fi's house. As we made our way there I noticed the lights were still on in the cricket pavilion.

Hannah banged Fi's front door like a woman possessed, slightly shaking as she awaited it to open. It seemed like five minutes had passed by the time Fi opened the front door. Hannah by this time was crying.

Fi: *Oh God, Hannah. Come in. Let's go into the kitchen so the kids can't hear. What is wrong?*

Hannah: *I need to talk to you. I have had these suspicions about Tristan and so I would go and sit outside this classroom, thinking that this is where he would be committing adultery. So this evening, I arrived outside of Mr Harbinger's classroom, half expecting to hear what I heard. I believed what I heard to be Tristan. The voice was so dramatic in his thrusts and the squeaky voice was enthusiastically receptive of his comparatively aged prodder. For a little while I had fantasised about that exact situation; me sitting outside his classroom door whilst he fucked a student. I assumed that I would storm into the classroom and confront him but I didn't and I don't know what to do now, Fi.*

Fi: *You didn't confront him then and there and now you think you have discovered his infidelity so you have come here for advice as to what to do next? I don't know what you should do, Hannah; unless you caught him, Hannah, in the act, then it will be difficult to prove; he is a clever man and well read; I don't believe for one minute he will now confess or that this is actually happening. You should have confronted him. Lies are the preferred allies to cowards at times like this.*

Hannah: *I didn't confront Tristan, Fi, I was confronted with Raymond.*

Fi: *Raymond was having sex with Tristan?*

Hannah: *No. Raymond was having sex with Letty Swallow.*

fLy: Hannah repeated herself, right from the beginning, and Fi drank her glass of white wine and Hannah's then poured two more glasses. I was expecting the front door to open and feet to rush in but there was no sign of Raymond that evening.

Hannah stayed with Fi until Fi passed out on the kitchen table. Instead of taking Fi upstairs to her bed, Hannah bought the duvet and pillows downstairs and made a makeshift bed for her on the long velvet sofa in Raymond and Fi's sitting room. Whilst Fi lay comatose on the sofa, Hannah wiped the eye bogey away from Fi's right eye, popped some slow-dissolving aspirin into her mouth, filled a pint glass with water, left it by her side and went.

When Hannah arrived home, Tristan was home. He was sitting and waiting for her in the chair by the patio window. Hannah was about to regale the evening's revelations to him but stopped as she saw the A4 white envelope with her handwriting scrawled across the front of it sitting on his lap.

As Shakespeare most definitely didn't say, "The shit has really hit the fan." And I have to say that I am delighted!